CANTIQUE

....

A NOVEL

JOANNA MARSH

Publisher's Note: This is a work of fiction. Names, characters, places, and incidents are a product of the author's imagination. Locales and public names are sometimes used for atmospheric purposes. Any resemblance to actual people, living or dead, or to businesses, companies, events, institutions, or locales is completely coincidental.

Book Layout ©2017 BookDesignTemplates.com

Cover Design ©2017 Beth Laird

Cantique / Joanna Marsh. -- 1st ed.
ISBN 978-0-9989788-0-2

For Michael Isaiah

Set me as a seal upon your heart,
as a seal upon your arm,
for love is strong as death,
jealousy is fierce as the grave.
Its flashes are flashes of fire,
the very flame of the LORD.

– SONG OF SONGS 8:6

The music which is too familiar to be heard enfolds us day and night
and in all ages.

–C. S. LEWIS

ACT I

Colette laughed and considered her options. When she and Sammy were in college, she would have gone with the margaritas, no question, but her love for ballet had supplanted most of her old interests. After all, her thoughts had wandered to *La* freaking *Bayadère* in the midst of losing the job she was supposed to want. She was almost 26 years old for goodness' sake, and she knew that such daydreaming was silly. But she also knew that it made her feel better. The music and the colors and the dance in her head—they all made her feel as though there were lovelier things to do elsewhere.

Tomorrow, she would begin to look for jobs like a responsible adult. But first, ballet.

CHAPTER TWO

Colette scrutinized her reflection in the closet mirror. Behind her, the bed was covered with dancewear. She had tried on several leotards before finding one that felt flattering. The farewell lunch she had eaten that afternoon was still sitting like a brick in her stomach. Yes, the black Noverre leotard was the only one that would do. Black leotard, black footless tights. Pink was reserved for special days of self-confidence. She would tie a chiffon skirt around her waist after she arrived at the studio. A skirt would help her feel like a real ballet dancer.

Long ago, Colette had found that if she *looked* the part, then she could *feel* the part. And if she *felt* the part, she could trick herself into dancing well. Those dancers with their track pants and loose T-shirts and socks—she didn't understand how they could manage it. Colette remembered how she had applied her "look the part" strategy while interviewing at Oleander. She had dressed to the nines that day, convinced that they would not offer her the job otherwise. A lot of good that did her now.

"Ready to go, CoCo?" Sammy asked.

"Just a sec." Colette opened the door with one flip flop dangling on her finger.

"You look so nice." Sammy looked down at her own tank top and leggings. "You make me look like a freaking hobo."

Colette laughed and rolled her eyes. "What are you talking about? You look cute."

As usual, Sammy drove them to class. Her car was the one with air conditioning, among other functional features. They had made this trip together hundreds of times during the last few years, but it never got old. At least, not for Colette. She couldn't wait to be in that studio. She wished she could go every day.

"Do you know where you'll start looking tomorrow?" Sammy asked.

"Ugh. No idea. I don't even want to think about it."

"Sorry. I'm sure you'll find something, CoCo. Things will work out."

"Yeah," Colette sighed. "I hope so."

"We don't have to talk about it anymore if you don't want to."

"Thanks, Sam."

They both knew that class would be a nice diversion. During that hour and a half, all of the adult students at the Westmoreland School of Ballet would temporarily forget their troubles. Women with demanding jobs and with kids at home were provided a much-needed mental escape in the midst of physical exertion. Ballet simply demanded too much focus. There was no room to think of anything else.

Trying ballet together at Westmoreland had been Sammy's idea, and Colette had obliged, enchanted by the prospect of shopping for dance wear. Colette never suspected that such a flippant decision would lead to her discovering an intense passion for ballet. She had felt awkward and physically challenged during that very first class, but she had a natural lyricism and aesthetic understanding that worked to her advantage. Instinctively, she knew what the steps were supposed to look like, though her body couldn't execute them yet.

Colette had worked hard since then and had greatly improved, but there would always be much to work on. For once, she was fine with this sense of hopeless imperfection. She simply loved ballet too much to let it make her quit. Dancing had given her a new sense of joy that she hadn't felt since childhood. She clung to that joy whenever she could, and there were secret moments when she wished that she could somehow make ballet the center of her life.

Sammy felt differently. Like Colette, she wanted to improve, but this desire came mostly out of frustration. Extremely fit and easily bored, she had seen the class as an opportunity to overcome a new kind of physical challenge. Now, three years deep and still in the beginner's class, she discovered that there was no overcoming ballet. There was always improvement, but dancing couldn't be conquered like the triathlons and muddy races she liked to do.

Since the 1960s, the Westmoreland Ballet had found a home in a sprawling, Prairie School building from the turn of the century. Colette thought it an odd choice for ballet. It was angular and rather plain, and it had been subject to several half-hearted renovations over the years, but its studios were large and light-filled and, Colette admitted, that's all that really mattered. There was nothing quite like an empty studio waiting to be awakened by the echo of music.

Colette and Sammy were the first to arrive, and they headed straight to the corner barre closest to the piano. This spot had always been Colette's favorite, even before she understood why. Eventually, she realized that she could feel the music and focus on the rhythm with fewer distractions. During each balance, she would stare straight ahead at the framed photo on the wall. The photographer had captured the great Jael Maier, one of Westmoreland's former prima ballerinas, dressed as Giselle from Act II and holding a perfect, 180-degree *arabesque penchée*. Such a feat still seemed impossible to Colette, but it didn't keep her from trying.

Other students trickled into the studio. One pregnant woman. Two academy mothers. One confident, elderly lady. Three newbies. The token male, and one retired professional dressed for snow skiing. The presence of an advanced dancer did not surprise Colette and Sammy, who both understood by now that the class label "beginning ballet" was completely relative.

Open class at Westmoreland was not so much for true beginners as it was for anyone. Most people who ventured there had some dance experience in the past, and if they didn't, they were the type who didn't mind being thrown into a completely foreign environment. Colette was not this type, but her love for ballet seemed to have brought out her courage. Instead of being intimidated, she was endlessly fascinated by the seasoned dancers who liked to take the beginning classes, sometimes entirely *en pointe*. Even in summer, they would be bundled up in sweatshirts, and Colette would stare as the patches of sweat spread across their backs during barre. She hoped that she could learn to work like these dancers, who saw the simplest combinations as opportunities to work every possible muscle. They knew how to take a *tendu* and break it down into a hundred, deliberate movements. And yet, somehow, all of this exertion would appear effortless in the end.

Colette pressed her calf back to stretch it out, her hands sticking to the duct tape wrapped around the barre. When she closed her feet back to parallel, she felt a lump on the bottom of her slipper. It was someone's used corn pad. Gross. Ballet studios were really quite disgusting sometimes.

"Hello, everyone!"

Marianne, their teacher, always greeted them with enthusiasm when she entered the studio. Twenty years of teaching clumsy, amateur adults somehow hadn't diminished her passion. Colette had tremendous respect for her.

"What the heck happened in here?" Marianne asked while kicking debris toward the trash cash. "Someone needs to have a talk with these summer intensive kids. Everyone, watch out for bobby pins! I don't want any broken bones today."

Everyone gave a courtesy chuckle.

Dunja the pianist arrived, arms full of bags and her standard liter of Diet Coke. She was a maroon-haired, plump woman with some sort of accent. Colette assumed she was Russian but was too intimidated by her to ask. Dunja plopped down on the bench and gave an abrupt wave as if to say, *I'm ready, bitches. Never mind that I don't have my music out yet.*

"Let's go ahead and start since we're running behind already. Facing the barre, from first, let's *tendu* front, turn it in, turn it out, close with a *demi-plié*. We'll do that *en croix* and take a little *relevé* balance and do the other side. Pretty simple. I'll call it out."

Colette wondered how Marianne could demonstrate the same, basic steps over and over again without a hint of impatience. And then after all of that demonstrating, people would still screw it up.

Marianne locked eyes with the pianist. "Okay, ladies... and gentlemen. Excuse me. First position. Thank you, Dunja, aaaannd *tendu*, turn it in, turn it out, *plié*. To the side. A little faster. Close first, *plié*. To the back..."

Colette paid careful attention to her alignment, trying to feel as many muscles working as possible. If she didn't, the class wouldn't be as productive. She wanted to be sweating by the time they did *dégagé*. She wanted this class to be awesome.

But that was a lot of pressure. Colette had found that if she demanded things from ballet, it would rarely accommodate her. The joy she had felt while dancing came from unsolicited, fleeting moments—from surprise breakthroughs and glimpses of artistry. So, she just tried her best. One combination at a time.

Sammy and Colette could tell that Marianne liked them. They might have even been her favorite students. Both were athletic and aware of their own bodies, something they had taken for granted until they saw the other students struggling to apply simple corrections. They were quiet and focused, receptive to instruction. And, as adult beginners, they had more natural talent than many of the women who had grown up dancing. Marianne was sure to push them when she could. Sometimes a mere glance would imply a challenge.

You could really be doing that en relevé.

You can hold that longer.

You should be trying for double pirouettes.

Sammy would try immediately. Colette, however, confused by a mixture of flattery and self-doubt, would act cautiously. If she tried to meet Marianne's challenge, it would often be at the last possible opportunity. She would rather fail at home, where no one could watch her.

The class moved on to the *plié* combination, which Colette loved. It was always simple and easy to follow, giving her the freedom to be a little expressive. She bent her knees in *demi-plié*, her arm gently floating from second position across to first. She began her *grand plié,* and the same thoughts persisted after years of taking class: *wrap your turnout, knees out, stomach strong, heels down through demi, follow the hand, shoulders down, elbows lifted.*

Marianne walked around, giving vague encouragements and general corrections.

"Keep it moving. Use the head. Very nice."

During *tendu dégagé*, Colette went on auto-pilot, not thinking of much but the rhythm—*and IN, IN, IN.* Out of the corner of her eye, she could see Marianne coming toward her with the dreaded "correction walk." To Colette's surprise, she stopped to talk to Sammy instead.

"You aren't quite closing to fifth in the back," Marianne said. "There's a gap here. Just *tendu* side for me. Heel to toe, heel to toe. No, now you're almost *rond de jambe*-ing. See what I'm saying?" Sammy nodded, looking slightly annoyed. "I know it's hard to the back. Try again. *Dégagé* in a straight line. Whoops. See, you're not closing all the way."

"It's because I have too much thigh meat," Sammy protested.

Colette laughed through her nose, her leg still swinging through *dégagés*.

"What?" Marianne asked.

"I have too much thigh to get around."

"Well, that's not a good excuse."

Sammy stared her down, unable to come up with a response, and Marianne simply walked away. Class time was too precious to hash this one out.

Barre went by quickly. By *fondu*, Colette could tell that this class would be good after all. Her body was cooperating. Her muscles weren't as stiff as usual. Her extension was noticeably higher. She had been working hard to pull up through her supporting hip.

When the class broke for center, it was clear that Sammy was still frustrated about the *dégagé* incident.

"Uh, *yeah*, it's a good excuse," Sammy whispered to Colette. "I have tight hips, lady. If I try to do it 'correctly,' I'll force my turnout in an attempt to get around my giant thighs and kill my knees and never be able to walk again."

"I know exactly what you mean," Colette replied. "I have the same problem. And you don't have giant thighs."

"Whatever. She never corrects you," Sammy teased. "Because you're perfect."

Colette rolled her eyes.

Center was a better experience for Sammy. She and Colette both danced well. Marianne, perhaps feeling guilty for singling Sammy out earlier, had her demonstrate *sissonne fermée* to the class. Sammy followed instructions. Her compact, muscular body sprung up and forward as her back leg snapped up and down. The students applauded. She was a good jumper.

At the end of the class, everyone settled in front of the mirror for *révérence*. This was Colette's favorite part, although it was almost always cut short due to time. She would have to make the most out of a sixteen count *port de bras* and the usual curtsies to the class, pianist, and teacher.

Quieting her tired muscles, Colette imagined herself on stage after a long performance, which she had never actually experienced. She filled her lungs with music and curtsied to her mirror audience. After accepting an imaginary bouquet of roses, she turned and gestured toward the orchestra, graciously folding her hands to her heart. The beautiful phrase ended, and everyone curtsied toward Marianne and clapped with a chorus of *thank yous*.

"Good job, everyone! Have a great week," Marianne said, smiling at Colette.

Colette smiled back and then remembered what her week would be like. She would probably be living in her pajamas, eating chocolate for breakfast, and scouring the internet for soul-crushing office jobs. What if she found something that would turn out worse than Oleander? What if she found nothing at all?

Cantique

In the mirror, she caught a glimpse of her face—glistening and suddenly pale with anxiety. Dread filled her heart as quickly as the class had calmed it. Even with all of its powers of distraction, the magic of ballet could not last forever.

CHAPTER THREE

After wasting most of the day, Colette stepped out into the sunlight. She had resigned to go for a run, although she'd rather be dancing. But Westmoreland didn't offer anything that time of day, and she couldn't blame them. Who else would be free at 3 p.m.?

Sammy had warned her about the heat earlier that morning—a typical thick July heat—the kind that soaked into Colette's dark hair and made it wavy. This type of weather prompted the local news anchors to advise folks to stay indoors with air conditioning and lots of water. Colette never drank enough water. Nor did she pay attention to the weather report. Sammy had become her only link to the outdoors.

Over a month had passed since the layoffs, and Colette had since faced an unsettling reality—there were no jobs to be had. At least, none that she wanted. There were decent positions elsewhere, in places like Chicago and Austin and Denver, but if she managed to land one of those jobs, she wasn't sure she'd even want to take it. Her attachment to her heartland city and to Sammy and to Westmorland Ballet had grown too strong to move over 500 miles away. Plus, she was beginning to regret her choice of career.

A fog gradually invaded her mind. Her days became tedious, and she countered her boredom with self-indulgence. Before she knew it, several weeks had passed in which—with the exception of ballet class—she had spent most of her time in bed.

This particular morning had been especially bad. She had found herself talking to the cat, which wasn't unusual, but then she became frustrated when he never answered back. That's when she decided it was time she left the house.

Colette had only reached the main road when she felt an ache under her ribs. The pain throbbed to the rhythm of the music streaming through her headphones. Running along to this music used to be a freeing activity, but it had since become a form of punishment. It reminded her of the endless time she had to waste. It gave her space to think of what she wasn't doing with her life. Once this happened, she redirected her thoughts to ballet.

It was easy for ballet to slip out of her during these jaunts along the sidewalk. She kept it restrained, though. Run, run, run, *glissade!* Nothing like the defiant street dance in *Billy Elliot*, she thought. Maybe one day—after she found a new job and could afford more classes—she could be good enough to pull off that kind of movie moment. She could put her angst into choreography and follow the *glissade* with a passionate *grand jeté*, arms reaching toward the sky and her head thrown back. People would stop and watch. Some passer-by would record her and post the video online. After a couple million hits, maybe she wouldn't need a job at all.

Lost in her daydream, Colette rounded the corner to the strip mall at full speed. This was her usual habit, as the sidewalk sloped downhill and she could feel Olympian-fast without much effort. This time, however, she was forced to come to a halt. The sidewalk had been demolished. Construction cones blocked her path like little orange and white striped soldiers.

What if someone were to put a tiny, green wig on one of them? An Oompa Loompa cone, right there on Rosewood Drive.

Walking carefully around the rubble, she observed the shops situated neatly along the block, an eclectic and ever-changing sample of commerce. Chinese restaurant, yoga studio, gun repair, and a tool shop named Tempe's. Across the street, the new Bread & Pan spanned the entire block. Sammy had complained about it robbing the historic strip of its quaintness, and she was right. The restaurant was always busy with people in suits and aspiring writers and teen-aged girls in track shorts giggling over iced coffee and muffins. Colette and Sammy missed the old cafe—the one that had been owned by a family down the road. And yet, even with all of this new development, the neighborhood still managed to retain its small-town charm.

Colette stopped to stretch and looked into the tool shop window. She had passed this shop a hundred times but had failed to notice it until now. It looked surprisingly clean on the inside, and she could see a middle-aged man sitting at the counter, staring at his cell phone. He was probably keeping quite cool in there, unlike the sweat-stained businessmen walking across the street. She laughed at the "Help Wanted" sign hanging in the shop window, considering how leisurely this man's job appeared to be. Did he really need the extra help? He looked nice, though. He'd probably make an excellent grandfather.

She decided to walk the rest of the way down the strip. The sun was beating down on her and she knew she was too dehydrated to be running. It was unwise, Sammy had said. *Unwise.* Colette had laughed and told her to shut her face, but Sammy simply stared at her in response, looking vaguely disappointed. She had known Colette too long to hope that her advice would have much impact. In fact, nothing Sammy said to her over the last month seemed to do any good.

About a half mile from home, Colette came upon another construction site. This time, there was no way to cross it without going farther out of her way. She stood there for a while, a nagging thought telling her to go back the way she came. Annoyed, she turned around. Her route would not be efficient today.

The strange nagging grew stronger as her steps slowed. Was it the ache in her side that was irritating her? Or the frustration of retracing her path? Or was it a combination of everything that had been troubling her during these idle weeks? Whatever it was, she wished it would leave her in peace. She wished she could be as calm and comfortable as that man in the tool shop.

The tool shop.

Her feet stopped.

Help Wanted.

It became clear that her gut was telling her to do something. Colette didn't want to do it.

Go into that store.

No.

Just go into it.

I'm not gonna work at a tool shop. That's the dumbest idea in the history of ideas.

But Colette was close now; she could just go in and look around. Then the feeling would go away. She could claim that she had tried. But what on earth would she say to the man?

Hello, good sir. I've never set foot in a hardware store. I don't even know what kind of shenanigans go on here, but I'm desperate for a job. Will you hire me?

She decided if she lost her nerve, she could pretend to be looking for something.

A hammer. Hardware stores have hammers.

Before she knew it, her feet were directing her into the shop. It was as cool and dry as she imagined, and she was suddenly aware of how sweaty she was.

The man looked up from his phone as the bell sounded. "Hello there," he said. "Sure is a hot one, ain't it?"

"Yeah, it is. I was just jogging by... thought I'd stop in," Colette said, wiping her forehead.

He nodded, unaffected by her news. Despite how awkward she felt, the man didn't seem the slightest bit surprised to see her there. Colette began to walk aimlessly from one aisle to the next, hoping he would go back to concentrating on his phone. Instead, he watched her.

"Can I help you find anything?" he asked.

"Um, no. Well, yeah. A hammer, I guess?"

"Sure, right up here. Up front."

"Oh." Colette pretended to concentrate on the display. She realized she didn't have any money with her. "I'll have to come back later. When I'm not jogging. And less sweaty."

"Sure thing."

Colette inched toward the door.

Nag, nag.

Before she could stop herself, she turned around. "Do you have an application I could take? I saw you're hiring."

"I do. We need a new sales associate. Have you worked in retail before?"

"Yes, I have."

"Great. Here you are, Miss. If you want, you can just fill it out now. It's real short."

Colette considered the alternative. If she took it home, she would have to come back later. She would have to talk to him again. And probably buy that stupid hammer.

She completed the application as quickly as she could, skipping over contact details of previous employers. It was not as if she would *really* want to work there, anyway. Why was she there in the first place?

After thanking the man, she left, wondering what had come over her.

COLETTE TRUDGED HOME, lost in thought. It was so late by the time she arrived that Sammy had already pulled into the driveway and was walking toward the mailbox. Her face fell as she saw Colette tiptoeing up the sidewalk.

"Seriously. You went running? I told you about the heat index. Here, take your trashy fashion mag." Sammy shoved the mail under Colette's arm.

"Okay, *Mom*. Dude, this is the neighborhood newsletter."

"Oh. I'll take that, actually. Come on, it's disgusting out here. Do you want to do take-out? I don't feel like making anything. Plus, it's *Friiiiiday!*" Sammy broke into a celebratory dance. "High fives!"

Colette had to laugh. "Sure."

Once inside, they both plopped down at the kitchen table. Sammy reached across the table for a jar of chocolate-covered almonds.

"Hey, you want some?" Sammy asked. Colette was staring into space. "Hey, weirdo, have some almonds."

"Oh, thanks."

"Are you doing okay?"

"Yeah," Colette replied. "I'm fine."

"No you're not," Sammy insisted. "Did someone die? Just tell me."

"*No.* I applied at that Tempe place on Rosewood." Colette found this embarrassing fact spilling from her, despite her intention to forget about it. Sammy had a knack for drawing out secrets.

"What?" Sammy asked, incredulous.

"You know. It's next to the antique shop."

"Like, applied for a *job*?"

"Yes."

"Um, isn't that a hardware store?" Sammy asked, trying not to smile.

"Yeah... Look, I realize I know nothing about tools. But they also have those big, cinnamon gummy bears there. So... there's that."

Sammy was laughing now. She couldn't help herself. "A *hardware* store, eh?"

"I know it's stupid. This is why I didn't want to tell you."

"Colette, is this about rent? Because I told you—"

"Stop. I can't just not pay you rent. I need to do *something*. And I had a weird feeling about this shop."

Sammy looked unconvinced. "A weird feeling?"

"Yeah," Colette said. She shrugged and waved her hand, as if dismissing the whole idea. "Anyway, I doubt they'll call me. I actually hope they won't now that you're making fun of me."

Sammy smiled. "Come on. You know you're capable of doing anything. It's just—you have to admit that the thought of you working there is pretty funny. What would you even wear? You have a closet full of lace dresses. And leotards."

"Yeah, yeah." Colette stood up to look in the fridge. "Are we still ordering out?"

"Sure," Sammy said. "Hey, I think your phone's ringing." She grabbed the jar of almonds and moved toward the living room, craning her neck to follow the sound. "Want me to get it? Is it in your purse?"

"Naw, don't bother," Colette said. She followed Sammy and joined Garçon on the couch. "You know, at least I wouldn't spend my paycheck at a hardware store. It would be a lot safer than other retail jobs."

"That's true," Sammy said. "Remember when you worked at Anthro?"

Colette frowned.

Sammy slunk down in her chair with her hand in the jar of almonds, which was balancing on her abdomen. She sat chomping and lost in thought until her face brightened. "You know, maybe you're actually a genius. You're right—you wouldn't spend your paycheck there. Plus, you could learn about home improvement stuff. And I bet you'd meet all sorts of hot guys."

Colette hadn't considered that possibility. "Yeah, and a lot of really old guys."

Sammy shrugged. "That's not necessarily bad—"

"Hold that thought. Sounds like I have a message." Colette sighed and forced herself off the couch.

"Your mom, again?"

"Probably." Colette went to find her phone. When she came back, her face had gone pale. "That guy at the shop called already. I—I think he wants me to start this week."

"Wow," Sammy said. "That was fast. Maybe it's a sign."

"I don't know." Colette shook her head. "He sounds like a redneck. Listen."

"Hi, this is Darrel over at Tempe's Tool. I looked at your application and can tell you right now—we'd love to have you work with us. I would like to meet with you for an interview of sorts, though, just as a formality. If you could come into the shop sometime this week, we could show you around and whatnot. Just give us a call".

"I really don't know what I was thinking," Colette said. "Maybe I just won't call him back."

"CoCo, you have to call him back now. Just tell him you're no longer interested." Trying to sound gentle, Sammy added, "That would be the adult thing to do."

"Ugh. I know. I'm such a loser."

"*Hey.* You're not a loser. Like I keep saying, this whole Oleander thing is not your fault. And I'm sure a better opportunity will come along. You're better than retail and *whatnot.*"

Colette nodded. "I'll just call him now so I don't have to think about it anymore."

"Good choice. I guess I'll go get the food while you take care of that." Sammy stood up and pointed at Colette, her arm fully outstretched like a rock star. "You better be ready to party by the time I get back."

Colette forced herself to dial the number quickly. She hated talking on the phone. It was best to do it before she could over-think it.

Just get it over with.

"Tempe's Tool, this is Reid."

"Hi. This is Colette Larsen. I was calling for, uh, Darrel?"

"Hold on one second."

Colette planned what she would say. *Hi, Darrel? This is Colette. I just got your voice mail. I know this is strange because I literally just applied, but I actually won't be able to work there. I had something else come up...*

"Hullo, this Darrel."

"Hi, Darrel. It's Colette Larsen. You just called me?"

"Oh, hey there. I sure appreciate you calling me back. Your application looks great. Are you free to come in at 10 o'clock on Tuesday? If not, we can work around your schedule."

"Um, yeah. Tuesday should work."

"Great. Wear something comfortable. Jeans and sneakers will do."

"Okay."

"We'll see you then. Take care."

"Thanks."

"G'bye."

Colette put the phone down.

"Damn it."

CHAPTER FOUR

Colette awoke early Tuesday morning, paranoid that she would oversleep on the first day of this rather unwanted job. Her stomach ached as she showered and changed into the outfit she had already planned in her head—a soft, yellow T-shirt, nice jeans, and a pair of white Converse. By then, she still had a full hour left for her hair and makeup. She worked methodically, hoping that looking good would help her feel better about whatever mess she had gotten herself into.

With just minutes to go, Colette sat on her bed to eat her breakfast, all the while staring at herself in the closet mirror and becoming drowsy again. After only a few bites, she set down her spoon and looked her reflection in the eyes.

You're such a stupid-head.

She sighed, forced herself up, grabbed her purse, and dumped her cereal in the kitchen sink. Garçon leapt up to lick the empty bowl.

"Well, kitty," she said, reaching down to pet him. "Here goes nothing."

The drive took all of two minutes and was over too quickly, although she did note that it was the most convenient commute she had ever had. When she pulled up to the tool shop, she was hoping to sit and finish listening to the song on the radio. That man Darrel, however, was already waiting for her. He opened the door before she was even out of her car.

"Thank you," she said, hurrying toward him.

"Colette, it's great to see you again. Come on in."

The shop was as calm as it was before and smelled faintly of top soil. This time, Colette realized that it seemed so quiet because there was no music. Where was the country radio?

"'Course I'm Darrel, as you probably figured out." He shook Colette's hand and followed her gaze as she observed the shop. There was no one at the cash register. "It's still pretty early, so we don't have any customers yet. There's only two of us here right now. Me and Travis. I'll introduce you a little later."

"Oh, okay." Colette tried to look interested, as if she were making an important mental note.

"How long's your drive?"

"Not long at all. Like two minutes. I live on Juniper, just down the street."

"Great! That's just great. I'm glad it's so convenient for you." Darrel stopped walking, faced Colette, and put his hands on his hips. He smiled and kept nodding his head as if to say, *"Good for you. Well done. Right on."* Colette smiled back, finally feeling more amused by this man than nervous. He sure was easy to please. Now that she was looking into his eyes, she noticed that they were a striking shade of aquamarine.

Finally, he clasped his hands together and said, "Well. Let's go on back to my office and talk business. Your first day might be a little boring. Mostly, uh, administrative stuff and such. Then we'll get you outta here early. I don't like to overwhelm anyone on the first day."

"Sounds good."

Darrel's office was full of junk in neat little piles. Stacks of merchandise boxes partially obscured the wood paneling, which was bare except for a few certificates that were hung in a displeasing cluster. Colette wanted to go straighten them out. He offered her a chair and she sat down, feeling awkward about where to put her purse. The floor would have to do.

Several framed photos sat on his desk, along with a set of antlers and a small nameplate, *DARREL BRENNAN, STORE MANAGER.* Colette watched as he emptied his pockets and lined up the contents on the desk. Phone, keys, wallet, change, more keys, pocket knife, ChapStick. His pants were like a magical Mary Poppins bag. She had never understood why men carried so much crap around.

"So, first things first. Store hours are 9 a.m. to 6 p.m., although we schedule an hour for open and close. So, shifts are generally eight to five or ten to seven. We're open Monday through Saturday. Now, at this point we can't offer you a set schedule. You'll get forty hours a week, but you might be working different shifts, and some Saturdays. Do you think that will work for your schedule?"

"Yeah, it shouldn't be a problem."

Darrel looked relieved. "Great. I'm sure that after the first few weeks, we could sit down and work out a regular schedule for you. That way you'll always know when you're working. I know it's tough to schedule weekends when work ain't regular."

Colette nodded. "How many people work here?"

"Well, there's five of us now. Plus you. If you're still up for it after today." Darrel winked and added, "But you'll see things are pretty laid back around here. You'll be just fine."

Darrel went on to describe what she would be doing at Tempe's—mostly working the register with some merchandise processing. They discussed the skills she had put on her application and her pay rate, which would be higher than she had expected. Darrel explained that having two degrees merited a starting pay increase, and he warned her that she would feel quite overqualified for this job. He looked concerned, maybe even a little embarrassed. Colette suddenly felt as if she was living in an alternate universe, and she didn't mind.

"Oh, I don't know. I mean, my degrees are in design, not hardware store management. If anything, I'm under-qualified."

Darrel smiled. "You're sharp and friendly," he said. "That will be more than enough here."

Colette spent the next hour filling out tax forms and reviewing store policies, all the while wondering why Darrel had decided that she was "friendly." She had barely spoken with him. Once she had finished her paperwork, Darrel gave her a tour. By then, the air conditioning was making the store feel frigid. Colette clasped her arms across her chest.

"'Course the offices are back here by the dock, where our shipments come in. Here's the staff restroom, but we have one for the customers in the northeast corner of the store. And here's where you'll clock in and out each day. I'll show you how to do that in a little bit. Automotive is back there. These three aisles are all hardware. Then you have the Power Tools, Hand Tools, and Lawn & Garden over on the other end. If you forget, you can always read the signs." Darrel paused to chuckle. "All right so far?"

"Yep."

"We do have some merchandise outside, which you won't have to worry about. If someone wants some mulch or something, you would have the person on the floor assist with that and give you the ticket."

"Okay."

"Oh," he said. His face turned somber. "I should show you something else. You see this back here? This is the utility closet, and that door on the other side leads to the back alley. That's where you should go if, God forbid, some sorta maniac comes in here. You just sneak in here and head out the back. And you grab yourself that old pickax back there. Just in case."

Colette laughed. "Have you had much trouble with maniacs?"

"No, not that I can recall. But you never know."

They had stopped to wait for the other employee walking toward them. He was a shorter man—muscular, balding, with piercing eyes and tight clothes.

"This is Travis. He's the assistant manager and is in charge when I'm gone, which isn't very often."

Travis greeted Colette, looking a little pleased with himself. He watched her intently while Darrel continued talking. Colette couldn't listen. She was too aware of the eyes lingering on her, and his face displayed the kind of judgment she had been afraid of. It was an expression of amusement at her expense and, in his case, lustful condescension. Colette guessed at his thoughts.

She must be stupid. I'd hit that.

"...of course, if you don't feel like bringing your lunch you can go across the street," Darrel continued. "We got one of those Bread & Pan Co.'s. They've got all these different soups and such. You can even get soup in, uh, a bread container of sorts?" He began to notice that Colette seemed distracted. "Like, it's a bread container that holds the soup, but you can eat it—the container, that is. Because it's made out of bread, you see?"

"Sure. Yeah, I've been there before," Colette finally replied, holding back laughter.

Travis had apparently found Darrel's culinary recommendation funny, too. He slapped Darrel on the back.

"It's the simple things in life. Right, man?"

"It sure is." Darrel nodded in approval, hands on his hips again. There was a long pause in conversation as Darrel, possibly dreaming of soup, stared toward the floor a few feet ahead of him. Thoroughly amused, Travis stood waiting and locked eyes with Colette, who couldn't help but smile at the situation now. One inside joke with the creepy guy would have to be okay. She cleared her throat.

"Well," Darrel finally chirped. "I'm gonna take Colette back to watch the training video. Let me know if you need anything."

"Will do. It was a pleasure meeting you." Travis bowed slightly. "See you around."

Over the next hour, she watched the training video in a daze, only remembering a few details from the history segment. The store was opened in the mid-1970s and was named after the original owner, Walter Tempe. Once it had reached the safety training section, Darrel came in and paused the video. He looked concerned.

"I think we should call it a day. I'm sure you're getting hungry, anyway."

Colette had only been there for three hours, and it had been an easy day so far. Regardless, she didn't want to stay longer than she had to. Her skin was starting to ache from the cold. She decided not to fight it.

"Okay," she said, trying to sound apologetic. "I am kind of ready for lunch."

"Sure thing. You'll have a full day tomorrow, so why don't you get on home and get rested up. Do you have any questions before you go?"

"I don't think so."

"Good deal." He guided Colette through the back offices, holding each door open for her. "You know, I have a son about your age."

"You do?"

"Yep. I bet you two would get along great." He stopped and faced her again, and Colette forced herself to smile. "Okay, then! We'll see you bright and early at 8 a.m."

"Sounds good. Thank you."

"You have a good one, Miss Larsen."

"You, too."

Colette managed to make her way across the shop floor without having to say goodbye to Travis. The bell sounded as she opened the door, and she was once again back out into the heat. What a relief the humidity was—like a familiar hug.

LATER THAT EVENING, Sammy came home to find Colette lying on the couch in the fetal position. Garçon was on top of her, sound asleep.

"Hey," Sammy said. "How was it?"

"Meh. Fine. Easy. Weird."

"Okay…" Sammy observed the trash-covered coffee table. "I see you had Taco Bell for dinner."

"No, that was lunch."

"Have you been home since lunch time?"

"Yeah, he let me have a short day. So I got me some lunch and have been on this here couch ever since."

"I see," Sammy said, gingerly picking up the burrito wrapper. "Let me just take care of this for you." When she came back, she set Garçon aside and sat herself on top of Colette in the same spot. "Ooh, it's warm right here!"

"What the heck? What are you doing?"

"Are you gonna tell me anything else about your day?"

"I sure ain't."

"Great," Sammy said. "Are you talking like what's-his-face now?"

"Darrel?"

"Yeah, Darrel. '*I sure ain't.*' '*This here couch.*'"

"I dunno. He's actually pretty nice. Like, really nice."

Sammy climbed down. "Well that's good."

"Yeah, I guess. The assistant manager is a tool, though."

"Most are. Little man syndrome, you know."

"That's funny," Colette said. "'Cause he's actually short."

"Really? So are you going back tomorrow?"

"I suppose I have to."

They sat in silence for a while, Sammy petting the cat slowly and Colette borrowing trouble in her mind. Finally, Sammy nudged Colette and said, "Come on. Let's do something fun. We still have that frozen pizza and a whole bottle of wine. You pick a documentary."

Despite her inclination to lie completely still forever, Colette obeyed orders and chose *On the Revolutions of Heavenly Bodies: Stars of the Astro-Ballet Conservatoire.* Sammy poured the wine.

"What's this about?" Sammy asked.

"Students at some conservatory of astronomy and dance in Los Angeles."

"You're kidding."

"Nope."

"That's too awesome for words. Why didn't we go there?"

Colette laughed and observed Sammy's expression, which was completely earnest.

"Sammy?"

"Yeah?"

"Thanks for all this—cheering me up and taking care of my trash and stuff."

"Don't mention it. We gonna start this thing or what? I'm ready for some intergalactic ballet!"

Colette shook her head. "Man, I love you."

"Aw, thanks. Love you, too, CoCo."

CHAPTER FIVE

Colette came to Tempe's bracing herself for a long and horrible day. Yesterday had been surprisingly painless, and she didn't believe she would be so fortunate a second time. When she arrived, she had to wait outside the locked door until a skinny, collegiate-looking kid let her in. He seemed to be half-asleep. The sound of the doorbell made him wince.

"Thanks," she said. "You must be Reid?"

"Yeah. Colette, right?" He paused to yawn. "I think I answered the phone when you called."

"Right. Um, is Darrel in the back somewhere? I'm not sure where I'm supposed to go today."

Reid led Colette back to Darrel's office, where she found him eating a breakfast sandwich. He wiped his hands and stood up to greet her, looking a little too enthusiastic.

"Good mornin'!" Darrel said. "Now, I hate to tell you that I have another form for you to fill out. Are you a morning person?"

"Not really," Colette replied.

"Well, let's get you some coffee, then."

"That would be great. Thank you."

Colette tried to start reading the form, but Darrel immediately reappeared with a Styrofoam cup and a Lamar's box in hand. He must have had it waiting for her.

"Now, I have a serious question," he said. "Do you eat donuts?"

"Sure. Why wouldn't I?"

"Oh good. I was worried you were on a special diet." He offered the box to her. "Everyone seems to be these days. Paleo and gluten free and whatnot."

"Nope. I'll eat pretty much anything."

"That's what I like to hear."

Darrel watched her carefully as she selected a blueberry cake donut and insisted that she take a second one. How different he was from Phil, one of her old bosses at Oleander. She remembered the smell of Phil's cologne and the way it used to saturate everything. It made her head hurt and her stomach turn. Darrel didn't smell like anything. Bless him.

"My breakfast was kind of sad. This is perfect," Colette said.

"Well, good! You just take your time and come see me when you're done."

Within a few minutes, Colette was in Darrel's office and offered him the form. She wondered if he would offer her another donut in return.

"Well, that was fast. Let's see. Why don't you follow me." Darrel brought Colette up to the front counter, where a leathery-skinned woman was breaking a roll of quarters. "Colette, this is Bonnie. She'll be training you on the register."

A fellow woman. Thank God.

"Hiya, hun," Bonnie said with a raspy voice.

"Nice to meet you."

"I'll leave y'all to it, then," said Darrel. "Oh, and make sure she gets a break at noon."

"Yes, sir."

Colette almost wished Darrel would stay. She wasn't sure about this woman, now that she had taken a good look at her. Bonnie's bleached hair looked like a starched relic from the '80s, and her teddy bear T-shirt smelled like cigarettes.

"Well, come 'round to this side, babe," Bonnie instructed. "You're gonna be captain today."

"Okay."

"'Course, I'll be right here, talking you through things. But you'll learn faster if you just do it yourself."

"Sure."

Bonnie explained the basics of the register. She spoke loudly, as if Colette had some sort of impairment, but began to relax once Colette rang up the first customer of the day. A frazzled-looking woman had come in with her toddler and decided on a single garden planter. Colette did everything Bonnie had instructed her to do. Before she knew it, her first sale was finished.

"Well, hun," Bonnie said. "You already got the hang of it. You're one a those quiet, smart types, aren't ya?"

Colette shrugged. "I don't know. I guess."

"You go to college?"

"I did."

"Well, there you go." Bonnie studied her, looking closely at Colette's designer sweater and winged eyeliner. "Boy, you sure got some different eyes. Real pretty. How 'bout that. Did you have one of them fancy majors?"

Colette laughed. "What's a fancy major?"

"You know," Bonnie said. "Economics. P.R. Sociology or whatever."

"I majored in Fashion Design and Merchandising."

"You can get a real degree in that, can you? Huh. What you doin' here, then? Why aren't you out in New York or L.A.?"

Colette took a deep breath. She knew this would be the first of many times she would have to relive her recent past. Funny, Darrel hadn't asked her about it.

"I got laid off a while ago, so this is really a temporary thing until I can find another job."

"Ah, shit," Bonnie replied. "Where did you work before?"

"Oleander. Their corporate office, not in a store." Colette added, "Not that there's anything wrong with retail—"

"Uh huh. What'd you do there?"

"I was just an admin assistant. There was a merger—"

"Did you like it?"

"I hated it."

Bonnie chuckled. "Well, you'll do just fine here. It's nothing fancy, but the work is easy and the people are nice. You'll catch on quick."

"Will I? I have to confess, I'm a little worried." Colette lowered her voice. "I don't know anything about tools."

"Oh, don't you worry about that," Bonnie whispered back. "You'll just be on the register. You've just got to ring things up. Whoever's on the floor will take care of questions and things. You usually won't even have to answer the phone."

"Really?"

"Really. Besides, no one expects you to know everything right now."

"That's good. I mean, I don't even own a hammer."

Bonnie threw her head back and laughed. She had a coarse laugh, something between a giggle and a cackle. "I like that," Bonnie said. "You're funny."

Colette felt relieved. Bonnie wasn't so bad.

The two of them spent all morning at the register. Colette was surprised to discover that Bonnie was quite comfortable with the computer. She had a background in IT, and Darrel depended on her to update the software. In between customers, Bonnie taught Colette how to process returns and print tags for markdowns.

When it came time for lunch, Colette ate by herself in the little break room next to Darrel's office. Her lunch consisted of deli meat wrapped in two slices of cheddar cheese, four pieces of dark chocolate, and one of Sammy's protein bars, which also contained dark chocolate. She vowed to get up earlier next time and make a decent lunch.

In the afternoon, she followed Reid around the floor and helped him stock a shelf with boxes of giant staples. Who knew there were so many different models of staple guns? Did people expect her to know about all of them? She tried to pick Reid's brain about regular customer inquiries. Even after Bonnie's encouragement, she was still afraid of having to answer questions about the merchandise.

Paranoia aside, everything was significantly easier than the work she had been accustomed to doing for the past three years. Toward the end of her stint at Oleander, she was juggling the schedules of her three difficult bosses and had begun to dread going to work every day.

She had to admit that she hadn't *always* hated it, though. She could remember being excited to begin her career and move in with Sammy that same week. When someone would ask, "So, what do you do?" she was relieved to have an answer and proud that it carried some prestige. Even people who had once mocked her choice of major recognized Oleander. They respected it.

Now, when people would ask her the dreaded career question, she would be back at square one. It felt much worse now that she was older—especially if she thought about what Sammy had managed to achieve. Not long after they had graduated from college, Colette realized that her dearest friend had already become a real adult. She had watched with wonder as Sammy cheerfully climbed the corporate ladder and simultaneously finished her CPA program. By her twenty-fourth birthday, Sammy had bought a house and Colette moved from their apartment with her, feeling rather childish in comparison. Now, she felt like a toddler.

Colette's last task of the day was to finish watching the safety training video. It was painful to watch, but at least she could sit quietly for a while.

Darrel came in toward the end and stood watching with his hands on his hips. A man with a thick mustache was demonstrating the proper way to climb a ladder when the credits abruptly appeared.

"Well, that sure ain't winning any Oscars." He ejected the VHS carefully, as though he were handling an ancient artifact. "But you get the point. Well, it looks like you're done a little early. Do you have any questions after today?"

"I don't think so. Bonnie was very helpful."

"Glad to hear that. She said you're picking everything up quick. But you just let us know if you need help with anything. Don't feel like you've got to figure everything out all by yourself. You're part of our team now." Colette nodded. "Why don't we go ahead and call it a day? Just mark the full eight on your time sheet."

"Okay, if you're sure. Thanks, Darrel."

"You're welcome. We'll see you on Friday, Miss Colette. Enjoy your day off tomorrow."

THE FOREIGN ENVIRONMENT at Tempe's had taken a toll on Colette. Meeting several new people at once could be dangerous; she could spend hours in her head replaying the various conversations she had with them and evaluating her responses. Not wanting to waste her time alone on her day off, she decided to take measures to avoid this self-inflicted torture. The best respite she knew consisted of the familiar—tea with chocolate, her favorite movies and music, and the promise of ballet class that evening.

Days seemed to fly by when Colette was alone in the house, yet she often couldn't even recall how she had spent all of her time. Sometimes, she would realize that she hadn't spoken a single word all day. Her voice would sound high and weak when she greeted Sammy in the evening.

Other times, she spoke and sang to herself, having hypothetical conversations and holding make-believe concerts. There were moments when she would stop suddenly, put her hairbrush microphone down and think, *what the heck am I doing? I'm a freaking adult. What if there are hidden cameras around here?* Then she would shrug it off, realizing that it really didn't matter. If she had a niece or nephew, or some other small children to mentor, they would probably think she was the coolest adult ever. She would give them a word of wisdom.

Remember, kids, only boring people lose their imaginations.

When she finally glanced at the clock, it was already 4 p.m. She frantically loaded the dishwasher and swept up the hair on the bathroom floor, hoping it would trick Sammy into thinking that she had been productive that day. Then, she started a hot bath.

It seemed pointless to take a bath before ballet class, but it was a necessary ritual for Colette if she had the time. She had to justify this strange behavior to Sammy on several occasions. For one thing, Colette claimed, she could shave her legs without getting her head wet. Her legs needed to be smooth so that she wouldn't have what she referred to as "cactus tights," and her hair needed to stay dirty so that it could be slicked back into a neat bun. Plus, soaking in the hot water prepared her muscles for dancing. It was science.

After finishing her bath, she popped a couple of ibuprofen and freshened up her makeup. Just a little mascara and lipstick would do, though. She never wanted to look too eager, though she was likely the most eager student in the class. Then, she began rolling out the muscles in her legs and feet with a foam roller and tennis ball, all the while thinking about which leo and skirt to wear. Class went better with this kind of slow prep.

By then Sammy had come home. Her mode of preparation was much lower maintenance and involved a quinoa bar, a quick change, and a ponytail. Colette was still getting ready until the last minute, when she would grab a water bottle and a mint on the way out the door.

"How was your day at work?" Colette asked Sammy on their way to Westmoreland.

"Fine," Sammy replied. "Although, this new client asked me why I wasn't married. And right in front of my boss, too. I'd never even met the woman before, and what am I supposed to say to that? 'Um, I don't know? I guess I'm hideous and unlovable?'"

"Ugh. People are the worst."

"Have the people at Tempe's asked you that yet?"

"Actually no, they haven't, now that I think about it. All my old coworkers did, though."

"Are you ever going to hang out with your Oleander friends again? Seems like it's been a while."

"I was supposed to tonight actually, but I canceled... What? We have nothing in common anymore. It's boring to listen to them now. Face it, Sam. You're my only remaining friend. But don't feel burdened or anything."

"'I shall help you bear this burden, CoCo Baggins,'" Sammy said. "'As long as it is yours to bear.'"

Once they entered the studio, they were surprised to find that one of their classmates had arrived before them. It was Tina, a forty-something woman who had been taking the Thursday evening class for a good five years. She had danced *en pointe* as a teenager and brought this fact up often, as if it made her special. Sammy had a strong dislike for her.

Colette noticed that Tina had a new leotard with an elegant, low back. She was naturally thin and looked like a dancer that day. Too bad she still couldn't quite get the hang of the classical aesthetic, despite her former years *en pointe*. She had stiff hands and a swayback, but she was under the delusion that she was an advanced dancer.

"Hey, girls!" Tina said.

"Hi. How are you?"

"Oh, I'm fantastic. *Swamped*, but fantastic. Are you going to any of the shows this season?"

Tina's husband could get her discounted tickets to the Westmoreland Ballet, the only major professional company in the area. Colette loved to go to the ballet, but always chose more classes over tickets when money was tight. She realized she hadn't seen a live production in well over a year.

"I don't know. I would like to," Colette said. "They're just so expensive."

Tina nodded with feigned sympathy. "Well, they are a lot cheaper than the big city companies. I will say that. Anyway, the first show is mixed-rep— the one in September. It should be fabulous. You should try to make it."

"Yeah, definitely."

Colette knew there was little chance of that happening.

When she and Sammy had first started dancing, the humble Westmoreland Ballet was conveniently emerging as one of the leading companies of the central United States. It had grown in the decades since the great Jael Maier, though it remained relatively small, and it had earned a reputation for its solid dancers and innovative artistic staff. The larger, coastal companies staged full-length classics and ambitious contemporary pieces, but Westmoreland had built a surprisingly diverse repertoire, and its freshness had attracted some of the most talented dancers in the world.

Fascinated by this new culture that she had stumbled upon, Colette had initially scoured Westmoreland's website and memorized the names of practically every company dancer. Since then she had fallen out of touch with the professional side, turning her attention to her own technique. As she fell deeper in love with ballet, she also learned that dwelling on the company dancers living a dream life that she could never attain could become a little depressing. The ever-present photograph of Jael Maier's *penchée* was reminder enough.

Class went by at the usual brisk pace, and Marianne was her usual, upbeat self. After *tendu* in center, she skipped several exercises and went straight to *petit allegro*, which was clearly her favorite section to teach. Her instructions became even more enthusiastic as she hopped along with the class. Despite her age, Marianne proved to be more fit than most of her students.

"And UP! UP! UP! *Pas de bourrée, changement, jeté*! And UP! UP! UP! *Pas de bourrée, glissade, assemblé!*"

Colette preferred the free-flying jumps of *grand allegro*. During that combination, Marianne had them dance across the floor one at a time. Colette volunteered to go first, even though she was aware that people would be watching her. At that particular moment, she knew the combination and wanted to go before she had time to forget it.

This strategy worked well. Free from the pressure of thinking about the choreography, Colette felt like she was actually dancing—not just stringing steps together but really dancing. She loved when that happened.

"Beautiful!" Marianne praised.

After Colette finished, she watched Sammy begin from the opposite corner of the studio. *Chassé, sauté arabesque, tombée pas de bourrée, glissade...* Sammy was doing well with the combination until the *pas de chat*, where she tripped over her back foot and missed the jump entirely.

"Mother *fucker!*" Sammy shouted.

Her fists clenched, she stood in an awkward pose in the middle of the floor, apparently unable to move. She had gone from genuinely graceful to the gruff opposite of a ballerina in a split second. After a brief moment of shock, Colette doubled over laughing, along with half of her classmates.

"*Ladies!*" Marianne scolded, trying to keep herself together.

Sammy finally scurried out of the way to avoid being trampled by the next girl. Colette wiped tears from her eyes and caught her breath. Had it really happened? Yes. Sammy had dropped the f-bomb in classical ballet class. Smirking a little through her fury, Sammy leaned against the barre next to Colette.

"I almost had it, damn it!" Sammy said. A few of the older women around them were frowning in disapproval. Sammy lowered her voice. "That freaking *pas de chat.*"

Instead of moving directly into the left side, Marianne stopped the music and walked over to her students. She was doing a poor job of looking stern. Everyone could tell that she was trying her hardest not to laugh.

"Now," she said. "Everyone makes mistakes, but let's try to keep the language PG, okay?"

Sammy nodded. "Sorry, everyone. Got a little carried away."

"Well, at least we know you're passionate!" Marianne replied. Several of the girls were still giggling. "Okay, everyone. Left side. And let's nail those *pas de chats!*"

CHAPTER SIX

Colette had been dreaming before her phone began to ring. She was performing a *pas de deux* on a stage flanked with marble pillars, and she was dancing remarkably well—far beyond her normal ability. Her costume was made of sparkling chiffons that seemed to change colors. Fiery, sunset oranges and Mediterranean blues swirled around her as she turned through a rapid *manège*. Exhilarated, she leapt blindly and was caught in a fish dive before being placed into an effortless arabesque *en pointe*. Strong hands steadied her waist as she turned multiple *pirouettes*. She had never felt so free and light. Although she could not see her partner's face, he seemed familiar, as if she had known him all her life.

"Hello?" Colette answered.

"Aw, you don't sound well. Are you sick?"

Colette glanced at the clock. "Mom, why are you calling so early? What's wrong?"

"Oh, sorry, honey. I just wanted to chat."

"Can I call you later?"

Her mother was silent. Colette could tell that she was beginning to cry, and her tears were manipulative, regardless of whether or not she intended them to be. Colette sat up.

"Hey, I'm sorry," Colette said. "I'm just really tired. It's early."

"I know, honey. But I miss you. Do you think you'll be able to come down to Houston soon?"

"I don't know, Mom. I have work. Plus, I don't think I can afford a flight right now."

"Oh, we'd pay for it. You know that."

"Why don't you and Craig come up here?"

"You know, we'd like to, but he has limited vacation time—"

"Only because you spend three weeks a year in Maui."

There was another long pause. Colette decided to stand her ground this time. She wouldn't apologize for this. It was the truth, after all.

Her mother finally broke the silence. "You're right. Maybe we can work something out in early October."

"That would be nice."

"Honey, I'm worried about you. This new job of yours—"

"Don't be," Colette replied. "I'm doing fine. Mom, I have to get ready for work now. I'll call you soon, okay?"

After a few more rounds of promises, Colette got her mother to hang up the phone. It was a rough start to the day. Thankfully, work would seem easy in comparison.

With over a month at Tempe's under her belt, Colette had begun to feel more comfortable there. By then she had met all of the staff, including Hal, an elderly man who seemed to be mentioned more than he actually worked. She began to wonder if Hal was really a ghost from the Walter Tempe era. Perhaps he had suffered a fatal fall off the ladder while doing the yearly inventory. Now his benevolent presence watched over Tempe's, ensuring that the workplace safety training video was shown to all.

Hal was probably not a ghost, but he was a bit irritable and generally kept to himself. Colette learned that if she needed him to give her a break at the register, she would have to factor in an additional four to five minutes to wait for him to walk across the store. When he finally arrived, all hunched over and huffy, he would grip the counter and dismiss her from her post with an abrupt nod.

"Don't you mind Hal," Bonnie told her in front of him. "He's so old he can get away with anything."

To Colette's surprise, Hal cracked a smile and said, "You aren't much farther behind me."

"Like hell I am, mister! I got a good twenty-five years before I catch up with you."

"That's nothing," Hal said with a wave of both hands. He turned toward Colette, addressing her directly for the first time. "You'd better watch out for this one. What you see is what you get with her."

Colette observed that Hal reserved these types of good-natured jabs for Bonnie, serious, albeit short, conversations for Darrel, and words of wisdom for Reid. Hal hated Travis, so he reserved no words for him. Colette wasn't sure where she fit in yet, besides having an inkling that she was an annoyance and just another name to learn.

Despite these occasional run-ins with Hal, Colette found that she was not bothered by him or anyone else at Tempe's—besides Travis. He had toned down the staring as the weeks wore on but was also inappropriately preoccupied with Colette's relationship status. Why was she single? Was there something wrong? Why was she always making that face? He was the type of man who would routinely tell women to smile and acted too familiar in conversation. Colette found herself rolling her eyes at him on an hourly basis.

Reid and Colette, however, were almost always scheduled together. This was fine with both of them, as they were the closest in age and got along easily. Colette was glad to have someone who understood her pop culture references, and Reid found Colette to be cool and beautiful. Reid was a senior in college and lived in town with his parents. He had continued to work year round, hoping to pay for school without any student loans. Colette admired his determination but felt sorry for him. She wouldn't trade the carefree fun she had in college for financial freedom. Not when she would be spending the rest of her life working anyway.

Within her first month, Colette and Reid had established an effective system. Like a loyal older sister, she would cover for him when he overslept in the mornings, and he would intervene quickly whenever Colette was cornered by an impatient customer. Colette could ask Reid anything without feeling embarrassed, which was a tremendous relief.

And then there was Darrel. He kept the shop together as if it were a walk in the park. She even heard him telling Travis once that the work they do should never be stressful. She wondered if Darrel ever bothered to worry about how Tempe's was doing financially. Saturdays were busy, but the shop was practically empty during the week.

During slow spells, Darrel would sit by the register and ask Colette questions in a genuine attempt to get to know her. She found this habit rather annoying at first, and his unfailing politeness was almost ridiculous. He reminded her often that he had a son about her age, as if she should immediately seize the opportunity to meet this mini Darrel. In time, however, she began to find him endearing and refreshingly uncomplicated. He was easy to talk to.

In the course of these chats, she told Darrel about Oleander—about how it had been great for a while and how it had slowly crushed her hopes and dreams. He listened patiently until he felt compelled to interject.

"It ain't right," he said. He shook his head. "That's not how you treat employees."

His words made Colette feel protected. Even at Tempe's, where she often felt out of place, she had the comfort of knowing that she could part ways on good terms. If she found something new soon, Darrel wouldn't hold it against her. He would probably congratulate her and wish her the best, convinced she would go on to do great things.

Until then, she would have to settle in as best as she could. When she wasn't busy worrying about her aimless life, she found that she actually enjoyed the slow, quiet atmosphere at the tool shop. Her work was easy and Darrel let her read if there was nothing else to do. She practiced a lot of *relevés* and *demi-pliés* at the counter and, when no one was around, would do *chaîné* and *piqué* turns down the aisles. One day, she lost balance and almost crashed into an end cap. She pictured what would have happened if she had—the entire row of shelves would fall over and knock the others down domino-style until debris busted through the front windows, killing some innocent pedestrians outside. Darrel would finally lose his patience.

"What in the Sam Hill were you doing?" he would ask.

"*Piqué* turns."

"Peek-a-what?"

"I was dancing. You know, ballet."

"At your age?" He would laugh maniacally until finally yelling, "YOU'RE FIRED!"

Colette would exit the store in tears, gingerly stepping over the bodies of those she had killed with her poor ballet technique.

After this imaginary incident, she was a lot more cautious with the aisle dancing. Instead, she would pace back and forth, studying the merchandise. By then, she had a general idea of what everything was used for and where everything was located. The first couple of weeks had been rough whenever a customer asked her for help, but she became adept at secretly Googling product names while maintaining eye contact. And if she really couldn't figure something out, it was not the end of the world. Reid or Bonnie would be there in a minute. Looking back, she didn't know what she had been so worried about.

CHAPTER SEVEN

"Is Tempe's still going all right?" Sammy asked. She poured more coffee and staggered back to the kitchen table. It was Saturday, and Sammy was still in her pajamas while Colette was already dressed for work and eating what she liked to call an "adult breakfast" of eggs, sausage and toast. She had to admit, a good breakfast made her days go a lot better.

"Yeah, it really is," Colette replied. "I actually don't mind it there at all."

"But you're still looking, aren't you?"

"Here and there," Colette lied. She hadn't searched for a single job opening since she started. "How about you?"

Sammy yawned. "Same old, same old. Oh, I actually got a raise this week after my evaluation. Forgot to tell you."

"That's great!" Colette said, smacking Sammy on the arm. "Congratulations."

Colette smiled and shook her head. There was Sammy, with her disheveled morning hair, continuing to make her way up in the world as if it were no big deal. From time to time, Colette would joke about Sammy's so-called "effortless overachievements," but she couldn't resent her if she tried.

"So, what are you gonna do today?" Colette asked.

"Not sure. Maybe go to spin class this morning."

"No ballet?"

"Naw." Sammy never went without Colette. "But, uh, I actually have a date tonight."

"What?!" Colette shrieked. "Since when? Who with?"

"Sheesh, calm down. He's one of our consultants. He asked me out to dinner as soon as the project ended."

"Really? What's he like?"

Sammy shrugged and stabbed her toast. "He's nice. Pretty cute. I don't know... We'll see how it goes."

"Well that's exciting," Colette said. She stood up to clear her dishes. "I'd better go. Text me if anything crazy happens."

"I will. Have a good day at work."

Colette thanked her and hurried out the door, actually looking forward to spending the day at Tempe's. Saturdays were generally busy, and while that meant she would have to deal with more customers, it also meant that the day would go by quickly. And Reid and Bonnie would both be there to provide entertainment. They had become her favorite co-workers.

Today's shift started at 10 a.m., which meant that she would arrive in the thick of the morning rush. That was good, because it would be lunchtime before she knew it. There was always a slight lull around this time and she could take a breather. Maybe get some *relevés* in before having her own lunch, and then settle back in for a steady stream of afternoon shoppers.

Bonnie left first to take her break, leaving Colette alone at the front of the store. Resting her hand on the counter, she bent her legs into a *demi-plié* and rolled through her feet before stretching up to *relevé*. She was checking her alignment when she heard the doorbell sound. Her heels snapped back onto the floor. Irritated, she looked up to see who had interrupted her. A young man had walked in and was heading straight toward the counter.

"Can I help you with something?" Colette asked.

"Oh, no thanks. I'm just here to see my dad. I'm James, Darrel's son."

Colette observed him more closely. He was rather good-looking and resembled Darrel in the eyes. Perhaps in coloring, too, if Darrel weren't gray-headed. She quickly surveyed his outfit—a navy blue track jacket, rolled-up sleeves, and ugly yellow sweatpants. His hands were strangely sinewy, and she detected a hint of a tattoo on his left forearm. He was obviously in good shape—but a weird kind of good shape, she decided.

Maybe he's an Olympic ski jumper or something. No, not skinny enough. A pole vaulter, maybe?

"So... is he in the back?" James asked, looking amused. "He should be expecting me."

"Probably. I'll call him up here..." After several rings, she began to fear that she would be stuck there with mini-Darrel for eternity. What would they talk about? "Sorry," she said. "It's still ringing. He's probably on the can again."

Why the heck did I say that?

But James was laughing. Darrel finally answered.

"He'll be up in a minute," Colette reported.

"Cool," James said. "Thanks."

An awkward pause followed. James tucked his hands into his jacket pockets and began to pace slowly in front of the register. Colette found herself mirroring his stance and avoiding eye contact, though she really wouldn't have minded looking at him again.

"So," James finally said. "Are you the new girl he's been talking about?"

"Yeah, guess so."

A faint smile appeared on his lips, and he stopped pacing. "You don't look like you belong in a hardware store."

"What do you mean?" Colette asked, unsure of whether she should feel flattered or insulted.

"I don't know," James replied. "Just not the type."

Colette stared in response. She couldn't exactly contradict him.

"Anyway," he continued. "I bet Travis is thrilled you're here."

"Oh really?" Colette rolled her eyes. "Why?"

James suddenly became interested in the gloves hanging by him. "Oh, you know how he is."

"No. How is he?"

He cleared his throat, and Darrel appeared before he had to think of a reply.

"Hey Jimmy! Good to see ya." Darrel embraced his son and left a hand on his shoulder, as if to present him to the world. "Colette, this is my youngest boy James. Isn't he handsome?"

"Ha. Yeah," Colette muttered, feeling her face flush. "He looks like you, Darrel."

"Well that sure is kind of you!"

James didn't look quite as pleased. He was studying Colette's face intently, as if trying to read her mind. Did he think she was being insincere?

"Did you bring the tickets?" Darrel asked.

"Huh?" James said, his focus shifting from Colette to his dad. "Oh, yeah. I've got two for you and Mom. I told Josh to call me if they end up finding a babysitter."

"Thanks, son. Wanna head out for lunch real quick? We can go across the street. Get a soup n' sandwich."

"Yeah, I was planning on it. I have about forty minutes."

Darrel turned to Colette, looking regretful. "I would love for you to come with us, but I know Bonnie has already gone out. I'm real sorry."

Thank you, Bonnie!

"Don't worry about it. I'll man the shop while you're out." Colette then saluted them military-style, an impulsive action that she immediately regretted. James looked as though he had never seen someone so strange.

DARREL RETURNED FROM lunch alone. Feeling relieved and miraculously having had no customers, Colette was uncharacteristically cheerful. She didn't mind when Darrel sat himself next to her at the counter.

"Looks like it hasn't picked up at all," Darrel said.

"Nope. No one's been in since you left."

"I'm not too surprised. There's a lot going on in town today."

Colette nodded and reached over the counter to grab a bag of cinnamon gummy bears. She scanned the barcode, threw two dollars into the till, and began to eat the red bears like popcorn.

"So," she said, offering the bag to Darrel. "What's with the tickets? Are you guys going to a movie or something?"

"Naw, those were for Jimmy's performance. Didn't I tell you? He's a dancer."

Colette stopped chewing. "...Oh."

"He's real good, actually. Got into the Westmoreland Ballet Company two years ago. Next week is his first big performance as a soloist. He's had some solos in the past, unofficially, I guess. I really don't get how it works. He used to dance in the... oh, what's it called—"

"The corps?"

"Yeah, that's it! Hey, how do you know that? ...Colette? You all right?"

She was staring off into the distance, her eyes full of confusion and her fingers still gripping a cluster of gummy bears.

"Huh," she muttered. "What did you say?"

"I asked how you knew about that," Darrel repeated.

"Oh. I—I kind of love ballet. I actually take class at the Westmoreland School. I can't believe he dances there... " Colette mumbled, still trying to wrap her mind around this shocking new information.

Darrel's son is a professional ballet dancer. It couldn't be. What were the chances?

"Well, isn't that neat!" Darrel said. His face lit up, and he smacked the counter in celebration. "You would get along well with my wife, then. You might have heard of her. She used to dance there, too."

"Um," Colette began, incredulous. "What's her first name?"

"Jael."

"No."

Darrel smiled. "Yes."

"*No,*" Colette repeated, now completely perplexed. "Your wife can't be Jael Maier."

"Sure is," Darrel said. He laughed and added, "Well, Jael Maier-Brennan."

"Seriously? You're married to *the* Jael Maier?"

"Yeah," Darrel said proudly. "Over thirty years now."

"You've gotta be shitting me."

"Whoa there, Miss Colette!" Darrel laughed again, now thoroughly amused and delighted by Colette's reaction.

"But she was a principal dancer for years, wasn't she?" Colette continued. "Her pictures are plastered all over the studio."

"She was. She retired and started teaching around the time we had Jimmy. I can see how it might take you by surprise. I still don't quite understand ballet, myself, but my wife and Jimmy—what they can do is just plain incredible. Me and Josh, we missed out on the artistic genes. Luckily, Josh has a good head on his shoulders..."

Colette had stopped listening. She couldn't believe it. Darrel was married to Jael Maier. Darrel, who manages Tempe's Tool and worships the bread bowl. His wife was a ballet legend and his son, possibly some sort of rugged, up-and-coming dance genius. And Colette had just rolled her eyes at him and his yellow sweatpants. If only she had known when James had walked in earlier. Or the first time Darrel implied a possible set-up. It would at least have made for interesting conversation. Why hadn't he told her about all of this before?

Right. Of course. She hadn't bothered to ask about his family.

WHEN COLETTE ARRIVED home, she went straight to Sammy's bedroom to share her news. Sammy, who was sitting on her bed and flipping through a fitness magazine, was surprisingly disinterested. She seemed distracted, maybe even melancholy. Puzzled, Colette moved from the doorway to sit beside her. Then she suddenly remembered the date with the consultant.

"Hey," Colette said. "What happened with your date? Why are you home already?"

"I cut it short after dinner," Sammy replied. "Told him I was having menstrual cramps."

"Seriously?"

Sammy closed her magazine. "For real."

"Wow. I guess it didn't work out, then?"

"He's nice, I guess, but super boring. He talked about CrossFit and his downtown loft the entire time. Then he invited me to come see it, at which point I told him I was having wicked cramps."

Colette laughed. "What did he say?"

"He looked slightly horrified," Sammy replied, smiling at the memory. "Then he tried to play it cool. He was like, 'Oh, yeah, okay. Next time, then.' As if there will be a next time. I'm glad we won't have to see each other at work anymore."

"Yeah. Sorry your date sucked," Colette said. She offered Sammy a hug.

"That's all right," she replied, patting her on the back. "I'd rather hang out with you anyway. That's so weird about your boss's family. What a small world."

Colette was glad she had reopened the topic. "I know! I can't get over it. I never would have guessed that Darrel had anything to do with ballet."

"Do you think he could get us tickets?"

"Maybe. Next time Tina asks us if we're going we can brag about our insider connection."

Sammy liked that idea very much.

THAT NIGHT, COLETTE lay in bed wide awake, thinking over the events of the day. She wondered how Darrel and Jael fell in love. She wondered what kind of dancer James would be and what he thought of her. What had Darrel told him about her?

She finally turned on her lamp, decided to give up the pretense of trying to sleep, and mindlessly reached for her phone. An advertisement for Westmoreland Ballet appeared, showing the image of a sultry dancer dressed in red—Alexandra Vukoja, if Colette remembered correctly. She was striking, with olive skin, large brown eyes, pillowy lips, and a perfectly lean body. *Support Westmoreland Ballet,* it said. She wondered if James would be dancing with Alexandra.

Before she knew it, she was buying a ticket for the Sunday matinee. Sammy would be at Mass with her family. Colette could go by herself without having to tell a soul, which is exactly what she did.

HAVING BOUGHT THE cheapest seat available, Colette sat in the very back row of the balcony. It was a mixed-rep performance, with several short ballets that she had never heard of. James would be featured in the first Balanchine selection. Before the show began, she read his mini-biography in the program.

> JAMES BRENNAN *received his training at the Westmoreland School of Ballet under the tutelage of Erik Sanderson, Irena Mansky, and Jael Maier. There, he performed principal and soloist roles for the Westmoreland Youth Ballet, including Prince Charming in* CINDERELLA *and Ali in* LE CORSAIRE. *As a teen, he was awarded full scholarships to summer programs at Joffrey Ballet and Houston Ballet before performing across the country with Quadrilogy Dance Group. At Westmoreland Ballet, his favorite roles include Second Sailor in Jerome Robbins'* FANCY FREE *and Philippe in Henri Lavoisier's* THE SUN KING. *This is Mr. Brennan's third season with Westmoreland Ballet.*

The lights dimmed and the curtain went up. Colette squinted to find James's figure onstage. While her spot was certainly not the most enjoyable, she could see well enough to tell that James was an amazing dancer. Like all of the company members, his dancing appeared effortless, but his solo was short and Colette soon lost track of him on the stage. Truth be told, the principal dancers, Alexandra Vukoja and her partner, stole the show. She was mesmerizing, and Colette felt a slight pang of awe and jealousy.

When Colette was back home, she stashed the program in her dresser drawer, not quite knowing why. She sat down on her bed, still pondering the fact that the man she had just watched in the performing arts center was Darrel's son. *Darrel's* son. Then she pictured Darrel leaping around the stage in steel gray tights and a bouncy tunic. Just the thought made her burst out laughing.

It is just too strange, she thought. *Life is so weird.*

ACT II

CHAPTER EIGHT

Colette awoke to a crisp October morning feeling delightfully cool. Her bedroom window was cracked open, and Garçon was lying next to her, squinting at the sunshine. Colette patted him on the head and settled back under the covers. Garçon's purring tempted her to stay in bed. She could get away with it, since it was her day off, but she had promised herself she would be productive from the outset. In fact, she was looking forward to making the most out of her day.

She stood up and immediately changed into her exercise clothes. She ate breakfast—yogurt and granola with black tea—and washed her face. Her skin had been looking brighter lately. She called her mom. It had been too long since they had spoken. She started a load of laundry.

It was only 8 a.m. by the time she started her walk. She took a deep breath and actually smiled at the morning, realizing that she hadn't felt this kind of prolonged contentment since her days before Oleander—since college, really. It was so strange to be feeling this way now, she thought.

College had been great because she loved what she was learning. She had spent her days in design classes, creating beautiful concepts. And she spent her evenings in the textile lab, learning how to turn those concepts into beautiful things. Although she had never particularly liked to sew, she was glad to have acquired a skill set—to have a command over some sort of craft. But she hadn't actually made anything since then.

Maybe she'd drag the sewing machine out when she got home. She could make a ballet skirt. That should be easy enough. Why hadn't she thought of that before? This new idea was so exciting that she regretted walking so far, and she began to jog home, eager to sketch out ideas and head to the fabric store.

WHEN SAMMY ARRIVED home that evening, she found a spotless house, a light dinner on the kitchen counter, and three ballet skirts draped over the dining room chairs.

"Wow, you've been busy," Sammy said. She pointed to the skirts. "Did you *make* those?"

"Yeah. I screwed up the first one big time. The seam is crooked. But I think these two are all right." She handed them to Sammy. "What do you think?"

"They're really pretty. Seriously. I'm impressed."

Colette smiled. "You can have one."

"When would I wear it? You know I don't wear leotards."

"Just wear it over your leggings. It'll be cute."

Sammy held one of the skirts—a black and white floral print—up to her to waist. "I do love this fabric. I guess I can try it tonight. But you have to be honest if it looks stupid."

"It won't look stupid."

"Oh, wow," Sammy said, pointing to the sketch book on the table. "Is this one you kept in school?" She picked it up and began to leaf through it. "I remember these! I forgot how awesome they are, CoCo."

"Aw, thanks." Colette looked over Sammy's shoulder. "You know, I used to be so critical of my work back then. But I don't think they're so bad now."

Sammy flipped to the most recent page, where Colette had drawn sketches of the wrap skirts. She smiled and handed the book back to Colette. "It's fun to see you doing this again."

They rode to class with the windows rolled down, cracking each other up by sticking their heads out of the car and letting the wind squish their faces into weird expressions. It was a beautiful evening, and they were particularly excited for class. Perhaps it was the new skirts.

"Doesn't it kind of feel like we're in college again?" Sammy asked. Her eyes were watery from the wind.

"I was thinking about that earlier today," Colette said. "It was so much fun, but, you know, I wouldn't want to go back. I'm glad we're here now."

"Me too." Sammy paused. "CoCo, it's good to see you so chill again. I know I wasn't the most supportive about your job when you first started, but I feel like it's—and don't take this the wrong way—like it's bringing you back to life or something. You seem more like your old self."

Colette nodded. "I know. It's so weird. It's not like I love the work there. I think it's just because I hated Oleander so much. And having good co-workers helps a lot."

"Minus Travis?"

"Minus Travis. But actually, even he is kind of growing on me."

The two of them proceeded to impersonate Darrel the rest of the way to Westmoreland, talking in exaggerated southern accents about Bread & Pan Co. Colette didn't feel too guilty about it; he would have laughed along with them.

Marianne's class went as usual, but Colette felt a new ball of energy pulsing inside of her. It seemed to grow more intense during each exercise, and she felt a sense of urgency spurring her movement. Then, during *rond de jambe,* something strange happened. The air in the studio suddenly felt electrified, as in the moments before a storm. As she took her circular *port de bras*, she found herself closing her eyes. She stretched out and down, circling toward the barre, back and away. The notes from the piano seemed to grow louder until they enveloped her, and she felt delicious chills dance up and down her spine.

"Getting lost in the music, are we?"

Startled, Colette opened her eyes and looked through the mirror at Sammy, who was laughing. She gave a nervous laugh in reply and then stumbled over the next step in the sequence. Whatever happened had made her forget the combination.

After settling back into the rhythm, Colette realized that the music itself was strange and beautiful. It reminded her of the Gustave Moreau paintings she had studied in Art History class—jeweled and mystical. Colette wondered what ballet it was from. She was sure she hadn't heard it before.

"Aaaaaand *relevé*, up to *soussus!*" Marianne instructed. "Hold, hold. Bring the leg up to *retiré*. Good ladies. Stomach strong, shoulders down. Keep lifting!"

Colette stared straight ahead, oblivious to how long Marianne was having them balance. She was still entranced by the mysterious music.

"*Good*, Colette! And *plié*, finish. Beautiful. Good, everyone."

Once the class moved to center, Colette made her way over to Dunja.

"Excuse me; do you know what that song was from?" Colette asked. "The one you played for *rond de jambe*?"

"Yes," Dunja replied in a thick accent. She pointed to the sheet music, which was terribly yellowed and bound with masking tape. "Is from *Cantique de Salomon Pas de Deux.*"

"Huh?" Colette squinted at the title. "Is that handwritten?"

Dunja sighed and pointed to the title again, pausing on each word. "*Cantique... de... Salomon.* You know French?"

"Just a little. *Un peu.*"

"*Cantique* is like… *chanson.*"

"Song. Yes."

"So, like 'song' but more holy. You know—from scriptures. *Song of Solomon.*"

"I didn't know that was a ballet," Colette said. She wasn't sure she had even heard of *Song of Solomon.*

Dunja shrugged. "Me neither, but I like it, this music."

"Me, too."

"Now, please." Dunja waved her on. "I must start adagio."

Puzzled, Colette joined the others who were stretching on the floor. Since she had first become acquainted with ballet, she had devoured whatever information she could find on the subject. Why hadn't she heard of this *pas de deux?*

Tina's shrill voice interrupted her thoughts. "*Where* did you girls get those skirts? I have to have one."

"Oh," Colette said, feeling a tinge of pride. "I actually made them."

"You're kidding! They're adorable. I would pay for those. Can you make me one with a floral print—like Samantha's?"

Sammy rolled her eyes.

"Sure," Colette replied. "I can do that."

She wasn't crazy about the idea of designing a skirt for Tina of all people, but a commissioned project sounded like fun. Sammy threw her a cautionary glance.

"Hey," Colette whispered, scooting close to Sammy. "Did you notice that music during *rond de jambe*? Did it seem strange to you?"

"No, I guess not," Sammy replied. "But you know, I did notice that I've been doing freakishly well tonight. That was probably the best barre I've ever had."

"Me too, actually."

THAT NIGHT, COLETTE had strange dreams, although she could only remember snippets of them. At one point, she was back in ballet class, but the studio looked different. There were huge windows with sheer, white curtains blowing in the breeze, and the air was filled with an energizing fragrance.

When she extended her leg forward *en fondu,* she saw that her foot was covered in henna tattoos. She searched for her reflection, but there was no mirror.

She woke up at 4 a.m. thinking of the *Song of Solomon* music and trying hard to remember how the melody went. She had forgotten it already. How could she have forgotten something so beautiful?

Now wide awake, she decided to search for the music online but found nothing. There was no mention of it anywhere. It was as if such a ballet had never existed.

Then, Colette had another idea. She crept through the dark house to the living room and felt for the bookshelf. Sammy's Bible was there somewhere. As her hands found the leather book, the glint of Garçon's eyes from across the room made her jump. He ran toward her, meowing for food.

"Shhh, kitty," she said, carrying him back to her bedroom.

The sky grew lighter as she sat in bed, reading until she had finished all of *Song of Solomon.* Just like the music, it was strange and beautiful and, Colette was surprised to find, quite erotic. She thought about the love story, the poetic rhythm and all of the vivid, colorful imagery. It really would make a wonderful ballet. Why had it disappeared? And where had Dunja found that music?

Colette set the Bible and Garçon aside so she could lie down. As soon as she drifted back to sleep, her alarm began to sound.

CHAPTER NINE

Colette trudged to Tempe's still half-asleep from her late night of reading. She hoped she wouldn't have to talk to anyone for a while. Maybe she could slip into the bathroom and throw some makeup on before opening.

To her horror, Darrel, Travis, Bonnie and Reid were all standing by the register when she arrived.

"What's going on?" Colette asked.

"Wow, you're not looking too good," Travis said. "You tired?"

Colette squinted at him.

"*Travis,*" Darrel said. It was the first time she had heard Darrel sound disappointed with someone. She liked that it was on her behalf. "What's going on is it seems we're overstaffed this morning. Minor scheduling error. So, I'm real sorry, but we'll need to send somebody home and shuffle the rest of the week around. I'll let the three of you settle it, but, Colette, if you're not feeling well...?"

She saw her chance. "Yeah, I'm honestly not feeling the greatest this morning."

"You should go on home, hun," Bonnie said. "Reid and I can stay."

Reid agreed. Colette knew he would want to stay, and Bonnie had a long drive. It made the most sense, anyway.

"Okay," Colette replied. "If you're sure you don't mind."

"I think that's settled, then," Darrel said. "You get to feeling better."

A smile crept onto Colette's face as she left the store. "Thank you," she whispered, not knowing if she was thanking God or the universe or what. Sometimes things just worked out too perfectly.

Once she had slept for a couple hours, Colette woke up feeling refreshed and decided she should do something nice for her coworkers. Cookies. She could bake them some cookies and deliver them in the evening, lest they be suspicious of her quick recovery time. The chiffon on her sewing table beckoned to her in between cookie batches, and she spent the rest of the day hammering out the skirt she had promised to Tina.

When she stopped back by Tempe's before ballet class, the crew looked as if they had never been more excited to see baked goods. And, of course, they were happy to see her looking better. Travis and Reid dove into the cookie container with both hands, and Darrel gave her two thumbs up, crumbs caught in his goatee. She was glad she had thought of them. Maybe she would do it more often.

COLETTE AND SAMMY waited at the barre, wondering who would be subbing that evening. It seemed to be the day for sick days. New instructors always made Colette nervous. After becoming accustomed to Marianne's teaching style, substitutes and their strange choreography brought in a whole new element of challenge.

Tina stood nearby, already wearing the red and black floral skirt that Colette had made, and proclaimed that it was the most beautiful skirt she had ever seen. She insisted on paying Colette forty dollars for it. Colette made a point of protesting but took the money. She *had* spent a long time on it.

"Look, there's our sub," Sammy whispered. "Damn. This could be distracting."

The teen-aged girls next to her giggled.

Oh no. Colette recognized those yellow sweat pants.

"Hey, everyone. I'm James Brennan. I'm subbing for Marianne today."

James smiled and searched the room for a place to station himself. He found a barre against the wall, lifted it with one arm, and hauled it to the center of the studio. Colette watched silently as he took his time squaring the barre to the mirror. It was only a matter of seconds before he would have to look in her direction. Would he recognize her? Should she say something?

"Uh, they called me sort of last minute," James continued, pushing up his sleeves. "So I apologize if I may seem a bit out of it. It's been awhile since I've taught a class, so I will try really hard not to be confusing. Just stick with me." He smiled again and assumed his first position. "So, let's start right away with *pliés*—oh—"

He locked eyes with Colette, and she saw both recognition and confusion in his expression. "Hey," he said. "Colette, right? You take class here?"

"Hey," she replied. She gave him a brief wave and felt her face turning scarlet. "Yeah, I do."

Sammy stared at her in wonder. "What the—"

Colette quickly bent over, pretended to stretch her hamstring, and whispered, "Tell you later."

"Cool," James said, still puzzled to see her there. "Anyway... Okay. So, from first, two *demi-pliés*. One *grand plié*. Down five, six, up seven and eight. *Plié, relevé, plié relevé*, hold, hold *plié, tendu*. Same thing in second, same thing in fifth. *Tendu* back to first, then we'll take a little stretch to the right and left. Oh. Does everyone know all of that? I mean, should I be explaining any terminology?"

Silence.

"We're good? Sweet. How about after that we take a stretch forward in parallel, too. I'll talk you through it. Any other questions before we start? Feel free to ask anything."

"What do we do with our arms?" Sammy asked.

"Oh, good question. Just keep them in second for this one. Actually, you can do it with the *port de bras*. Or just do whatever feels comfortable to you."

Sammy nodded and turned around for preparation. Colette stared straight ahead, focusing on a tiny dent in the piano instead of the photo of Jael Maier. As she prepared, her sweaty palm slipped off the barre and her knees began to wobble.

Great, she thought. *Class is ruined. Fancy ballet James will know how bad I am and he'll tell Darrel. I'll never dance again.*

As soon as the music started, however, Colette settled into it. Dan the pianist was playing a medley from *Phantom of the Opera* and Colette loved him for it. It was hard to be stressed while dancing to "Angel of Music." Her spirits already slightly elevated, she found a new resolve. Who cares what James would think? There was nothing to prove to him. She would just try her hardest. She would do her best.

James walked around observing, neglecting to call out the steps as he had promised. When he came around to Colette's spot at the barre, he stopped to watch.

"Nice straight back on the *grand plié*," he said. "Very good."

Colette smiled shyly, never knowing whether an audible "thank you" was appropriate during combinations. James's simple comment gave her a surge of confidence. She began to hope that the class might be good after all.

She was not disappointed. As they worked their way through barre, it became evident that James was a decent teacher. The combinations he created were simple with a fun, contemporary feel. Colette watched him demonstrate with great fascination. He managed to have a style that was both precise and boyish. His pointed feet were not elegant but sharp, and he restrained his extension to 90 degrees, his leg shooting out like a threatening arrow. Everything appeared to be ridiculously easy for him. He was wearing a long-sleeved T-shirt and hadn't broken a sweat.

When it came to corrections, James was laid back and generous with compliments. He noticed Sammy's winged feet and steady balance. He took pains to fix Tina's alignment in *passé*, which was something that Marianne had ceased to do. He gave the true beginners extra pointers and praise. And while he encouraged everyone in the class, Colette could tell that he was paying her particular attention.

"See how she actually lifts up to go back?" James said while Colette demonstrated *cambré*. "Nice job... Everyone, watch her head as she comes into arabesque. That's what we're looking for... Great. Nice *développé*. Don't forget to turn out that standing leg—oh, see you're already on top of it... Colette, would you mind moving to the front so the others can follow?"

Colette was extremely relieved to be doing well, especially in the eyes of a professional dancer. There were a few moments when she paused to think about the fact that this was Darrel's son. *Darrel's* son. She could picture Darrel right now, hunched over the counter and staring at his cell phone, his giant fingers pressing the tiny buttons on the screen. She tried to imagine him in the ballet studio, dressed in his Wranglers and Carhardt jacket, watching a tween-aged James during parent observation week. Nope. Then, she tried to picture James dancing through the aisles at Tempe's. She couldn't see that either. He probably wouldn't ever think to do that; he was too busy dancing in real studios and in real performances.

Toward the end of class, James danced a combination with them full out. Colette saw him nail a perfect quadruple *pirouette* like it was no big deal. Although she knew he was probably conserving his energy, she wished she could see him dance more. She wanted to see how high he could jump. Some strange confidence bubbled up inside of her, and she decided that if he didn't demonstrate *grand allegro* for them, she would ask him to.

Before she had the chance, James divided them up and declared that he would go with the last person since the numbers weren't even. Not wanting to miss a prime watching spot, Colette pulled Sammy up to the front with her. Colette rushed her way through the combination and hit her final *grand-jeté* too early, but she didn't care. Out of breath, she and Sammy jogged to the opposite corner and waited to watch James.

He was amazing. He seemed to move to music as naturally as his father conversed with strangers, and his dancing made Colette forget the choreography. There was no *sauté arabesque, failli, contretemps.* No *tombée pas de bourrée, glissade, saut de chat*—just seamless dancing. His strength disguised itself as nonchalance, and his face was calm, as if he were thinking, *no big deal, just dancing here.*

When James repeated the combination to the left side, he added elaborate beats and changed the last step to some sort of Russian leap that Colette had never seen in person. Sammy looked astonished and leaned toward Colette, whose eyes were still glued to James.

"Are you kidding me?" Sammy said. "What *was* that?"

The class erupted in applause when he was finished. He laughed and thanked them, looking a little embarrassed. Perhaps he felt like he had been showing off. No one minded.

"Shoot. Looks like we're out of time," James said. "Thanks, everyone. Thanks for letting me teach. This was fun."

James bowed to the class and everyone curtsied back, thanking him enthusiastically. As the students gradually left, Colette noticed Tina lingering, pretending to mark the *grand allegro* combination and sizing up James for a chat. Realizing that she better thank him while she still had a chance, Colette hurried over to him. Sammy followed, sat down to change her shoes, and watched them with impatient curiosity.

"Hey, thanks for class," Colette said. "That was great."

"Sure," James replied, grinning. "I hope I did okay. I'm on the list of subs, but I'm not really used to teaching."

"No, it really was great. Thank you."

"No problem. I had a lot of fun." He paused and cocked his head to one side. "Hey, how long have you been dancing here?"

"Um... about three years?" Colette glanced at Sammy. "Yeah, a little over three."

"Where did you dance before?"

"Nowhere," Colette replied. "I've only had the three years here."

James looked skeptical. "Three years, altogether? You didn't dance when you were younger?"

"Nope," Colette said, feeling another surge of confidence.

"Wow. You're doing really well," he replied, glancing at Sammy. "Both of you are—"

"Oh, sorry—this is my friend Sammy."

Sammy stood up to greet him. As James extended his hand, Colette caught a glimpse of the tattoo on his forearm, poking out from under the sleeve he had pushed up. She could see that it was text of some sort—something ending in –*ightly*.

Brightly? Unsightly? Does he have to cover that thing up for every performance?

"You know, it's funny," James said. "My dad never mentioned that you took class here."

"I'm not sure we've talked about it," Colette lied. "I usually keep pretty busy at work."

Sammy looked at Colette with raised eyebrows, finally making the connection. They both tried to play it cool.

"Huh. Well you guys should keep dancing. You obviously have a good understanding of ballet. You should probably be taking intermediate."

They both laughed and pretended to be scared, but James insisted they give it a try.

"Okay, we will," Sammy said.

By this point, Tina was tired of waiting her turn. She stuck her head into the little triangle they had formed and looked at James with a saccharine smile. Colette and Sammy stepped back.

"I just wanted to tell you that you gave a lovely class and you are just a joy to watch. Just marvelous. It's so wonderful to see a true artist."

Sammy closed her eyes.

"Oh, thank you," James said, glancing at the clock.

"You know," Tina continued. "I was wondering if you could tell me about your experience with *Don Q*. I've been watching various versions and am intrigued by the changes in the variations over the years. Do you think one version is preferable? Only, I've been telling my friend Deb about them—you know Deb Foster? Her son Aiden is in the youth ballet, top of his class. Anyway, so he is set on dancing *Don Q* for his spring performance, and he needs to have a strong style like yours, you know, very aggressive—very masculine. And I told Deb, I said 'make sure he does the right version' because end of the year performances are so crucial, at least they were when I was in school, which was longer ago than I care to divulge, ahaha…"

Colette and Sammy exchanged looks and decided it was time to leave. Despite wanting to save James from Tina, they knew that this could last a while. They quietly left the studio, and James stood listening politely. Who knew how long he'd be stuck there.

As soon as they were safe in the dressing room, Sammy punched Colette in the arm.

"Dude!" Sammy said. "He is *beautiful.* He even had his sleeves rolled up. You know how I like a good rolled-up sleeve on a man."

"I sure do," Colette replied.

"Did you see him adjusting my *fondu*? He can adjust my *fondu* any day, *if you know what I mean.*"

Colette couldn't help but laugh. "No, I have no idea what you mean."

"How come you didn't tell me he was so handsome?"

"I don't know." Colette shrugged. "I guess I didn't really see it since he reminds me of Darrel."

"He seemed really nice, too."

"Yeah, I guess he did, didn't he?" Colette's gaze drifted, and she began to smile at nothing in particular.

"Uh oh," Sammy said, smirking. "Are we developing a little crush?"

Colette laughed and shook her head. "He's my boss's son *and* a professional dancer. I don't stand a chance."

"Those sound like lame excuses to me."

On the way home, Colette continued to think about James and his parents. She had decided that he was named after the lead in *La Sylphide* but wondered why Jael would name her child after that character. In the ballet, James abandons his fiancée in pursuit of the sylph and, like a moron, unwittingly leads the sylph to her death by following a witch's advice. Sure, he dances well and looks good in kilt, but he's definitely not a hero. What was *the* Jael Maier-Brennan thinking?

"How tall do you think he was?" Colette asked suddenly.

"James? I don't know—six feet? Six foot one?"

"Yeah."

Sammy chuckled to herself, and Colette went back to staring out the window.

CHAPTER TEN

"So, your son taught my ballet class last night," Colette said. She had debated about when she should divulge this information to Darrel. She figured she better lead with it, and there was nothing else to do at the moment. The morning had been painfully slow, and both she and Darrel were sitting by the register as usual, eating the donuts that he had bought from the shop down the street.

"He did?" Darrel replied. "Well how about that!"

"Yep. It was a fun class. He did a good job."

Darrel nodded. "I'm sure he did."

"He seemed surprised that I take class there. Did you not mention it to him?"

"I thought I did?" Darrel thought for a while and then shook his head, apparently annoyed with himself. "You know what? I think I just told Jael. I must be getting old."

Colette smiled at the idea of Darrel talking to Jael Maier about her. It was still too strange to wrap her mind around. And then there was James—how had these polar opposite parents raised such a person?

"How did James get into dancing?" Colette asked. "I mean, I'm sure he kind of inherited it from his mom, but what made him interested in it?"

"Well, he was always dancin' around as a kid, trying to make us laugh." Darrel paused to chuckle. "You know, I can't rightly remember how the serious ballet started. Jael didn't put him in dance class until he was, oh, probably twelve or so. He was always into sports before then, but he was just so good at ballet. 'Course, what he does now is plenty athletic. But you know all about that."

"Yeah," Colette replied. "People don't realize how hard ballet is until they try it."

Darrel nodded. "I'm sure that's true."

"What did he do before he got into the company? I think I remember you saying he only started a couple of years ago?"

"Let's see. After he graduated, he danced with a touring group for several years until he got into Westmoreland. He had to do some serious training for that, and the group he was with—Quadrilogy it was called—hardly paid him anything. I think at one point he was dancing full time, training for his audition and bar-tending at night. I remember I hardly ever saw him."

"Wow. Was Jael ever one of his teachers?" Colette asked, even though she already knew the answer.

"Oh, just for a little while. She quit teaching several years back. It's just too hard on her arthritis. That reminds me. I have something for you. I'll be right back."

Colette wondered what in the world he could have for her besides more donuts. He promptly returned and presented her with a card—an invitation to his 60th birthday party.

"I told Jael she didn't need to go to the trouble," Darrel said. "But it'll be nice to visit with everyone. We'd love to have you if you can make it."

"Aw, okay. Thanks for inviting me. That's really nice of you."

Colette read the invitation. It was next Sunday. She didn't have anything going on that day. No immediate excuses. She wanted to be nice to Darrel, but the thought of being in his house, meeting his celebrity wife, and being faced with James again filled her with anxiety. She would have to find some sort of excuse.

"Time for my break," Colette said. Darrel's phone rang as soon as she got up, but he motioned her on. He had no qualms about talking on his phone loudly in front of whomever, even customers.

"Jimmy," Darrel said. Colette felt her stomach drop. She slowed her pace to listen. "Sounds good. See you in a bit."

With that, she bolted to the break room.

Those thirty minutes passed too quickly. Colette came back from her break to find James hunched over the counter, still talking with his dad.

"Well, there she is now," Darrel said. He switched places with Colette.

"Great. Were you guys gossiping about me?" Colette joked. She typed her code into the register and plopped down on the stool. She was determined to look as nonchalant as possible.

"Now, we wouldn't do that," Darrel replied. James's eyes quickly met his dad's. "Well, I've got to go take care of some markdowns. I'll see you later, buddy."

Colette felt a pang of nervousness as she watched Darrel walk away. Instead of leaving, James lingered and tapped his fingers on the counter, as if drumming to some imaginary music. Colette picked at the tape on the *No Personal Checks* sign until she felt compelled to break the silence.

"So, do you know if you'll be subbing for the adult classes again?" Colette asked.

"I'm not sure," James said. "Probably only if no one else is available. Do you take that class every week?"

"Yeah. I usually take at least three classes a week. I've become a little obsessed."

James smiled. "I get it."

"I guess I'm trying to make up for lost time." She paused to laugh at herself. "It's a little silly, I know."

"It's not silly. I think it's cool that you started as an adult. You're doing really well."

Colette smiled. "Thanks. I just wish I had started earlier. I feel like I could have been better when I was younger, but I don't know. Regardless, I really love it."

"I could tell in class that you love it. You should stick with it."

"I will," Colette promised. "I'll just have to resign myself to never being as good as you are. Darrel is sure proud of you."

James smiled again and looked down at the counter. Colette watched his lips part and close again. Finally, he looked her straight in the eyes and asked, "Does *Darrel* give you a lunch break?"

"Well… yeah," she said, feeling her pulse quicken. "I just had mine."

"Oh."

Colette's face flushed as she searched for something else to say. "What—what about you? Do you have time to eat when you're dancing all day?"

"Yeah, I have to grab something or I'll pass out. Do you eat at noon?"

"…most days."

James nodded. "That's when you'll go tomorrow?"

"Oh," Colette replied, completely confused. "I don't work tomorrow."

"Oh, right." James took his phone out of his pocket. "Shoot, is it one o'clock already? I'd better run."

"Okay," she said. "See ya."

"Bye, Colette."

James gave a brief wave and glanced back at her as he pushed open the door to leave. After hesitating a moment, he was gone.

Colette felt her body relax.

Do you eat at noon? That's when you'll go tomorrow?

Did it mean what she thought it meant? Surely not.

Colette texted Sammy.

Had another run-in with fancy ballet James. Must tell you about it. My pits are sweaty.

SAMMY: *WHAT?!?! DO TELL. Wine and doc party tonight?*

COLETTE: *Um, yes! I'll have to recite the conversation in person. So strange. I think maybe he was trying to ask me out...?*

SAMMY: *OMG! Now I really can't wait!!*

CHAPTER ELEVEN

It was Sunday, the day of Darrel's birthday party, and Colette stood in front of the bathroom mirror curling her hair. Her hands were jittery, and she felt a knot in her stomach. By this point, she and Sammy had re-hashed Colette's conversation with James several times. Sammy assured Colette that it was clear that James was interested in her, no matter how many times Colette half-heartedly denied it. Deep down, she knew that it was true, and it made her nervous.

Sammy insisted that she go to Darrel's party and refused to be used as an excuse.

"Will you go with me, then?" Colette pleaded.

"Let me think about it," Sammy said. "Nope."

So Colette prepared to go. She had made Darrel a birthday card and wrote, *Happy Birthday to the world's best boss!*

To her surprise, she actually meant it.

It didn't take long to get to Darrel's house, which was a small craftsman-style painted hunter green and cream. As she expected, the landscaping was perfectly manicured. Darrel loved a good lawn. She walked up to the porch, took a deep breath, and rang the doorbell.

The exquisite Jael Maier-Brennan was not what Colette expected her to be, although she really didn't know what to expect. It was immediately apparent that Jael was a calm, quiet spirit. Her voice was low and sweet and she moved as deliberately as she spoke. It was as if she were born for adagio. No wonder people admired her dancing so much, Colette thought. It was beautiful, but humble. There was nothing conceited about her movement or her manner.

"I am so glad to meet you," Jael said upon their introduction. She clasped both of Colette's hands and gazed at her warmly. Darrel, looking quite proud, kept glancing back and forth between the two of them. "Darrel has told me such wonderful things about you," Jael continued. "He likes you very much, and I trust no one's opinion more than I do his."

Colette suddenly felt a little choked up. "Oh," Colette stammered. Jael waited patiently. "Well, I'm so excited to meet you. It's an honor, really. I see your photos all over Westmoreland."

"Do they still have those up? I should hope that pictures of James and his friends would replace them by now."

"But they're beautiful."

Jael smiled. "That's kind of you to say. Now, Darrel tells me that you are an excellent dancer."

"Oh, no! Not at all," Colette replied, mortified. "I mean, I've taken classes for a few years but I wouldn't call myself a dancer, let alone an excellent one. I've never even performed or anything. It's just for fun. I'm what you would call an 'adult beginner.'"

"Colette, the most freeing thing about dance is that you don't need to perform to be a dancer. If dance is in your soul and it comes out through your body, you are a dancer. It's as simple as that." Jael squeezed Colette's hand. "And I can tell that you are. You're a beautiful dancer."

Now, Colette was choked up, for sure. She could find nothing to say in response, and Jael suggested they move into the living room to wait for the others to arrive. James, it turned out, was upstairs showering and his brother Josh and his family, Darrel informed her, were always late. It occurred to Colette that no other guests were mentioned besides these immediate family members.

"Darrel," Colette whispered. "Is it just your family and me? Am I the only one coming?"

"Oh, well I invited everyone at Tempe's. They were all busy, it turns out. I sure am glad you could make it, though. I especially wanted you to meet the family."

Colette was both confused and honored. Why did this old man like her so much? What had she done to earn his respect?

While Darrel started a fire "for ambiance," Colette sat alert, observing her surroundings. The Brennan home was neat and clean and flooded with light. Sheer, white curtains obscured the windows, and the rooms were painted in tranquil shades of green and gray. Jael's aesthetic was simple. Clean lines, earth tones, fresh flowers, and oak furniture. Nothing alluded to the fact that she had once been a great dancer. The only hint of ballet was a picture on the mantle. From what Colette could see, it was a photo of James dressed in a stretchy prince costume, mid-*cabriole.*

Colette watched Jael as she came back from the kitchen carrying two glasses of iced tea. Her body, which had remained willowy, looked effortlessly elegant as she placed the glasses down on the coffee table. Colette wondered if she still went through her ballet checks—shoulders down, stomach strong, neck long—or if these habits were just ingrained in her. Maybe she couldn't break them if she tried.

"I know how much you like tea," Jael told her. "This is my favorite Irish Breakfast tea. I first had it in Dublin and recently found that I could order it online. I was so delighted to have some again. Do you take sugar?"

"Wow, thank you. Unsweetened is fine."

I know how much you like tea. What the heck?

Under normal circumstances, Colette would have found this familiarity utterly creepy. But these people were special. They had some sort of hold over her that she didn't mind, for once. She felt lucky to be invited into their home—to catch a glimpse of this family and to be known by Jael Maier.

"I love this coffee table," Colette said. It was rustic, yet contemporary, with oxidized copper hardware. "I've never seen anything quite like it."

"Oh, James built that. Isn't it beautiful? He's quite the carpenter."

Suddenly, the tranquility surrounding Jael, her tea, and her spotless home was interrupted by shouting coming from outside. The front door burst open, and two small children came barreling toward Jael and Darrel.

"Oh my goodness!" Jael laughed as she was bombarded by the smaller of the two, a red-headed boy with a sticky face. "Well, hello Hunter. And how are you?"

"Gramma J, see my new shoes?" He stomped one foot against the floor.

"Wow! Those are amazing! Did Daddy buy those for you?"

"Pshh, no. I can't keep track of their sizes for the life of me." Colette turned around to see who this new voice belonged to—a tall, jovial man in his early thirties who had Jael's amber eyes. He extended his hand out to Colette. "Hey, I'm Josh. You must be Nicole?"

"Colette."

"Colette!" Josh grimaced and bonked himself on the head. "Right, sorry."

"That's okay," she replied, laughing at his penitent expression. "Close enough."

"Where's Audrey?" asked Jael.

"Oh, she's getting Molly out of the car," Josh replied.

"Hadn't you better help her, Josh?"

He threw his head back. "Yes, mother!"

Colette chuckled. Josh didn't seem to care that his mother was *the* Jael Maier-Brennan, but he made Colette feel more at ease already.

The older child, a girl with bright eyes and long hair, was sitting on Darrel's lap and laughing hysterically. He had a shiny, pink plastic cuff on top of his head.

"No, Pa," she said. "You can't wear my bracelet!"

"Why not?"

"Because you're a boy!" She grabbed it, hopped off his lap and almost tripped over Colette as she backed away.

"Watch out, sweetheart," said Darrel.

The girl looked up and was startled to see a stranger.

"What a pretty bracelet," Colette said.

She grinned and whispered. "You can wear it."

"Aw," Colette said, smiling as the girl daintily placed the bracelet on her wrist. "Thank you."

Josh and Audrey entered with a baby carrier and several bags. Audrey gave orders as she made a beeline to the kitchen. Colette heard a muffled exclamation, something like, "Well, why didn't you say she was here?" and she reappeared, her hand extended as she walked over.

"Hi, I'm Audrey! So sorry—we're so rude!"

"Not at all. I'm Colette. Nice to meet you."

"Rose, Hunter, have you said hi to Miss Colette?"

"They have," Colette responded, hoping to save them some fear. She remembered what it was like to be a kid. "Your children are adorable."

"Oh, thank you. Molly is our four-month old—"

"Hey, where's Jimmy?" Josh interrupted.

"Showering," Jael replied.

"What? Why? Did they turn his water off or something?"

"No. He didn't have time to go home. He ought to be done by now."

"He's such a woman! Oh, wait, I see... " Josh chuckled and winked at Colette. "He's getting all dolled up for our company."

She blushed, despite her best efforts to play along with the joke. Crap, was this Darrel's birthday party or a legit set-up? How would she act normally at all, now?

It was too late to speculate, however, as James himself was coming down the stairs. He was running his hands through a scruffy pile of hair, which was still damp. The yellow sweatpants were gone, thankfully, and replaced by dark-washed jeans. Colette noticed that his pale turquoise T-shirt matched his eyes.

"Hey, Mom?" James shouted. Jael hadn't heard him. Should Colette say something? "Mom! Oh, hey—good to see you again."

"Good to see you, too," Colette said.

"It's cool of you to come. My dad is really happy about it."

"Ha, yeah... Did you have a good shower?" Colette cringed. *Why the heck did I say that?*

"Yeah, although the water pressure sucks here."

"Oh, that does suck." *Someone save us.*

"Hey broseph," Josh said. "Don't you smell nice."

"Joshua. How's it going?" The two exchanged a brotherly hug. Quick embrace, double pat to the back.

"Good, good. Colette and I were wondering if you were shaving your legs in there."

Colette nearly choked on her tea. "We were?"

"Male dancers do that, right?" Josh asked. "Better air speed velocity and whatnot."

"Naw, not really," James replied, shaking his head. "I hear you shave your chest, though."

Josh leaned in closer so only the three of them could hear. "That was *one* time, dammit."

"Does Audrey even know about that?"

"Know what?" Audrey called from the kitchen.

"Seriously? How come you always hear *everything*? Hunter, stop that!" As Josh left to keep his son from jumping on the couch, a thought occurred to Colette. She had something she could talk to James about.

"Oh, so James..." Colette tried to sound nonchalant again. "Have you heard of a *Song of Solomon* ballet? Actually, it would be *Cantique de Salomon.*"

"Hmm... No, I don't think so."

"The pianist played a piece from it in class recently—a *pas de deux*. I've been intrigued by it ever since. I can't seem to find anything out about it, though."

"Huh. Yeah, I don't think I've ever heard of it. Hey, Mom?"

Jael poked her head around the kitchen entryway.

"Have you heard of a *Song of Solomon* ballet?" James looked at Colette for help.

"*Cantique de Salomon,*" she added.

"It doesn't ring any bells," Jael replied. "I certainly never danced it."

"Maybe I'll ask Lavoisier," James said, turning back to Colette. "He's—you know, been around for a while. I'm sure he knows about it."

"Really? That would be great."

Henri Lavoisier was the artistic director of the Westmoreland Ballet, and he was rather ancient. Colette received newsletters supposedly written by him; they would always end with a photocopy of his wobbly signature and a head shot that was probably ten years old. Even then, his hair was solid white, but Colette had found him to be a handsome older man. He reminded her of Christopher Plummer or some other old movie star.

"Is he easy to talk to, then?" Colette asked. "I mean, is he approachable?"

"Oh, yeah. He's one of the reasons I auditioned for Westmoreland. He's not stuffy at all. I'll let you know what I find out."

James uncrossed his arms, and Colette noticed that his whole tattoo was finally visible. The words *Freely & Lightly* ran the entire length of his forearm in Old English script. She wanted to ask what it meant but couldn't bring herself to.

Jael called them into the dining room to eat, and Colette continued to watch James as he walked before her. The fabric of his shirt was wearing thin, clinging to his lean muscles. She could see every slight definition in his back and shoulders. Maybe he wasn't *that* much like Darrel.

After settling in and passing food around, Colette felt the surreality of this new environment begin to wear off. She was sitting down to dinner with a very tangible family. Dance aside, there was nothing immediately extraordinary about them, save that they were kind and rather funny. She was glad Darrel extended the invitation, regardless of how awkward she had felt about it twenty minutes ago.

"All right. Will y'all pray with me?" Darrel asked as he bowed his head. Colette followed, hoping she wouldn't be expected to contribute. But Darrel's prayer was short and heartfelt, like most of his communication. He even thanked God that Colette had joined them that evening. She felt rather honored.

"So, Colette," Audrey said. "Tell me how you ended up at Tempe's? Are you in school?" Colette paused to swallow the bite of salad in her mouth. "Oh, I'm sorry!"

"No, you're fine! Um, no, I sort of just wound up there. I have a degree in fashion design, which isn't the most practical thing in the world. So, I haven't had much luck finding a job. Tempe's is just down the street from me; I used to jog by it all the time. One day, I just felt like I should apply. So, I did."

"Just like that?"

"Yeah, it was on a whim. Everyone thought I had gone a little crazy. I mean—I'm obviously not too experienced when it comes to manly tools."

This inspired some laughter from the family, but James studied her silently. Their eyes met, and one corner of his mouth turned up into a sly smile.

"Anyway," Colette continued, her eyes still resting on James. "I'm glad I did."

"She's doing such a great job," Darrel added. "She picked things up faster than the manly men."

At this, Hunter and Rose started giggling. They repeated "manly men!" over and over again until they were cracking themselves up, along with everyone else.

"Well, thank you, Darrel," Colette said, talking over the laughter. "Lucky for me, I have a great boss."

Jael seemed to greatly approve of this comment.

Colette stayed longer than anticipated and, by the end of the evening, felt quite comfortable with the Brennans. She felt genuine and particularly quick-witted, and she was proud to have made them laugh on several occasions. She couldn't remember ever feeling that way with so many new acquaintances.

As Josh and his family prepared to leave, Colette thanked Jael for hosting and wished Darrel a happy birthday once more. They both gave her hugs. Then, she said goodbye to James, feeling awkward about not hugging him.

"Talk to you soon?" James asked. "I'll let you know what Lavoisier says."

"Yeah, that'd be great."

"Cool. Have a good night."

Colette looked down to find Rose by her side.

"Are you coming back?" Rose asked.

"Sure, I'd like to come back sometime. Oh, this belongs to you, doesn't it?" She stooped down to return the bracelet.

Rose grinned and wriggled her hand into hers. Colette felt her heart melting. Rose's little hand was warm and chubby, and it gripped hers tightly until Josh told her that it was time to get into the car.

CHAPTER TWELVE

Tempe's was strangely quiet for a Saturday. At the moment, there was no one in the shop except Colette. Travis had left her with a violent-looking garden cultivator for protection while he went across the street. She had to admit, it was a funny gesture.

Now, she stood alone with a notepad in hand, staring at the air compressors. She had put a customer on hold while she tried to find a particular model. After only a minute, she was overjoyed to find one that matched the number she had written down. *Yes*. It was such a relief when phone calls were easy.

As she made her way back to the front, her stomach leapt. James was outside, crossing the street. She was sure he had come to see her and, this time, she was glad. Thank God she had decided to wash her hair that morning.

"Sir? Yes, we do have that model. I can put it on hold for you if you… $159.99. Yes." James was now in the shop, grinning and keeping his distance as he waited for her to finish. Colette smiled back, hoping this man on the phone would shut up soon. "Sure, we can do that. Monday at 9 a.m. Uh huh… Until 6…. Yeah. Okay, sounds great. Thanks, we'll see you then! Uh huh... No problem. Take care. Bye bye."

James had made his way to the front and was resting his elbows on the counter, leaning in toward her. "Hard to get off the phone, huh?"

"Yeah," Colette replied. "What brings you here? Darrel's not in today."

"Well, I actually wanted to see *you*," James said.

Colette's stomach fluttered again. *Man, he smells good.* "You did?"

"Yeah. I talked to Lavoisier about that *pas de deux*—the *Song of Solomon* one."

"Oh, yeah? Had he heard of it?"

"He hadn't, but he talked to some people he knows at some dance archive. There's hardly any information about it, but it's super old. Like, eighteenth-century old."

"Wow."

"Yeah. I guess it was performed briefly in Paris, but it wasn't well-received, which makes sense. You know, considering all those Enlightenment ballets were about Greek myths." Colette nodded and smiled, certain that James was quoting Lavoisier at this point. He didn't seem like the type of dancer who would be terribly familiar with ballet history. "Anyway, there were no choreographers or composers listed. It's really weird."

"So, *no one* knows where it came from? That's bizarre."

"Right? Obviously, Lavoisier was crazy fascinated by the fact that you saw the sheet music for it."

"No kidding. I wonder how Dunja got a hold of it."

"I have no idea. He seems really curious about it, though. He asked if you wouldn't mind finding out more, if you could. For some reason he was hesitant to bother her about it, but since you already had the conversation—"

"Sure, I can do that," Colette said. She could guess why even Lavoisier would want to postpone a meeting with Dunja. "Huh. Thanks so much for asking him."

"No problem. I'm pretty intrigued, myself. You said you liked the music, right?"

"I did. I loved it. There was something really unique about it. It would be awesome to see it performed."

A customer suddenly appeared in the doorway, startling the two of them out of their conversation.

"Hi, how are you today?" Colette asked.

The man gave a half-hearted smile in response and disappeared into the automotive section. They both chuckled, and James saw his opportunity.

"So, what are you up to tonight?" he asked.

"Not much, really. Might just stay home. You?"

"Well, I actually wondered if you'd like to have dinner with me," James said, his expression sincere and hopeful. "That is, if you're up for it after you get off."

Colette was pleasantly surprised by his directness this time, although, she also hadn't prepared herself for it. She was trying to mask the grin that was creeping onto her face. After a couple of seconds, she decided to let it go. She liked him, so why pretend otherwise?

"Sure," she said, smiling her brightest smile.

JAMES HAD COME back to Tempe's and was waiting outside. They had agreed to walk together to the Mexican restaurant down the street once Colette finished her shift. Seeing him waiting especially for her made Colette giddy. She was anxious to join him, but Travis was counting down the register at a snail's pace. He eyed James suspiciously.

"What's Darrel's kid doing out there?" Travis asked.

"He's waiting on me," Colette replied. "We're going to dinner."

"You're kidding. With *that* guy?"

"Yeah. What's wrong with that?"

"Hmph," Travis snorted. He shoved a stack of dollar bills back into the register. "You sure he's not gay?"

Colette rolled her eyes. "Not all dancers are gay, you know. And yeah, I'm pretty sure. Besides, why should it even matter? We're just going to dinner."

"I don't know, sweetheart. I'd be careful with that one."

"Yeah, well, thanks for the advice," Colette said, throwing her purse over her shoulder. "Are you done with me? I should have been off like five minutes ago."

"Okay then." He waved her on. "Go on, have fun."

"Thanks," Colette said, already walking away from him.

"Be safe!" Travis called after her.

Colette gritted her teeth and let the door slam behind her.

"You okay?" James asked.

"Yeah, I just—ugh, I hate that guy sometimes."

"What did he just say to you?"

"He said to 'be safe,'" Colette said, rolling her eyes again. "And, um, he was trying to convince me that you're gay."

James laughed. "What a jackass. I'm not, by the way. In case you were wondering."

"I wasn't. Why did Dar—your dad—hire him, anyway?"

"You know how he is. He likes to give everyone a chance."

Colette supposed he was right.

They arrived at the restaurant early for a Saturday night, and they seemed to be the only guests under the age of sixty-five. That was fine with Colette. It felt less like a serious date. James asked if they could eat outside if it wasn't too cold, and Colette was glad he had suggested the idea. The patio was quiet and isolated, and the sky had already begun to morph into a collage of oranges and pinks. When the waiter asked for drink orders, Colette went with water to be safe. James ordered a beer.

Surprised, she asked, "Can you drink during the season?"

"Normally I try not to—especially when a performance is coming up. But we're between shows. Plus, tomorrow's my day off."

"Oh, I see," Colette replied. She looked down at her menu and added, "I um, I actually made it to your last show. The first Sunday matinee."

James smiled. "You did?"

"Yeah. It was amazing. How did the other performances go?"

"Good," he said, nodding and squinting at the menu. "No major fails."

They sat in silence for a minute, both contemplating their orders, but Colette's eyes wandered back to James. She took in an assortment of details—his bruised thumbnail, his black Adidas jacket, the sunset glow on his face—and felt what remained of her nervousness give way to curiosity. Suddenly, she wanted to know everything about him, and there he was now, sitting right across from her.

The waiter appeared again. "Are you two ready to order?"

"Sure," Colette said. She had thought about getting a salad but decided James might as well know about her eating habits from the get-go. "I'll take the *carne asada* tacos with a side of guacamole. And, um, could I actually get a margarita as well? On the rocks, with salt."

"Certainly. And for you, sir?"

"Yeah…" James was still studying the menu. "Could I get the ranchero salad?"

Crap.

"Of course."

"And also the steak quesadilla platter. Plus, could we get some more chips and salsa? I'm gonna knock these out here in a minute."

"No problem. We'll have that right out for you."

"Dude," Colette said, laughing. "Did you just order two meals?"

"Yeah. I'm starving," James said. He began to devour tortilla chips as if his life depended on it.

"I'm actually relieved. I thought you were just going for a salad, which would make me feel like a fatty." Colette was surprised at her own honesty. Was that a weird thing to say? But James was already laughing and coughed on the chip he had begun to swallow.

He cleared his throat. "You're definitely not a fatty."

Colette figured she better change the subject. "So, were you named after the guy from *La Sylphide?*"

James laughed again. "No. Why?"

"Oh. I just thought maybe you were."

"Nope," he said, polishing off the rest of his salsa. "What about you? I've never met anyone named Colette before."

"Yeah. My mom was learning French when she was pregnant with me. She found the name in her textbook. Nothing too exciting." She paused and slid her bowl of salsa over to James. His eyes lit up, as if she had just offered him a small fortune.

"Really?" he asked, holding a chip at the ready.

"Sure," Colette replied, laughing. "Oh, I meant to ask you the other night if you ever worked at Tempe's?"

"I actually never did. Josh did for a couple of summers, though. Do you think you'll stay there for a while?"

"I don't know. It was supposed to be temporary, but I really don't know what I want to do. I need to figure that out."

"Dad told me about what happened at Oleander," he said. "I'm sorry. That really sucks."

"Yeah." Colette nodded. "But, you know, I don't care so much anymore. Tempe's is way less stressful. Your dad is really great. Does he ever even get angry?"

"Not very often." James paused. "Oh, there was this one time when Josh and I took his truck to a party outside the city. Josh hit a deer with it. He was pretty pissed then. But then we brought the deer back with us and he made jerky out of it, so he got over it."

Colette laughed. "Seriously?"

"Yep. He still talks about how good it was. He kept the rack, too. It's in his office."

"That's hilarious! I totally thought that was a hunting trophy. Turns out he has roadkill on his desk."

"That's my dad." James chuckled and sat back in his chair as if his hunger had been temporarily satisfied. He watched Colette, saw her shiver and began to unzip his jacket. "Here—"

"Oh, no. That's okay—"

He had already stood up and began to drape it over her shoulders. "No, really. I should have given it to you sooner."

"Well, thank you," Colette said, feeling the warmth soak into her skin. She looked around them and realized that the sky had already turned dark. "I was fine before the sun went down. You sure you'll be warm enough?"

"Oh, yeah. I'm good," James replied. The self-assured expression on his face seemed to produce an instant calming effect—something that reminded Colette of both Jael and Darrel.

"So," she said. "I'm kind of fascinated by your parents. Is it ever weird to you to think about them getting together? I mean, it obviously works, but they seem so... well, different in a lot of ways."

James shrugged. "I guess I haven't thought about it much. I don't know. I mean, Mom was this great dancer, but she has always had a level head. She was okay with giving it up for a family. I think she actually prefers having a simple life. They're both similar that way."

Colette took a sip of her margarita. "How did they meet?"

"Um, night school or something. Yeah, they were both taking a college course and had to do a project together. I think they bonded over their blue-collar jobs. Dad was on a road crew at the time—"

"*Blue-collar?*" Colette set her glass down. "Your mom was a ballerina!"

"Yeah, which is manual labor."

She thought for a minute. "Oh my goodness... you're totally right. It *is* manual labor—made to look easy. I've never thought about it that way."

"I have the missing toenails to prove it."

Colette laughed. "Gross."

James smiled, sat back and rested the beer bottle on his knee. "What about your family? What are they like?"

"Well, my mom and stepdad live in Houston now, so I don't see them very often. Although, they're actually coming to visit tomorrow. And my dad died when I was four, so I don't see him much either. That's probably a good thing."

"Shoot," James said. He sat up straight. "I'm so sorry."

"It's okay," she replied, struck by the expression on his face. It was a look of concern without the discomfort that others sometimes had upon broaching the subject. His eyes had grown bigger and softer, and they peered into hers without a hint of embarrassment.

"Can I ask how he died?"

The waiter appeared with their meals, but James didn't glance at his food. He sat still, with his hands on his knees, and waited for Colette to answer his question.

"He had a heart attack," she replied, digging into her dinner. "I barely remember him, but he was pretty cool."

"Do you have any siblings?"

"Just Seth, my stepbrother. He and his wife live in California. We get along well but aren't close at all. I actually can't remember the last time I talked to him."

"Do you have *any* family around?"

"Nope, not really."

"Wow. That must be hard," James said. The same, soft expression fell upon his face—a look of compassion, rather than pity.

She smiled and shrugged. "I'm used to it. It's neat how close your family is. You're very lucky."

James agreed.

"So," she said, eager to move on to a new topic. "I've noticed your tattoo. Is there a story with it?"

"Oh, yeah." James turned his palm up and observed his own arm. "It's just a good reminder to myself. You know, to live freely and lightly."

Colette couldn't decide if his answer was extremely obscure or extremely simple, but she decided not to press the matter. "Cool," she said. "I like it."

"I have another along my ribs here. It's of a phoenix. It's pretty bad-ass." James paused to laugh at himself. "No big deal."

They continued talking for over an hour, though they spoke very little of ballet. Colette was curious about his life at Westmoreland but was careful not to bring it up too much. She assumed that he probably got tired of talking about his job. Plus, she was just enjoying his company. Like Darrel, he was easy to talk to, but also much cooler and more attractive—the perfect genetic combination of his parents.

When the waiter brought the check, James quickly grabbed it and refused Colette's offer to split the bill. She found his insistence to be quite chivalrous, considering he was already paying for his own two meals. He couldn't be making much money, could he?

Colette checked her phone and found a message from Sammy.

B!tch where u at?

Colette laughed and remembered that Sammy had been out with co-workers that evening. She had probably had a few drinks already.

"I forgot to tell my roommate that I was going out. She's kind of protective. Oh wait, I forgot you've met Sammy before."

"Oh, yeah. I remember."

"Um, would you mind giving me a ride home when we're done? I actually walked to work today."

"Yeah, no problem. Did you want to go now?"

No. Yes. Come with me. Or not.

"Either way," Colette said. "I'm up for hanging out longer if you are... Would you want to come over for a while?"

"Sure." James nodded. "That sounds good."

"Great. I'll just let Sammy know."

Been having dinner with James. Bringing him home now. Please check the bathroom trash for visible tampons.

CHAPTER THIRTEEN

Colette sat in the living room, waiting for her mom and Craig to arrive. It had been over a year since they had come to visit, yet they were only staying for the day on their way up to Lincoln. Colette was too happy—and too sleepy—to care much, though.

She and Sammy had stayed up hours after James left. He had become visibly tired by 10 p.m. and had gone reluctantly, hoping Colette wouldn't think he was too lame. She assured him that she understood. He had had Saturday class and a rehearsal earlier that day.

When they were alone, Sammy had hugged her and squealed, "Oooh, I'm not ready for you to get married yet!"

"Married?! You're getting way ahead of yourself."

"I don't think so," Sammy said, staring down into her wine glass with one eye shut. "He's *so* much better than what's-his-face—your last boyfriend. Or Chad! Oh man, do you remember Chad?"

Colette cringed. "Of course I remember him. I threw away my V-card with that loser."

"Well," Sammy said. "I can tell you right now. James is perfect for you. You seem so cozy—no, what'stheword—*comfortable!* You seem comfortable around him."

Colette realized that Sammy was right; she had certainly come a long way from wanting to hide from him. She felt that she had been uncharacteristically bold by inviting him over, and yet, nothing felt unnatural. Although she had a lot to learn about James, she sensed that she already understood him. It was as if he had always been around.

COLETTE HEARD THE *thunk* of a car door. They were here. She took a deep breath and went outside.

"Sweetheart!"

"Hey, Mom. Hi, Craig. It's good to see you."

Colette hugged them both and led them into the house. As usual, they were impeccably dressed. Lillian had always been stylish, even during her years as a poor single mother. As a child, Colette was enchanted by her mother's peony pink lipstick and breezy floral dresses, and she remembered insisting on playing with Lillian's Estée Lauder samples over her waxy play makeup.

"My Colette already has a sense of luxury," Lillian would tell her friends. "She has better taste than I do. And she *always* carries a handbag."

"Oh, she will be just like you when she grows up," they would say, smiling down at the ecstatic Colette. "What a little fashionista."

With her green eyes and delicate freckles, it was true that she had grown up to resemble her mother, whose face was starting to sag a little. Colette's dark hair, however, had come from her father. She remembered Craig complimenting her on it when they first met, unwittingly winning her over. She was an awkward thirteen-year-old at the time and, by then, had grown to feel a little inadequate next to her blond bombshell of a mother. Craig had offered few praises since then, but he had at least earned her loyalty. He was the second love of Lillian's life, and Colette knew it couldn't be easy for him.

"Oh, honey, it's so good to be with you again," Lillian said.

"Thanks for making the trip."

"It's about time we came by," Craig said. He leaned forward to stretch his back. "I'm glad we didn't drive the fourteen hours. The trip from the airport alone nearly did me in."

"It's not *that* far," Colette laughed. "How long is your conference?"

"A week, but we'll try to head back early—"

"Sweetheart," Lillian said. "We were thinking of taking you out to brunch. What do you think?"

"That sounds good, Mom."

"Is Sammy here? Does she want to come with us?"

"No, she's gone."

"Oh, that's too bad. I always like visiting with her. Is she seeing anyone?"

"Not at the moment."

"I don't see why not," Lillian replied. "She's such an attractive young lady. Takes good care of herself." Craig nodded in agreement. "What about you, honey? Anyone new?" Colette didn't want to talk about James. Not yet. But she had hesitated too long. "Oh, yes there is, isn't there?! Who is he?"

"It's nothing serious. We only had our first date last night."

"Oh!"

"Calm down, Mom."

"But it's so exciting! What's his name? How did you meet?"

"His name is James and he's my boss's son."

"What does he do?" Craig asked.

Colette grinned in disbelief of what she was about to say. She cleared her throat. "He's a professional ballet dancer."

"Oh, how neat!" Lillian exclaimed.

Craig looked horrified. "He's a ballerina?"

"They're called ballet dancers," Colette replied flatly. "Or *danseurs,* if you want to be fancy. Anyway, he's a nice guy and he has a really great family. They're really close."

Her mother's face fell a little, as if this were a personal dig at her. She lowered her voice. "Well, I think that's great, sweetheart. He sounds lovely."

"How's your car running?" Craig asked. To his credit, he always became aware of Colette's practical needs when they were face-to-face.

"Fine."

"When's the last time you took it to the shop?"

"I don't know. Whenever I needed an oil change. I barely use it now that I work so close."

"I'd like to take it out for a spin, if you don't mind. Make sure everything's in order."

"Oh, you don't have to—"

"It's no trouble," he insisted. "I'll only be a few minutes."

"Well, okay, I guess. Thanks, Craig."

"Be right back. Look after your mother while I'm gone." He winked without smiling, and Colette gave him her keys.

Lillian sat close to her daughter, happy to have a moment alone with her. She stroked Colette's hair and said, "My, it has gotten long."

"Yeah."

"You just get more and more beautiful, sweetheart."

"Ugh. Thanks, Mom."

"So, do you really like this young man?"

"I feel weird talking about it... I barely know him, but yes—I like him. I wouldn't have gone out with him, otherwise."

"And his dad is your boss? What is he like?"

"Darrel? He's a little backwoods, but he's a really good guy. Super nice. I think he's been wanting me and James to go out for a while."

"Well of course he would!" Lillian began to dig through her purse.

"But I'm not getting my hopes up. Like I said, I barely know him yet."

"I know, honey." She produced a small stack of cash. "Here, I want you to take this."

Colette could see that the stack contained $100 bills. She shook her head. "No, Mom. I don't want to take your money."

"No, no. You listen. I know you must be a little low on cash what with your—you know—temporary job situation. Craig and I want you to have it. We insist."

"Seriously. I don't need it. I don't want to take it. I'm too old for this."

"You sound just like your dad," Lillian said. She smiled, and her eyes began to water. "Please, honey. I'm not around to take care of you. It's the least I can do."

Colette shook her head again. "I would rather you visit longer than give me all this money. I know Craig's busy, but why can't you come without him?"

"I know," Lillian whispered, tears now running down her cheeks. "I should. I just feel like I can't leave him. I have to keep him healthy."

"Mom, he's a surgeon. I'm sure he can take care of himself while you're gone a few days."

Lillian laughed at herself and let out a sigh. "I suppose you're right."

Colette nodded. As she watched her mother cry, she began to cry, too. It had been a while since she had felt empathy for her, rather than frustration. She had always been impatient with her mother's fragility, and she resented the way she seemed so content to live a life of easy luxury on Craig's salary. Colette had been both envious of her freedom and repulsed by offers to "take care of her" in the same way, should she ever join them in Houston.

Now, Colette found herself wondering if she had been a little too hard on her since they had moved away. She and Craig seemed happier, as if finally entering the honeymoon phase they never had. New city, new memories. Maybe Colette couldn't blame her for not visiting; she probably didn't want to leave her life of domestic bliss.

The front door swung open, jarring the two of them. Craig had come back and looked startled to see them in such an emotional state.

"What happened?" he asked.

"Oh, nothing," Lillian said. She dabbed her face. "We just miss each other. Honey, I'm going to put this on your dresser." Looking determined, she held up the money.

Colette sighed. "Okay."

"Your car looks good," Craig said. "You've been taking care of it."

Colette smiled. The joke was on him. "Good. Thanks for checking on it. We ready for brunch?"

"I am. Let's make your mother decide on the place."

FOR THE DURATION of her parents' visit, Colette's mind often wandered to James. Would he text her that day? Should she text him? She didn't want to look too eager.

To her surprise, he called her while they were out that afternoon. She felt giddy as she listened to his voice mail. He wanted to see what she was up to. He had a good time last night. Oh, and he might have left his jacket in the living room. He would try to catch her later.

Colette found his jacket on the love seat and smiled as she remembered Garçon curling up on it the night before. She had apologized, but James hadn't minded. He had said something about Garçon looking comfy, had sat down close to him, and patted him on the head.

Colette smiled again and picked up her phone.

Hey, James. Sorry I missed your call! I've been out with my parents. I had fun last night, too. I'll call you as soon as they leave.

JAMES: *I forgot. No hurry.*

COLETTE: *I found your jacket. Do you need it soon?*

JAMES: *Might be nice. I can stop by today. Don't want to interrupt, though.*

Colette suddenly had a crazy idea. She looked at Lillian and Craig and asked, "Hey, would you guys want to meet James before you go? He left his jacket here."

Lillian's face lit up.

"I would," Craig said sternly.

"Okay. I'll see if he can stop by."

Colette stepped into the hallway to call him.

"Colette?" James answered.

"Hey. Um, I just had an idea and thought I'd call real quick. Feel free to say no, but I wondered if you'd want to stop by while my mom and Craig are still here. I know it's kind of soon to meet them, though. I understand if you feel weird—"

"Sure. Should I come now?"

"Okay, yeah." Her palms began to sweat. "Now would be great."

Colette and Lillian chatted nervously until James arrived. He came in without knocking, letting a cool breeze into the house. He was wearing another soft T-shirt—a gray one this time, and his face was clean-shaven. They had only locked eyes before James walked over to Craig, hand extended. Colette had the sudden desire to kiss him.

"This is my stepdad, Craig," Colette said. "Craig, this is James."

"Hey man," James said. "Nice to meet you."

Craig observed him closely. "You've got a good handshake."

"And this is my mom, Lillian."

"So nice to meet you," she said. "My, aren't you handsome?"

The four of them visited long after Colette had returned James's jacket. Craig interrogated James about his career and worldly possessions, which he endured patiently. Colette learned a few new things about him thanks to Craig's thoroughness, mainly that he was interested in choreographing. In fact, he had already been creating small pieces for the company's showcase performances. The more Colette thought about this, the more it made sense to her. He seemed to be too laid back to be a serious performer for long. And it was clear that he enjoyed constructing things—from the combinations in class to Jael's coffee table.

James made a point of reciprocating Craig's questions and seemed genuinely interested in his tales from surgery. Colette was relieved. Craig told his story about the patient who died mid-sentence and promptly finished his thought as soon as he was resuscitated. James laughed right on cue.

Colette and James were sharing the love seat. She felt strangely at ease next to him. Her mind started to drift, imagining what it would have been like if they had met in high school or college, before Colette realized that Lillian had been talking at James for several minutes. She was praising Colette's wit and listing her talents.

Colette cringed with embarrassment, but James looked at her with genuine admiration. They locked eyes again, and he reached for her hand. She smiled slightly, trying not to look like this was a big deal to her. But it was. She squeezed his hand back and settled in closer to him.

"You two are just adorable," Lillian said. She looked as if she might cry again.

This comment annoyed Craig, but it was clear that he had been impressed by James. As they got ready to leave, he nodded solemnly at Colette as if to say, *I approve for now.* James and Colette walked them out, hugging, shaking hands and making vague plans for future visits.

Lillian held Colette tightly and whispered in her ear. "He's *wonderful.* I love you so much, sweetheart."

"Love you, too, Mom."

AS THEY DROVE away, Colette realized that she was about to be completely alone with James for the first time. That is, if he even wanted to stay.

James held the door open for her. "Mind if I stay here a while?"

"Of course you can," Colette said. "What do you want to do?"

"Just be with you," he said, plopping down on the couch. His clear, aqua eyes were at once serious and playful. Colette's stomach fluttered. She sat close to him, smiled, and tucked her legs in toward her chest.

"I like you, you know," she said without thinking. It was the first time she had ever disclosed her affection so freely.

James grinned. "I like you, too. It's weird—I feel like I've known you for a long time."

"I know what you mean."

They sat still, gazing at each other for a while. Colette felt comfortable with the silence. Now, it was strange to remember how awkward she had felt with him before. How had things changed so quickly?

"You know, that first time we met at Tempe's," she said. "I thought you didn't like me."

James laughed. "Why?"

"You were glaring at me."

"No, I wasn't!"

"Yeah, you were! I remember your dad asked me if I thought you were handsome, and I said that you looked like him. And then you stared at me like you hated me."

He laughed again. "That's ridiculous. I didn't hate you. I do remember staring at you, though."

"You do?"

"Of course. Who wouldn't?"

Colette tried to restrain a smile. "What do you mean?"

"Well, you are really beautiful."

Colette actually believed him. A strange boldness possessed her again, and she gave him a quick peck on the cheek. Before she knew it, James was lifting her chin and staring deeply into her eyes. She smiled, and his gaze moved to her lips. His face began to close in toward hers when Sammy opened the front door.

"Shit!" Sammy said, immediately stepping back outside.

"Wait, Sam!" Colette called. "It's okay, come back!"

Sammy turned around reluctantly. "I'm so sorry. The *one* time I use the front door—"

"It's okay, really."

"Hi, Sammy," James said, looking more startled than embarrassed.

"Heeey, James. Again, *so* sorry. I'm just gonna..." she motioned back to her room and disappeared.

"Well, that was—" Colette began, trying to ease the tension. But James was gently pulling her face in toward his, and he kissed her as if he were already in love.

CHAPTER FOURTEEN

Colette and Reid sat in the lawn and garden section, reclining in the patio chairs. They were silent companions, Reid having closed his eyes out of sleep deprivation, and Colette lost in her own thoughts. She could not stop thinking about last night, after her parents had left. Every detail was vivid—the glint in James's eyes, the faint smell of his aftershave, and the way his lips felt foreign and familiar at the same time. She could feel the strength in his hand as it gently pulled the back of her head, guiding her closer to him.

Colette jumped as her phone sounded. Reid grimaced and opened his eyes.

"Sorry," she said.

It was James.

Can you call me when you get a chance? I want to hear your voice.

It was possibly the most romantic message she had ever received. She read it again and grinned like an idiot.

"What's your deal?" Reid asked.

She handed him her phone. "Is this real, or am I imagining this message?"

Reid looked at her like she had gone insane. Colette thought maybe she had. "Huh," Reid said. "He must really like you."

"I think he does," Colette whispered.

"Looks like someone's here. Hey, she's kinda hot."

Colette looked up to see Sammy walking in, carrying an over-sized fountain drink and a paper bag.

"Yes! My iced tea is here." Colette jumped to her feet. "Sam, you're the best!"

"I know."

"I love you so much right now."

"Okay, calm down. Keep it in your pants."

Reid stood up slowly and put his hands in his pockets.

"Oh, Reid, this is my friend, Sammy."

"Hey," Sammy said. "How's it going?"

"Good."

"Anyway," Sammy set the bag on the counter. "I got you some cheddar peppers, too. Figured you could use some."

"Aw, ched-r-peps! You're awesome. Thank you!"

Sammy watched Colette as she sipped her tea. "You sure are in a good mood today."

"Well, it's a beautiful day."

"Uh huh," Sammy said, smirking. "Well, I'd love to stay and chat, but I've got to go meet Mom at Ikea."

"Taking a long lunch today?"

"Yeah. Don't tell my boss. I hope your day goes well."

"Thanks, Sam. You, too. Say hi to your mom for me."

Once Sammy was out of sight, Reid turned to Colette and crossed his arms. His face was red. "You're not gonna tell your friend what I said, are you?"

"Huh?"

"You know…"

"Oh. Right. I won't tell her. On one condition."

"What?" Reid asked, looking nervous.

"Can you cover me while I go call James?"

His shoulders relaxed. "Sure."

James answered right away and asked if she would be able to watch his rehearsal that evening. Colette suddenly realized that, over the last two days, she had ironically forgotten about ballet. Now, she began to consider just how much insider access James could provide her. Attend rehearsal at Westmoreland? She told him that she would *love* to, provided that she wouldn't be in the way.

Before Colette got back to the register, Darrel had come out and gestured to her. He wanted to see her in his office. She felt a tinge of panic and thought, *I made out with your son last night.* Was Darrel upset that she hadn't said anything to him? She meant to mention her weekend with James, but Darrel had been on the phone all morning. She hadn't had a chance—

"So," Darrel said as he shut the door. "I hear Jimmy is quite taken with you." His face was beaming. Colette relaxed and smiled down at her lap.

"I guess so," she replied. "I hope you don't mind. I'm quite taken with him, too."

"'Course I don't mind! I think it's great. I've got a real good feeling about this."

"Me, too."

"Are you wanting to go to his rehearsal tonight?"

"Yes," Colette said, surprised. "But only if it will work out."

"'Course it will. We'll cover so you can leave a little early. I can't refuse that boy when he really wants something."

"You mean, he already asked you to let me go?"

"Sure did. But I warned him that he can't get away with too much of this. You let me know if he's interfering with your work. I'll remind him who's boss here." Darrel winked, thoroughly enjoying the situation.

"Thanks, Darrel. I appreciate it."

COLETTE ARRIVED AT Westmoreland feeling strange about coming in street clothes. She had only had time to grab her dance bag for class later that evening. When she explained why she was there, the usually jovial receptionist eyed her blankly. Colette thought maybe she didn't recognize her. She had never worn her hair down there.

"Looks like they'll be in studio four," the receptionist said. "But let me just call up there to make sure. One second."

Colette waited, thinking maybe she had made a mistake. She felt like she wasn't supposed to be there—not unless she was there to pay for class.

"Okay. You can go on up. Enjoy."

"Great," Colette said. "Thank you."

A portly woman dawdled in front of Colette as she climbed the steps up to studio four. She was growing impatient when she noticed a bottle of Diet Coke poking out of the woman's tote bag.

"Dunja? Excuse me, Dunja, right?"

Dunja turned around, looking irritated. "Hullo."

"Hi. I, um, have a weird question for you…"

Colette reminded her of the night she played *Cantique de Salomon,* explained how James and the artistic director would like to see the sheet music, and could she make a copy?

"Anything for M. Lavoisier," Dunja said. "You take class tonight?"

"Yes."

"I bring you copy."

"Great! That would be great. Thank you so much."

"I do not understand why he does not ask me himself."

Colette shrugged, and Dunja resumed her trek down the hallway. Colette slowed her pace to walk beside her.

"I really enjoy your playing in class," Colette said. Dunja only nodded. "Especially the *Song of Solomon* music. Where exactly did you get it, if you don't mind me asking? It seems like it would be rare."

"It belonged to my grandfather," Dunja replied. "He was collector of Soviet ballet music."

"So, it was a Russian ballet?"

"No, French. But composer was Russian Jew."

"How do you know that?"

Dunja sighed, as if she were already tired of answering questions. "Is what he told me. They destroyed his work, but my grandfather found copy."

Colette's eyes widened. "Where?"

"Eh—" Dunja shrugged. "People. Mafia."

"The *mafia*?"

"Yes," Dunja said curtly. She opened a studio door.

"Do you know his name? The name of the composer?"

Dunja shook her head, and the door closed behind her.

Colette was more intrigued than ever, and she was relieved that their exchange had gone so well, all things considered. She couldn't wait to tell James.

Once she had found studio four, she hesitated to go in. She couldn't see James, but two female dancers saw her peeking in. One looked amused, and the other completely indifferent to her presence. It was too late to turn back now.

Colette took a deep breath and walked in, consciously standing tall and straight. She scanned the room for James and was relieved to find him crouching by the piano, rolling out his quad with a tortuous-looking stick.

"Colette!" he called, dropping the strange device. He jogged over and—to her delight and embarrassment—lifted her off the ground as he embraced her.

"Hey!" Colette laughed. "James, put me down."

"We're about to start, so I'll introduce you to people later. Do you want to sit in that corner over there? I'll grab you a chair."

Colette nodded and headed toward the back of the studio, acutely aware of the pairs of eyes following her. She looked forward and pretended not to notice but once rehearsal began, she watched everyone closely, soaking in every possible detail.

In her excitement, Colette had forgotten to ask James what exactly they were rehearsing. The music sounded familiar, but she couldn't place it, and she began to feel unqualified to be there. She tried to divert the thought by focusing on the row of ballerinas in front of her.

They were all so tiny in real life. Not one was over 5'7", and they were incredibly thin up close. Their legs appeared alarmingly fragile underneath their rehearsal tutus, though she knew they had to be strong. Colette looked down at her own legs and felt like a giant in comparison.

One dancer in particular stood out from the rest—the tallest one who had looked disinterestedly at her. Eventually, Colette recognized her as a bare-faced Alexandra Vukoja. Her features were still beautiful without makeup and her body perfectly proportioned; it wasn't so much skinny as impossibly lean. Nearly every muscle and sinew was visible beneath her glowing olive skin, as if her body had never known excess. Had she ever craved a dessert in her life?

Alexandra did a slow *soutenu* with the most graceful *port de bras* Colette had ever seen. Then, she extended her leg behind her in a high arabesque with complete control. A second before lowering, she arched her back and lifted her leg even higher, looking like some exotic contortionist. Colette was in complete awe. She could never do that.

The men entered gallantly and paired off with the women. To Colette's surprise, James was partnered with Alexandra. Westmoreland's ranks must be more fluid that she thought, or maybe James was quickly climbing his way up. Whatever the case, he wasn't doing much dancing at the moment—mostly assisting. His hands held Alexandra's tiny waist while she turned multiple *pirouettes*. He dropped to one knee and took her hand to steady her in *arabesque penchée*. Colette could tell that James was concentrating, but he looked calm. It seemed easy for him.

The ballet master, a Chinese man dressed in black, had been counting off and on during the run-through. He stood up when they were done.

"That's looking good guys. I'd like to do this again. Before we do that, a couple of notes—Alex?"

James shifted to let his partner step forward.

"Yeah?"

"Could you lower your arabesque? It's lovely, but I want to keep it even with the rest of the group. Right now, it's looking pretty high. It's like, thirty degrees too high."

A couple of the dancers groaned.

"Okay." Alexandra nodded.

"And—for the first one out of the *soutenu*—remember to get completely down on seven. You were just a teeny tiny bit late."

"Got it."

"Actually, that goes for everyone, ladies. Start thinking *down* almost on six, otherwise you'll have to rush into the transition. Okay, can we take it from the top and maybe just kick up the energy a little bit? I know it's the end of the day and we're all tired, but the arms are looking a bit droopy."

They ran through it again, and Colette could tell that it really did look better the second time. Alexandra modified her arabesque, briefly checking the mirror to make sure she was in sync with the other dancers. James assisted her with no discernible flaws that Colette could see. He looked so natural, so unpretentious—especially next to Alexandra, who seemed to be quite satisfied with her own dancing. But how could Colette blame her?

After rehearsal was finished, James quickly made his way over to her.

"I'm sorry," he said. "That was kind of a boring one to watch."

"No, not at all. I really enjoyed it."

"You gonna introduce us to your friend, Brennan?" A lanky dancer with a thick accent and ice-blonde hair was walking toward them. James introduced him as Andreas the Scandinavian.

"Our company is like a little United Nations," Andreas told her. Colette stared at his eyelashes, which were pale and feathery—the kind that women would immediately coat with mascara. Andreas pointed at the other dancers. "See, look. Brazilian. South African. Japanese. Canadian—wait, Canadian, does that even count? Just joking, Iris."

"I suppose you're right," Colette said, relieved to see that the others were laughing along with him. A few of them came up to introduce themselves. Nathaniel, the dancer from South Africa, was soft-spoken and gentlemanly. He had luminous eyes and was the most muscular person Colette had ever seen up close. Helena, a petite blond, was the first of the women to introduce herself. She bounced over and waved at Colette.

"Hi!" Helena said cheerfully. "I would shake your hand, but I'm all sweaty."

In a few minutes, the other dancers meandered their way into the forming group. She met Iris, who was married to Nathaniel. She met Yumi, Timothy and Keith, and then started to lose track of names. Almost everyone had left the studio when Alexandra finally came over, now drowning in warm-ups. Helena lingered nearby.

"Oh, this is Alex," James said.

"Hi," Colette said. "You're such a beautiful dancer."

"Thanks," Alex replied, still looking at James.

"This is Colette," James said, resting his hand on the small of her back.

Alex finally took more than a passing glance at her. She nodded and then touched James on the shoulder.

"See you tomorrow, partner."

"Yep," James called after her.

"Don't pay attention to her," Helena whispered to Colette. "She's got issues."

Colette actually didn't mind. She was preoccupied by the feeling of James's hand on her back—of how comfortable it felt there already, and how she hadn't known she had been missing it all her life.

"Can we hang out a little longer?" Colette asked once they were alone.

"Duh," James teased. "I was about to ask you the same thing."

CHAPTER FIFTEEN

"How do I look?" Colette asked, adjusting her dress from Sammy's doorway.

"Hotsville," Sammy said. "I wish I could pull off knee-high boots. Is he taking you somewhere nice?"

"I don't know. He said he'd take care of dinner, but I'm not sure what that means. Dude, I don't know why I'm so nervous."

"'Cause you'll be all alone in his apartment. It *is* kind of a big deal. What if he's actually a serial killer? Or worse, what if his place is a complete dump?"

"Oh, no. Don't say that."

"Meh, I'm sure it'll be fine."

JAMES LIVED BY himself in midtown. When he had told her of this fact, Colette secretly hoped that he wasn't in one of the party neighborhoods—those were overrun with college frat boys. Surely he had outgrown that.

To her relief, she pulled up to a quiet street and found that he actually lived in an old house that had been converted into apartments. She walked across the huge porch and buzzed up to his apartment. In the seconds that followed, paranoid thoughts raced through her mind.

Did she have the wrong time? Was he even home? Did he even exist?

"Hey, come on up! Up the stairs on your right."

Maybe he did exist, after all.

James's place was in decent shape, with dark woodwork and original 1920s floors that constantly creaked. He had done little in the way of decoration, except for the living room, which had wooden bookshelves, a luxurious-looking leather couch, and a coffee table with a glass top. Splashes of teal in the couch pillows and bamboo rug jumped out against the room's predominant browns and grays, and two framed blueprints flanked the book shelves.

"The living room looks really nice," Colette said. "Did you decorate this yourself?"

"Yeah. This room took me forever, so I kind of gave up after that. I um, I built the bookshelves and the coffee table."

"Really? I wondered if you did. They're beautiful, James." Colette inspected them more closely. "How did you get into woodworking?"

He paused to consider the question. "Shop class was the only class I liked in school. Well, that and P.E. Even after I starting homeschooling, Dad sent me to woodshop classes—"

"Wait. You did home school?"

"Yeah, just for the last two years of high school. So I could train full-time."

"Oh, right. I bet that was nice."

James smiled. "Yeah, it was. But it was also pretty hard. I didn't have much of a social life." He ran his hand across the bookshelf. "My dad actually helped with these."

"Is that something you guys like to do together?" She pictured James and Darrel in some sort of shed, wearing safety glasses and bonding over wood grain and dovetail joints.

"Yeah," James said. "We've spent a lot of time building stuff together. It's always a good way to get my mind off of work. Plus, I have to use his tools. It would be nice to have my own someday. Or at least a table saw." James looked around the room. "Don't have anywhere to put it, though."

The rest of his apartment was plain and bare-walled and not particularly inviting. Colette noticed a stack of framed prints and photographs coated with dust. She wondered how long ago he had abandoned his plans for that project.

"So, what are we doing for dinner?" Colette asked.

"I actually picked up some pizza. I have some salad and wine, too. I hope that's okay."

"Yeah, that sounds great."

"I wanted to cook for you, but—I'll be honest—I can't really cook."

"Me neither," Colette said, laughing. "I mean, I *can* cook, but I don't like to. It just takes so long."

"Right?" James said. His face lit up, as if this small exchange of understanding meant the world to him. "I'm always too hungry by the time I get home."

Colette helped him set the table, and he had her sit down while he served dinner. She watched with amusement as he darted back and forth from the kitchen an inordinate number of times. It was the first time she had seen him the tiniest bit flustered.

"James," she said. "This looks great. Thank you for doing all of this for me."

His shoulders relaxed a bit. "It's no problem."

He grinned and took a giant bite of salad. Colette watched with fascination. He could eat large quantities of food faster than anyone she knew. After inhaling his salad and first slice of pizza, he sat back and wiped his face with a paper towel. He looked as though he had an announcement to make.

"What's up?" Colette asked.

"Well, I have some news. It's pretty exciting."

"Yeah?"

"You know the *Song of Solomon* music you gave me?"

"Uh huh," Colette replied, her mouth full of salad.

"It's kind of a big deal. Lavoisier has been talking to people about it. I haven't heard much yet, but he wants to use it for a *pas de deux* to show at the New Year's Gala. And, uh, he wants me to choreograph."

Colette swallowed, her eyes wide with disbelief, and set down her fork. *"Seriously?"*

"Yep."

"James, that's *awesome*! I can't believe it!"

"Me neither," James mumbled, grabbing a second slice of pizza.

"Aren't you excited?"

"I am, but I'm also pretty nervous. I've never done anything this involved before."

"Well, he obviously has faith in you," Colette replied, returning to her food. "He knows you'll be great."

"I don't know. I do have a bunch of ideas already, so that's good, I guess. You were right about that music, by the way. It's so... I don't know, just different. I've never heard anything like it."

"Yeah. Kind of other-worldly?"

"Right."

"I still can't believe it," Colette said, shaking her head. James would be creating a new ballet, all because *she* had noticed the music. *She* had told him about it. "Do you know who will be dancing it yet?"

"Well, I am, actually. And we've already cast Alex."

"Wow, *James*. That's a big deal. This is a huge step for you, isn't it?"

"Yeah, I guess it is. Honestly, I'm more excited about choreographing."

"But dancing a brand new piece with the prima ballerina—that seems like it's huge."

Colette was happy for him, but she couldn't help but cringe at the thought of Alex playing his bride. Of course she would be perfect, but a *Song of Solomon pas de deux*? It would be intimate, to say the least.

"Colette," James said. "I was wondering if you wouldn't mind helping me brainstorm a bit, since you're familiar with the music and have read the book and everything. You wouldn't have to do much. I have a lot of ideas for the choreography, but I want to figure out how to incorporate the text—you know, the story—more. I'm just not much of a reader."

"Of course I'll help. I would *love* to help." Colette couldn't believe that she could be involved in something like this. It was too good to be true.

After dinner, they retired to the leather couch with James's Bible. Fascinated, Colette peeked through it while James scribbled on a notepad. The inside cover bore an inscription:

To James Ryan Brennan, our dear prince and warrior. Love, Mom and Dad, Christmas 1995.

In the middle pages, she found a bookmark made out of blue felt—a relic from James's childhood, she decided. A verse was written on it in thick marker.

"For I know the plans I have for you," declares the Lord, "plans to prosper you and not to harm you, plans to give you hope and a future."

To her horror, Colette had begun to cry. She had no idea why. Keeping her head down, she quickly wiped her eyes and concentrated on searching for *Song of Solomon*. James hadn't noticed.

"The whole thing will only be about eight minutes," he said. "I just don't know how much story to cram in there. Like, should it be this abstract *love, conflict, marriage* type of thing?"

Colette thought for a while. "Maybe it would be easier to find one particular passage and base it just on that. You know, make it more focused."

James liked the idea.

"It's listed as *Song of Songs* in here," Colette said. "Is that the same thing?"

"Uh, yeah, I think so."

They began to search through the text, all the while laughing at the strange imagery.

"Colette," James said. "'Your hair is like a flock of goats.'"

"Oh, yeah? Well, 'your breasts are like two fawns.'"

James cupped his chest. "Really? *Thank you.*"

Some of the poetry no longer seemed ridiculous, though. Her perspective had changed since she had read it alone in bed. Now, she found herself stealing glances at James, who had gone back to sketching in his notepad.

> *My beloved is radiant and ruddy,*
> *outstanding among ten thousand.*

She noticed flecks of gold in his hair and in the scruff covering his jaw. She could see a subtle flush in his cheek—the blood pulsing beneath his skin.

> *His arms are rods of gold*
> *set with topaz.*

The veins in his left hand protruded as he gripped the pen, and her eyes followed them up the length of his arm.

> *His mouth is sweetness itself;*
> *he is altogether lovely.*

Colette thought back to that first kiss on the couch. They hadn't kissed since then. Would it happen again soon?

She took a deep breath and kept reading, feeling increasingly unhelpful. She had no idea how people went about creating dance pieces. And now that she was re-reading *Song of Solomon*, she had no idea how it could translate to ballet. She was nearing the end of the book and about to give up hope when something stopped her.

"James," she whispered. "I think I've found it. Read this."

> *Place me like a seal over your heart,*

like a seal on your arm;
for love is as strong as death,
its jealousy unyielding as the grave.
It burns like blazing fire,
like a mighty flame.
Many waters cannot quench love;
rivers cannot sweep it away.
If one were to give
all the wealth of one's house for love,
it would be utterly scorned.

"Wow," James said. He had been staring at the text for quite some time. "Yeah. I could work with that."

"Really?"

"Yeah. Um, this may sound weird, but would you mind reading it to me?"

"Sure," Colette said. James closed his eyes, and she read each line aloud carefully, as if they were the most important words she had ever spoken. She felt like maybe they were. That phrase, *for love is as strong as death.* It was so simple and powerful, and what if it were true?

"I really like it," James said. "I think this will work."

"Good. I like it, too. Although, I'm glad you know what you're doing, because I have no idea how you'd turn this into choreography."

"It'll happen one way or another," James said, yawning. "Oh, shoot. It's probably getting really late, isn't it?"

Colette looked at her phone. It was almost 2 a.m.

"Crap. I'd better go."

James paused. "You can stay if you want."

The offer caught Colette off guard. As she stood there, considering its implications, a look of realization appeared on James's face. "I mean," he added. "I can sleep on the couch."

Colette smiled. "Thanks, but I'd better not. I have to be at work in six hours."

James looked concerned. "You sure you'll be okay?"

"Yeah, I'll be fine." She chuckled and, as she reached out to touch him on the arm, he pulled her in closer to him.

"Hey," he said. "I'm sorry if I was moving too fast the other night. You know, when we were on the couch. When Sammy walked in—"

"Yeah, I remember," Colette said, laughing. "I didn't mind, James. Obviously."

He grinned and wrapped his arms around her. Colette could feel the strength within them; they could probably crush her if he'd let them.

He seemed to be waiting for her, so Colette summoned her boldness. She gazed up at his bright eyes and gave him a goodnight kiss, which lasted about fifteen minutes, before finally heading out the door. She glanced back at him once more and smiled at the sight of him there, sleepy-eyed with his disheveled hair. He looked extra boyish when he was tired, but he was still so strong. The strength in those arms—Colette would keep thinking about it until she finally crawled into bed, exhausted and divinely happy.

CHAPTER SIXTEEN

Working on little sleep had become the usual for Colette. She stood leaning against the old soda machine by the register, sipping her break room coffee out of a Styrofoam cup. Her breath was slow and deep, as if she were about to drift off to sleep, but she was actually intensely focused on the previous night's search through *Song of Songs*. There in the quiet shop, an extraordinary thought had occurred to her, as if she had been gifted a secret rush of inspiration—she knew she could separate the chapters of the book into scenes for a full-length ballet. And she knew exactly where James's *pas de deux* would go.

Her intuition urged her to get these ideas down on paper before they disappeared. Almost frantic, she began to read through the book on her phone, jotting thoughts on sticky notes and arranging them on the counter. After several minutes, a shopper began to linger nearby, and she could feel him watching her with curiosity. She looked up from her project, trying not to appear annoyed by the interruption, and asked, "Ready to check out?"

"Yes, ma'am," the man said, glancing at her notes. He was buying a ton of outlet covers—practically their whole stock. Did he live in a mansion? Not one to force small talk with customers, Colette scanned the multitude of items in silence. The man must have grown tired of it. He pointed to the train of yellow squares and asked, "What you working on there?"

"Oh just a project," Colette said. To keep it sounding work-related, she added, "for the manager's son." She wasn't about to discuss her amateur and unsolicited attempt at creating a ballet with a complete stranger. Her exchange with Sammy that morning, during which she shared the news about the *pas de deux,* had been difficult enough.

"*The Song of Solomon*?" Sammy had asked, looking confused.

"Yeah. What?"

"That just seems like it would be really... you know... *sexual*. How would that work?"

Having expected Sammy to be excited for her and James, Colette was disappointed at such an underwhelming reaction, and she felt embarrassed that she had not considered the erotic imagery to be such a problem. Should she have been more worried about it? She had finally made up a response, hoping that it would prove to be true.

"It's *sensual,* maybe. But there's no ballet sex, if that's what you're thinking. No flesh-colored unitards."

"Oh, okay." Sammy laughed. "That's good."

Colette continued bagging outlet covers, trying to make it clear that she was not going to divulge any further information. The man craned his neck to read one of her notes.

"*Daughters of Jerusalem,*" he read. "*Do not arouse or awaken love until it so desires—*"

Colette blushed and snatched the note away.

"Well, well," he said, winking. "Can't see what that has to do with hardware. For the manager's son, you say?"

"It's just an idea for a ballet he could be in. He's a dancer. It's just an experiment, really. It won't actually happen."

He snickered. "Why you bothering, then? Sounds like you're wasting your time."

She had had about enough of this guy. "Well," she said, "It's fun and the idea just came to me. Why do you need so many outlet covers?" She handed him his bags. "Have a good day."

As soon as he was gone, Colette went back to work, writing in a frenzy and still compelled by the strange need to make her ideas manifest. Once she had laid out all of the scenes, she combined her notes and copied the contents onto an old piece of Tempe's letterhead. Within an hour, she had created an outline for a three-act ballet:

CANTIQUE DE SALOMON

CAST:

Solomon's Bride* (The Shulamite Woman) - Alexandra Vukoja
King Solomon/Shepherd - James Brennan
Daughters of Jerusalem - 7 females
Watchmen - 4 males

Cantique

Mighty Men - 7 males
Townspeople - Corps de ballet

ACT I

IN JERUSALEM,
AT A COURTYARD OUTSIDE THE ROYAL CHAMBERS OF
KING SOLOMON

The people of Jerusalem dance to welcome young King Solomon, who has returned home after a supposed journey to visit the King of Tyre. In truth, Solomon has been absent courting a beautiful Shulamite woman, whom he now desires to marry. While in the company of her friends, the Shulamite woman confesses her love for King Solomon. They implore her to tell her love story, and she obliges, describing how Solomon wooed her in secret, dressed as a humble shepherd before revealing his true identify. She warns them not to awaken love until love so desires. Afterward, Solomon reunites with his bride-to-be, and they promise to be sealed to one another in eternal love. Solomon's bride dances to honor him, praising his wisdom and strength. The lovers part, and the bride is left alone to sleep.

SCENE 1 - DANCE TO WELCOME KING SOLOMON
Divertissements: Mighty Men, Daughters of Jerusalem, Townspeople, Solomon

SCENE 2 - THE BRIDE CONFESSES HER LOVE
 Variation: Bride, Divertissements: Daughters of Jerusalem

SCENE 3 - SOLOMON AND HIS BRIDE DELIGHT IN EACH OTHER
Grand pas de deux: Solomon and Bride [James's pas de deux]

SCENE 4 - THE BRIDE ADORES HER BELOVED

Variation: Bride, Solomon present

ACT II

IN THE BRIDE'S CHAMBERS
AND THE STREETS OF JERUSALEM

The Shulamite woman dreams that she has heard Solomon's knock upon her chamber door, but he has disappeared. She wanders the streets in search of him and mourns that she has lost him to another. In her grief, she bitterly warns her friends again not to awaken love until it so desires, and she falls into despair. She awakens haunted by the dream but remembers the promise Solomon has made to her.

SCENE 1 - THE BRIDE'S DREAM
Ensemble: Bride, Daughters of Jerusalem, Watchmen, Solomon

SCENE 2 - THE BRIDE AWAKENS
Variation: Bride

ACT III

IN JERUSALEM, AT THE TEMPLE OF KING SOLOMON

The royal wedding is about to take place, and Solomon celebrates with his subjects. When his bride arrives, Solomon praises her beauty and purity, and the two are wed. The lovers delight in each other as husband and wife. They vow that their love will be as strong as death, likening it to an unquenchable flame. Afterward, the couple and the people of Jerusalem celebrate the royal marriage, and all is well.

SCENE 1 - SOLOMON ARRIVES FOR THE WEDDING

Variation: Solomon, Divertissements: Mighty Men, Daughters of Jerusalem, townspeople

SCENE 2 - SOLOMON ADMIRES HIS BRIDE'S BEAUTY
Variation: Solomon, Bride and townspeople present

SCENE 3 - TOGETHER IN THE GARDEN OF LOVE
Pas de deux, Solomon and Bride

SCENE 4 - FINALE (CODA)
Ensemble: Solomon and Bride, Mighty Men, Daughters of Jerusalem, townspeople

*Note – Solomon's bride needs a name!

She filled in the margins with sketches of costumes—one with flowing chiffons for Solomon's bride and details for Solomon's golden headpiece. Having no watercolors to fill in the sketches, she settled on labeling the fabric colors—royal purple, sea-green and cerulean.

Colette realized that she had written her synopsis almost exactly like Westmoreland Ballet's program notes. She didn't know how else to do it. Did people write librettos for ballets? She felt silly that she didn't know, but what did it really matter? It wasn't as if her idea would amount to anything. After all, they only had music for one *pas de deux*. She resolved to show James anyway, knowing that he would at least appreciate the thought she had put into it.

AT WESTMORELAND THAT evening, she presented her work to James, who had been working late in the studio. He was shirtless and sweaty as he sat down on the Marley floor, reading slowly with what seemed to be unnecessary concentration. Colette stared mindlessly at his phoenix tattoo as she waited. While seated, his obliques folded over one another, slightly distorting the image. Colette had been observing it for a while when she realized that he was still silent. She began to worry.

"I know it's silly of me," she said. "It's awful, isn't it? That's okay, you can stop—" she reached for the paper.

"No," James said, pulling it away from her. "I'm not done yet."

Colette suddenly understood. He really hadn't finished reading it, even though most people would have finished minutes ago. *I'm not a great reader,* he had told her. His struggle with text was quite literal.

Colette continued to wait patiently, and when James had finally finished, he looked stunned.

"This is really good, Colette," he said.

"What? I doubt that."

"No, really. You just thought this up at work today? Like, how long did it take you?

"I don't know. An hour, maybe? I had to do a little research."

James shook his head. "I'm impressed. Seriously."

"Thank you. Of course, I just did it for fun. I don't know anything about creating ballets. Obviously."

"But it's a good start, and I could see how this structure would work." He studied the page again.

"Well," Colette said. "I took some liberties with the story. Half of the time I don't know what's actually going on with that book. It's kind of confusing—"

"No, I like what you've done with it," James said. He held up the paper. "Mind if I keep this for a while?"

"Sure, if you want."

"Thanks." His eyes wandered off into the distance, and they sat in silence until he grunted and struck the floor.

"What's the matter?" Colette asked.

"Nothing." He shook his head again and smiled. "I just wish I could do this."

It was the best compliment he could have given her. Now Colette wished the same, but a pestilent voice inside of her, which sounded a lot like the customer from earlier, reminded her that such a wish was unlikely to come true.

CHAPTER SEVENTEEN

Colette and Sammy peeked into the studio window. They were killing time before class by watching James and Alex rehearse. He was constructing the *Cantique Pas*, as he and Colette had begun to call it. At the moment, Alex was standing there in her warm-ups, listening to James's instruction and watching him mark the steps. Colette noticed that Alex's hair looked completely secure in its tight, shiny French twist. How on earth did she manage that?

Sammy glanced at Colette, whose eyes were wide and still fixed on Alex.

"Is this kind of awkward for you?"

"Yeah. A little, if I'm honest. I know he has to partner people all the time, and I totally trust him, but she's just so *good*. And so… well, *beautiful*."

Sammy shook her head. "Dude, if beauty is a competition, you're winning. Hands down."

"Ha! Beauty isn't a competition, Sammy."

"Yes it is. We're in America. I'm telling you, you're way prettier."

"But you haven't seen her dance yet. See, *watch*."

They began to move slowly through the choreography, and the piece seemed to be coming together nicely. Now that Alex was filling in the gaps, James's solitary marking in the studio began to make a lot more sense. Colette was relieved. Until now, he had looked a little insane, like some delusional inventor wearing institutional sweats.

Colette and Sammy scrutinized Alex's every move. She was retreating from James with little *bourrées,* her slender arms outstretched toward him and her face betraying a longing that seemed to be a bit beyond the theatrical. James followed her and lifted her into the air from behind, her torso draping back toward him. Alex's back was so flexible that their faces almost met in an upside-down kiss. As she descended, her leg wrapped around him in *attitude* and there was an unmistakable gleam in her dark eyes.

"Huh," Sammy said. "I see what you mean. She's, uh, really getting into character already, isn't she?"

"Yeah," Colette replied. "She sure is."

Although she couldn't see James's face, she trusted that his expression was one of stoic concentration. She hoped he wasn't looking Alex in the eyes, although she knew that at some point—once they had mastered the choreography perhaps—he would have to. He would have to play the part of a lover romancing another woman, and Colette began to wonder about the line between fantasy and reality. James would be acting in character, but the body intertwined with Alex's still belonged to him. The eyes that would have to gaze at her were still his, as was the soul within them. Colette thought about how she could trick herself into dancing better—about how she could *dress* the part to *feel* the part. If James played his role long enough, wouldn't some small piece of him have to fall in love?

It was time to go to class but, for the first time in a long time, Colette really didn't feel like it. She struggled her way through barre, gripping her muscles and finding it difficult to remember the combinations. Class usually went by quickly, but she found herself glancing at the clock, wishing it would tick faster. She just wanted to be home.

During center, Colette waited to the side to watch the second group dance while lazily marking the steps with her hands. Her eyes were naturally drawn to the best dancer in the group, a tall, slender, red-headed girl. She looked young enough to be a Westmoreland academy student but was also dancing with mature technique. Clean double and triple *pirouettes*. Calm. Serene. She was the type of dancer who wore those plastic shorts—the kind that suggest, *I know what I'm doing. I'm so good, I can get away with wearing trash bags.*

Colette kept an eye on her for the rest of class, which was a mistake. The girl seemed to get better and better, and Colette felt chubby and clumsy in comparison. When it came time for *grand allegro*, she had put undue pressure on herself. She waited in position for her turn, thinking through the combination as if her life depended on it.

"Next group get ready," Marianne called to Colette and Tina. Colette's shoulders tensed. "Five, six, *piqué* seven—whoops, whoops! You missed your cue. You have to get that *piqué* on seven. Dan, can we start again? Thank you."

Colette felt a pang of embarrassment, but she ignored it and reset herself. At least Tina had messed up, too.

The music started. Colette nailed the *piqué arabesque* this time, but her first *tour jeté* went horribly wrong somehow. She wasn't even sure if she had made it off the ground. Before she could try again, Marianne clapped her hands twice and asked the pianist to restart the music a second time. Colette was mortified.

"Do you know what you did wrong?"

Colette froze, unsure of what to tell her. She finally muttered something about starting on the wrong foot. The real issue, however, was that she was thinking too much. Instead of listening to the music and trusting her body's movement, she was telling it, *left leg, right leg*. Her mind was wrong this time. Her muscles knew better.

Marianne marked through the step again and Colette went back to the corner, trying hard to concentrate despite her embarrassment.

"And five, six, *piqué* seven, eight. And *tour jeté*! And *tour jeté*! Much better. And *tour jeté, piqué, failli* through, step, hold..."

Colette knew she could make it through the rest, but she wasn't giving it her all. She was containing her movement, hoping it would make the class notice her less. Would they ever forget? They probably already had, but Colette wouldn't.

She walked to the other corner as soon as she could. Sammy and the redhead were about to take their turn. The girl was especially amazing at *tour jetés* and finished the combination without any discernible flaws. Colette sighed. While Marianne had marked the combination, the girl had sat fiddling with her pointe shoes. She hadn't even been watching. What was it like to absorb choreography like that? Colette wondered why she even bothered trying to dance.

Jael's words fluttered through her mind. *"You are a dancer... I can tell you are a beautiful dancer."*

Screw Jael. What did she know?

On the way home, Colette was teetering on the edge of despair, replaying her *tour jeté* disaster in her mind on an endless loop. She imagined Alex peeking through the studio window at her, smirking as Colette stumbled through the simple combination. She couldn't help but pour salt on her own wound.

"Did you notice that red-headed girl in class?" she asked Sammy.

"Yeah, she was good."

"Do you ever get... I don't know... weirdly jealous of people like that?"

Sammy thought for a second. "No, I don't think so. It makes me a little mad at myself for sucking, but I don't really care that much. I mean, that girl has probably taken class every day for her entire life. We can't afford that shit."

"I wish I didn't care," Colette said. She turned her face toward the window.

"Well, can you imagine having to be that disciplined at that age? We can enjoy the benefits of ballet and then go home and eat a whole pizza if we want. We don't have the pressure of being perfect. You know?" Colette nodded, still looking out the window. Sammy hunched over the steering wheel, trying to see her face. "CoCo... this isn't your *career,* so you don't have to be so hard on yourself. Would you have loved it this much if you had started so young?"

"Probably not."

Colette had thought out the scenario before.

Say she started dancing as a child and say she, somehow, had enough talent to even *consider* a career in ballet. Would she have been dedicated enough, smart enough—ambitious enough—to have made it? Could she have moved away as a teenager? Could her mom have afforded all of it in the first place? No. She couldn't have. At least, not until Craig came along.

Say, in a more likely scenario, she started young and *didn't* have enough talent to consider dancing professionally. Or even to dance really well. She would have quit and never gone back. She would have become bitter and shut ballet out of her thoughts. She would have missed out on the joy it brought her now.

No, this was how it was supposed to be.

Colette relaxed and looked forward. "You're right. I just love it so much that I want to be as good as I can. It gets frustrating sometimes."

"I know," Sammy replied. "When it gets frustrating, just think of my *pas de chat* indiscretion."

Colette burst out laughing, feeling a brief release from her own perfectionism. At times like these, she wished she could be more like Sammy, who never seemed to dwell on her own mistakes. For though Colette felt better at the moment, she knew that later that evening—while she tried to prevent the same harsh thoughts from returning—Sammy would be alone in bed, sound asleep with a smile on her face.

CHAPTER EIGHTEEN

It was Colette's day off, and she sat in her car, bracing herself for the cold. She had come to Westmoreland to bring James some lunch between rehearsals. Gathering her bags and their two drinks, she opened the door and stepped out into the shrill wind. She walked briskly with her head tucked down and realized that one of her black, suede boots was covered in cat fur. There was nothing she could do about it; her hands were full.

The security guard opened the door.

"Thank you!" Colette said.

"No problem, ma'am."

Ma'am? Am I really looking that old?

The Westmoreland building was especially comforting during the winter; its warmth and the constant, faint *Nutcracker* music felt festive. Colette was thinking about finally wearing her leg warmers to class when she turned a corner and almost crashed into an oncoming dancer. It was Alex, who had been distracted by her reflection in the display glass.

"Phew! That could have been bad," Colette said.

"Yeah. Excuse me," Alex muttered.

"Hey, do you know if James is on break yet?"

"He didn't tell you? He's meeting with Henri." Alex glanced down at Colette's furry boot. A subtle, smug expression ran across her face, and she lowered her voice to a whisper. "I would just—you know—stay out here." She nodded toward the break area. "It will be quite a while."

"Okay then."

They studied each other's faces until Alex's eyes turned resolute. She reached for Colette's bags and said, "Or I can get his food to him if you don't feel like waiting."

Colette clutched them tighter. "That's all right. I'll just wait."

"Suit yourself," Alex said. She shrugged and went on her way.

Colette had only just set her things down at one of the tables before she saw James heading her direction. He was accompanied by someone—Lavoisier himself.

Alex had told her it would be a while and yet there he was, right on time. Colette frowned. Had Alex been trying to get rid of her?

James greeted her with a hug, and Colette tried her hardest to look cheerful.

"I want to introduce you to someone," James said. "This is Henri, our Artistic Director. Henri, this is my girlfriend Colette."

Colette smiled at the sound of her new label. She still wasn't used to it.

"A pleasure to meet you, my dear," Henri said, taking Colette's hand and giving it a gentle pat. His eyes were kind and seemed to sparkle. "James has just shown me your wonderful work."

"My work?"

"Yes, your outline for a full-length *Song of Solomon.* I found it quite charming."

"Oh!" Colette widened her eyes at James. "That was just for fun. I don't know how realistic it is—"

"But you've shown a good understanding of the story-ballet. And, I have not forgotten that we owe our little *Cantique Pas de Deux* to you. What an extraordinary find that was. You have no idea what you've started."

James beamed and put his arm around her.

"Um, what have I started, exactly?"

"A whole host of scholarship, my dear. And it appears as though my colleagues are onto something. I've urged Dunja to keep her music safe until it can be appraised."

"Oh, right… I didn't even think about that."

"Yes. It is *quite* rare. Really extraordinary."

"Huh. And I just liked the music!"

Henri smiled. "What about it struck you so?"

"Um, I'm not quite sure. It's just so beautiful and, well, creates this kind of exotic atmosphere. That's it—it's atmospheric. Kind of dreamy. Then I started thinking about what an interesting ballet it would make and how stunning the costumes could be."

"Colette studied fashion design," James added.

"Oh, fascinating. So you love costumes, do you?"

"Yes, I do."

"Me, too." Henri leaned forward and lowered his voice, as if he were about to share a secret. "During my dancing days, wearing the costume was sometimes the only way I could pull off a performance. That's when the magic happens. Once the costumes are on—that's when ballets really start to come together." He turned to James. "Have you introduced her to Myra?"

"I haven't. I should do that."

Someone beckoned to M. Lavoisier, and he took his leave, again thanking Colette for her contribution and promising that he would be in touch. It felt nice to be recognized by someone so important, although she felt that she had done little to deserve such attention.

Once they had sat down for lunch, Colette asked James, "Is Myra the costume designer?"

"Yeah," he replied, his mouth full of chicken sandwich. "I'll take you down there sometime."

"That would be fun." Colette held up her carton of fries. "Do you want these? I didn't mean to get them."

"Mmm, no, better not. I can't eat too much. I have to do a crapload of double *tours* later."

Colette was quiet as James sat preoccupied with his food. She felt like she should be happier. It sounded as if *Cantique* were turning out to be a real discovery, and how amazing was that? She should be ecstatic, really.

"What's wrong?" James asked.

"Huh?"

"You look stressed or something."

"It's just—" Colette began, her face looking increasingly mortified. "Why did you have to show that to him?"

James laughed. "You don't have to be so embarrassed about it. I told you—it's a cool idea. I knew he'd enjoy it."

"Well, I just wish we could have discussed it first," she said. "I have to prepare myself for these things."

"Sorry," he said, still chuckling at her seriousness. "I'll be sure to ask your permission next time."

"Next time I write a libretto?" Colette asked, smirking.

"You know what I mean," he replied. Still seated, he gathered what remained of their lunch and chucked it into the trash can. "So, do you want to sit in on *Nutcracker* rehearsal after break?"

Colette's face lit up. "Really? Are you sure I'm allowed to be there?"

"Yeah, it will be fine. Lang is directing again. He'll be cool with it."

They had time to kill before rehearsal, so they decided to get coffee down the street. Once they were outside in the cold, the cafe seemed to be a mile away. In reality, it was just three blocks down the long sidewalk beside the Westmoreland building. Colette clung to James for warmth, feeling rather thankful to have him in her life.

Then she saw her again—Alex, with coffee cup in hand, strutting toward them as if the sidewalk were a runway. Her eyes were already fixed on James, willing him to look at her.

"Hey Jamesy," Alex said sweetly. "It's freezing out here."

Making it a point to ignore Colette, Alex tucked her arms into herself and pressed her body against James, as if trying to siphon his body heat. James looked surprised, although he didn't seem to feel as awkward as Colette believed he should. She pulled his arm to keep him moving.

"Yeah, well, that's why we're hurrying," he said. He slid past her. "See you in a bit."

They were silent as they entered the shop. Colette ordered a black coffee, too indignant to put forth the effort for a more elaborate order. Once they sat down, she felt her "nonchalant girlfriend" façade deteriorating. She couldn't help it. It was bound to happen sometime.

"Um, that was really weird, James."

"Yeah, I guess so."

"I don't know how it works in the ballet world," Colette joked, "But in the *real* world, that would be called *flirting*."

James shrugged and sat quietly. Colette thought he was contemplating the situation until he asked, "So, what do you want to do tonight?"

"Hey," Colette said. "You can't just change the subject. This is a problem."

James laughed. "It's not that big of a deal."

"Yes, it is. James. She is clearly into you. Can't you see that?"

At that, he grunted, looking both annoyed and embarrassed. He sat quietly, avoiding Colette's stare, and the frustrating silence sent more words spilling from her mouth.

"Have you not noticed the way she looks at you?" Colette asked. "How she touches you all the time? The way she completely ignores me? I mean, she has been pretty rude to me ever since we met and you're totally oblivious." James gave no response, and Colette felt her patience already wearing thin. "Don't you have *anything* to say?"

"What do you want me to say?" James asked. He shifted in his seat. "You're turning it into a bigger deal than it is. Can we please stop talking about it?"

"Why are you so uncomfortable talking about it?"

As she waited for him to respond, Colette's mind drifted to Alex's beauty and talent and the fact that she and James shared the same passion as a vocation, not just some cute pastime or pipedream. Despite the fact that Alex seemed to have no sense of humor or general civility, perhaps she and James really would make a better couple. It would make sense. Of course it would.

Colette expelled a sardonic laugh at her own expense, looked James in the eyes and calmly asked, "Is it because you're in love with her, too?"

"Of course not," he replied, thoroughly disappointed. Splotches of red appeared on his cheeks. "How can you even ask that?"

The sincerity in his voice snapped Colette out of her despondent daydream. There was nothing to worry about on his end. He didn't feel that way about Alex, and if he had, something would have happened between them by now. A feeling of relief came over her, though she also sensed that he was truly angry with her for the first time.

"Okay," Colette said. "I just had to ask. I'm sorry."

James gave a brief nod, took a drink of his coffee and asked, "Can we move on now?"

His attempt at dismissal produced the opposite effect. Colette felt anger rush back inside of her. How could he just brush this off so quickly?

"Um, *no*," Colette said, not bothering to restrain her attitude. "We're not done here."

James laughed again and threw his hands up. "What do you want me to do about it?"

"Well, you can start by acknowledging it, for one. Instead of acting like nothing's going on." Colette rolled her eyes and added, "Are you really that stupid?"

His shoulders fell. He sat back and stared at his coffee cup. Silence passed between them, giving Colette time to feel the regret settle inside of her. Her eyes filled with tears.

"James," Colette whispered. "I'm—I'm so sorry. I didn't mean that."

The muscles in his jaw tightened. Colette sat still, thinking hard about what she could say to explain herself. For some reason, she pictured Darrel and Jael witnessing their conversation and felt mortified. Had she ruined everything?

"You're *not* stupid. I'm really sorry I said that."

James nodded. "I know."

"You must think I'm a terrible person. God, what is wrong with me?"

"I know you didn't mean it, Colette. Let's just forget it." James stood up. His face was still flushed and his eyes distracted in thought. "Can we get out of here?"

Colette agreed, and they went back out into the cold, this time walking slowly. The wind had died down, and neither of them was in hurry to get back under this unpleasant circumstance.

It was clear that James wanted to forget the whole thing and, if she really thought about it, Colette couldn't blame him too much. It had to be awkward—speculating about his colleague's feelings for him. But Colette also knew that something would have to be resolved. She wouldn't be able to function otherwise, and, despite James's indifference toward Alex, there was still the problem of her behavior. His silence must have been giving her hope when there was none.

Colette reopened the topic as gently as she could.

"About Alex," Colette said. "I just don't like how it looks. It may seem to her—and to other people—that you're enjoying the attention. Can't you just, I don't know, gently put her in her place? You know, so she'd take a hint."

"I get what you're saying. I do talk about you at work. But I guess not really when she's around. I just don't talk to her much, in general. Except in rehearsal." James took a deep breath and stopped walking. He turned to face Colette and stood rigid as if he were about to say something especially important. "I'll try to be more direct with her, but I do have to dance with her pretty much every day. Is that gonna be a problem for you?"

Colette was surprised at his tone. He had sounded as if he had a choice in the matter. Would he do something drastic if she said yes?

"No, it's not a problem," Colette answered. She saw his body relax and added, "I know it's your job. Although, I can't pretend it's not a little awkward for me—you dancing with her when it's obvious that she wants you. I mean, it's *Song of Solomon* we're talking about. Major seduction opportunity. " James laughed and shook his head, and Colette quickly added, "I know it's juvenile. I'll try to get over it."

They continued to walk slowly, side by side, down the long sidewalk. Colette silently vowed to drop the subject. She began to wonder how she might have approached it differently in the first place. Of all the clichés, being jealous of her new boyfriend's dance partner was the most embarrassing. What must James think of her now?

She glanced at his face, which was contemplative and ruddy from the cold. The silence had given him space to think, and he finally began to say the words that Colette needed to hear.

"Helena mentioned it to me before," James said, gazing at the sidewalk a few feet ahead of him. "But I guess I'm good at ignoring things. I didn't think about how it might affect you." His eyes turned to rest on her face. "I'm sorry, Colette."

She nodded. "Thank you. It's okay."

James stopped walking again and took her by the hand. "You have nothing to worry about. I want to make sure you understand that. This is just work to me. And you—you're the only person I'm interested in." He paused and began to smile—the type of sly grin that made Colette want to hug him— and added, "I pretty much haven't stopped thinking about you since that day I taught your class."

Colette smiled. "Really?"

"Really."

"Despite my terrible dancing?"

"*No.* Your dancing is beautiful. Why are you so hard on yourself?"

It was a good question, and it stung a little. She remembered her similar discussion with Sammy and decided to be honest with him. "Because I see you and Alex and Helena and Iris and everyone else in the company and I see how it's *supposed* to look. I wish I knew what it felt like to dance that way."

James was silent for a few moments. He stared at Westmoreland ahead of them until his eyes lit up with sudden excitement.

"Hey," he said. "I have an idea. Why don't you learn *Cantique* with me?"

Colette laughed. "Now you're just being mean."

"No seriously. Will you try it at least?"

"I can't dance *en pointe*!"

James shrugged. "It doesn't matter."

"Um, yes, it does," she said, incredulous.

"We'll adjust it. Come on. It'll be fun."

Colette sighed. As nervous as the idea made her, she also didn't want to pass up an opportunity to dance with him. The two of them alone in the studio—that would be fun.

"Well..." she said. "I guess we can *try* it, if you really want to. Although, you'll probably be disappointed."

"No, I won't."

They had reached the door to the Westmoreland building. James opened it for her, but she didn't feel right going back in.

"Do you mind if I sit this one out?" Colette asked. "I'll come again some other time."

"Oh, okay," James said with a little disappointment. "That's fine. See you tonight, though?"

"Sure," she said. She could see dancers in the lobby through the open door—Helena and three others, maybe even Alex. James, practicing his promised directness, threw his arms around Colette and planted her with a theatrical kiss. She heard laughter from the lobby and, seeing Helena waving her direction, she waved back and covered her face in feigned embarrassment.

"Too much?" James whispered, grinning.

Colette laughed. "Nope."

CHAPTER NINETEEN

Colette and Sammy sat on the couch, both eating cereal for dinner and trying to keep Garçon at bay. Sammy was bundled up in her running clothes—her cheeks red and wind-burned from the cold—as she listened to Colette discuss James's idea of teaching her the *Cantique Pas*. As usual, Colette was having second thoughts about the whole thing.

"Why not? Of course you have to do it," Sammy insisted. "If you don't, I'll tell him all of your secrets."

"What secrets?" Colette asked.

Sammy paused to crunch her shredded wheat. "You know. Like that time you farted during barre stretch."

"What?!" Colette laughed. "That wasn't me."

"Whatever. It *so* was."

"I couldn't help it. You know barre stretch forces it out. Anyways, he's a guy; he farts *all the time*."

"Alright, well then I'll tell him about the program you kept."

"How do you know about that? Do you go through my dresser when I'm gone?"

"No," Sammy retorted, looking offended. "Remember the other day, when you insisted that I borrow your wrap sweater?"

"Oh, right. Okay, so the program was a souvenir. No big deal."

"Sure it was. There's also that time you had to Google what a socket set was."

"...fair enough."

A sudden pounding on the front door made them both jump. James entered the house before they could answer, bringing the cold in with him. Garçon ran to greet him.

"Hey there, little buddy," James said, reaching down to pet him.

"What's going on?" Colette asked.

"I tried to call you. Why don't you ever have your phone with you?"

"Sorry."

"The big studio is empty tonight and I got the okay to stay after hours. You want to come dance with me?"

Sammy shot Colette an expectant glance. Colette sighed and stood up. "Sure, okay. Let me just go throw up my cereal—I mean, go change."

As she walked toward her bedroom, she heard James chuckle and say, "She's such a goofball."

"Tell me about it," Sammy replied. "I had to blackmail her into doing this. She was about to bail on you."

"Thanks, I owe you one. I don't know why she's being so stubborn about it."

"I can still hear you," Colette called from her bedroom.

"Self-sabotage," Sammy answered, even louder. "The frustrating part is that she's pretty much good at everything and she doesn't even know it."

"She is, isn't she?"

"Yeah. Except parallel parking." Sammy shuddered. "Don't ask her to do that."

"Hey, I'm not *that* bad," Colette said, reappearing with her coat in her hand. She turned to James. "How hard are you going to work me? Do I need a water bottle?"

"Don't worry about it. I've got you covered."

"All right. Bye, Sammy."

"Bye, guys." Sammy pointed at Colette. "You have fun."

WHEN THEY ARRIVED at Westmoreland, the air had gone still and quiet, as if it were about to snow. James looked excited and quickly ushered Colette into the main studio, which was more of a little theater than a class space.

"Wait here," he said. He jogged to the opposite corner and flipped a few switches. The giant shades covering the floor-to-ceiling windows rose, and snowflakes began to fall softly, as if on cue.

"Oh, wow," Colette said. "It's beautiful."

James looked up from where he now sat fiddling with his iPod and the stereo system. "Pretty magical, huh?"

After a few minutes, the *Cantique* music began to fill the air. It sounded different against a snowy backdrop. Until then, Colette has associated its entrancing melody with the heat of the Middle East. It had brought to mind the smell of spices and of exotic botanicals. It was why Alex, with her beautiful bronze skin and dark eyes, looked like the perfect casting choice.

Cantique

Now, paired with a Midwestern winter, the music sounded personal and romantic, as if it were their own secret song.

James showed her where to start. She was to stand in *effacé devant*, both legs in *plié*, with her head in profile instead of being tilted toward the audience. Once James had approached her, she would step into *piqué arabesque*, and he would immediately lift her in a *presage*. Colette's heart sank. This did not bode well.

"Once you get up there, your lower leg will come into *passé.*"

"Oh, no. You shouldn't try to lift me. I weigh a lot more than those Westmoreland girls."

James rolled his eyes. "Colette, I don't know if you've noticed, but I'm like *freakishly* strong."

She laughed. "I just don't want you to hurt yourself—"

It was no use. James had already begun to lift her.

"See?" he said.

"Okay. But can you wait until I'm ready this time?"

"Yeah. So, *effacé*. Yep... and now *piqué!*"

James began the lift, but Colette was off balance. He quickly set her down.

"Sorry."

"That's okay. Let's try again."

They tried twice more, each time improving only slightly. Colette's assumption that this was a terrible idea was already being confirmed. James was starting to look fatigued.

"One more time?" he asked. She nodded. "Really hold the position. Okay, ready. *Piqué* and hold it! Hold it."

Colette held her strongest arabesque and looked in the mirror. While her lines were far from perfect, she felt like she looked quite elegant as she drew her leg up into *passé*. She and James looked good together, with their reflections framed by the falling snow. And the feeling of weightlessness was one she could definitely get used to.

James put her down. "Good," he said. "That was way better."

He continued marking through the next few steps with her. They were tough. He was already teaching Colette new terms she had never heard of, which made her feel even sillier for attempting to dance with him. They spent about twenty minutes on these steps before she started to grasp them. She could have stopped there and spent an hour perfecting what she had learned, but James insisted they move on.

"Okay, so from here, *fouetté* to *pirouette*." He demonstrated as he spoke, but Colette stood still. She had never done that without the barre. "Just try it. I'll be holding you here—extend front, yep, carry it side, turn!" Colette turned a wobbly *pirouette* at half speed. "Try again," James instructed. She spotted herself in the mirror, looking determined, and tried again, but her turn was even worse the second time.

Colette cringed and asked, "Can I just do it from fourth?"

James stared at her for a second. "Yeah, okay. Sure. From fourth."

They reset themselves, and she turned a decent *pirouette* but stopped too late. He caught her by the waist. "Good," he said. "Now try a double." Colette gawked at him. He was turning into quite the taskmaster. She prepped in fourth position.

Spot, lift, float.

To her surprise, she turned a better double than the single, but James didn't pause to celebrate. "Okay," he said. "Do you want to finish out the phrase and call it a night?"

"Sure," Colette replied. "But this is just... kind of embarrassing. You must feel like you're dancing with a five-year-old."

"No. I'm glad I can share this with you. I know this is advanced, but you're doing great. Trust me."

Colette sighed. "If you say so."

Still hyper-focused on the task at hand, James taught her what remained of the phrase and asked if they could run through everything she had learned. Colette was overwhelmed. This thing was eight minutes long and she had barely learned any of it. James studied her face.

"Colette, I just want you to have fun with me, okay? That's why we're doing this. Don't try to be perfect. I'm not asking you to be."

She wanted to cry. It took all of her focus to prevent it.

"Babe," James said, his voice softening. "What's wrong? We can stop if you want."

Colette shook her head. "No. Let's go over it. I want to go over it."

"Alright," he said. "Just focus on the music, okay?"

He smiled and restarted the track. Colette took a deep breath, and imagined herself in the Shulamite woman costume she had designed in her head. It wouldn't do; she felt ridiculous. Instead, she watched James walk to his starting position. How was she really there with him? How had it all happened? And why couldn't she just enjoy herself?

The music started, and she took her *effacé* position, trying to listen without thinking too much. It helped. She slowly began to feel what *Cantique* wanted her feel—to be noble, beautiful and completely in love. Miraculously, she made it through everything James had taught her without having to stop, though she knew her dancing was laughable compared to his. She couldn't help but picture the steps as they were meant to be danced—the way Alex would dance them. Or the way Helena would dance them. Or Iris. Or that red-headed student from class. Heck, maybe even Tina would do it better. At least she would be easier to lift.

"Yes!" James said, looking thrilled. "You see? That was great."

"It felt okay." Colette sat down on the floor. "But I can't imagine doing a full eight minutes of that, let alone a two-hour ballet. How do you guys do it?"

"A crapload of practice." James joined her on the floor and began to change his shoes.

"Oh man," Colette said. "Your feet are *disgusting*."

"Yeah. You haven't seen them yet?"

"*No*. You've always had socks on. For the love of God, put them away!"

James laughed and rubbed his shoulder. "Sorry I'm so hideous."

"Are your arms going to be sore tomorrow?" Colette asked.

"I'm sore *every* day. Just wait. We haven't gotten to all of the press lifts yet."

"James…"

"Yeah?"

"Don't feel like you have to keep teaching me this. It's a ton of work for you. You're already so busy. And if this is already hard for me, well, I doubt I can do much of the rest."

He nodded, seriously considering her point. Colette knew that the whole thing had been more difficult that he anticipated, as if he had forgotten that she was still a beginner. "We can see how it goes," James said. "I just thought it could be something fun we could do. I like dancing with you."

"I thought I would, too," Colette replied. "But it kind of just makes me sad."

"Why?"

She sighed. "It's frustrating that I can't be better. It took me about twenty-three years to find something that I'm actually passionate about. I *love* ballet, but what am I supposed to do with it?" She sensed that she should stop there, but words continued to fall from her mouth. "I'm too old, too inexperienced to offer anything to this world of yours, yet I would give anything to be a part of it. Now, here I am with an education that I don't care about and an entry-level job that has nothing to do with it. Still, all I can think about is *ballet,* of all things! And I'm twenty-six! How dumb is that?" Colette was crying now. She couldn't help it. "Do you know what it's like to be so passionate about something that you can do absolutely *nothing* with?"

James, surprised to finally see the depth of her frustration, took her hand and shook his head. "I'm sorry. I don't know what that's like. But, Colette, you can still do something with it. You *are* doing something with it. Remember that dance you were just learning? You're the one who made it possible. And, you can always keep dancing, no matter what."

"Not dancing *well.* I'm too poor to afford more classes and I'm only getting older. Plus, *Cantique* was a fluke. It's a one-time thing."

James focused on the floor, lost in thought and unable to counter the points she was making. Colette followed his gaze and wiped her tears with her sleeve, waiting for him to speak. She wished that she could take back her neurotic speech. Coupled with their fight about Alex, she wouldn't be surprised if she had freaked him out for good. What must he think of her now?

She watched his eyes grow even more pensive, and he finally broke his silence. "Obviously, God gave you this passion for a reason," he declared. "Something will come of it."

Colette faced him, astonished. "You really believe that?"

"Yeah, I do. Don't you?"

"I guess I haven't thought about it. But, you know, I *want* to believe that... Is that why you're so confident about everything? Seriously, you never seem to get anxious. How can someone so talented be so steadfast?"

James laughed. "I don't know. Maybe because of my dad."

"And your mom!"

"Yeah."

"Your family—they're just amazing. You don't know how lucky you are."

"They can be your family, too," James said, reaching for her cheek. "They love you, you know."

His words touched Colette deeply. She hadn't done anything to deserve such love, but now she would do anything to keep it. Her tears fell faster, each one dispensing a tremendous feeling of relief. An invisible weight lifted off of her chest, as if there had been some creature latched to her for her entire life, whispering poisonous words to her face. The self-doubt, the anxiety, the fear that had muddled her decisions—it had all come from this parasite's mouth and she was too exhausted to keep fighting it by herself. Sammy had called it self-sabotage, but Colette understood now that there was something else—some force trying to hold her down. And if that were the case, well, then there had to be something else trying to lift her up.

The music changed. James stood up and extended his hand. "How about a waltz?"

"Alright."

They glided along the studio, Colette catching glimpses of the persistent snow. She had never waltzed with someone who knew what he was doing. Once she was comfortable with the rhythm, she barely needed to do anything. He was leading her gently and she simply responded. It felt like floating.

Every man should learn how to do this.

At the end of the song, James led her through a series of exhilarating turns. She spotted a sign on the wall instinctively and danced before she had time to think. He caught her in a dip.

"You're a natural," he said.

"That was amazing. We should do that all the time."

"Okay, we will," he replied, looking mischievous.

James hurried her out into the still night and insisted that they waltz their way back to the car. Their footprints made circular patterns in the snow as he flung them wildly around the parking lot. She had to hold onto him by the arms, her hand covering the ampersand in his tattoo. Colette could barely catch her breath from laughing so hard. From now on, she would try to live like this—freely and lightly.

CHAPTER TWENTY

A s much as she hated to admit it, Colette would need to find a way out of Tempe's sooner rather than later. The realization came as she sat in the back office processing new merchandise. She was happy to have a break from the register, but the mindless, repetitive nature of her task was becoming old. During the summer, she hadn't minded this kind of work. Now, she felt her brain turning to mush as she opened package after package, printed tag after tag, and stuck tags to box after box.

To keep herself occupied, she thought about the *Cantique Pas*. She tried to imagine what it would feel like to dance it properly—like how Alex would dance it. They would be in rehearsal right now, her hands all over James.

Colette stopped herself from further daydreaming on that subject. Her phone had been lighting up next to her, and she resolved to finish her project before letting herself check it. She printed another row of price tags, feeling a sense of urgency to complete her work, and then laughed at the absurdity of it all. What was she doing? What good did it serve? She was too smart for this.

Darrel appeared in the doorway. "Now, I understand you're coming over for dinner tonight?"

"Yep. Is Jael sure I don't need to bring anything?"

"Oh, I think she's got it covered. I'm actually gonna head out here in a bit, so I'll see you later tonight. Travis is coming in to close."

"Okay. See you later, Darrel."

She finished her tags. When she finally checked her phone, she couldn't believe the words that were waiting for her.

Costume assistant went on early maternity leave. They need extra help for Nutcracker. You interested?

She had to be interested. And the timing was too impeccable. Colette felt a jolt in her stomach. Maybe the time to move on was now.

James texted again.

Need your resume asap. Send to myrak@westmorelandballet.org

139

She could pull it off. As soon as Travis arrived, she told him she would need to run home. She knew she would have to send her resume before she could over-think the matter. Lately, opportunities like this—the kind that seemed to fall into her lap—proved to be worth taking. And this particular one seemed too good to be true.

LATER THAT EVENING, Colette arrived at the Brennans' house before James. This was not unexpected, as he had been consistently rehearsing late, squeezing in all of the extra work for *Cantique Pas* in between *Nutcracker* chaos. Darrel answered the door.

"Jael is around here somewhere," he told Colette. "Make yourself at home. I'm sure Jimmy will be here soon."

She wandered into the kitchen, where she found the source of the delicious aroma that was filling the house. Jael had made a giant pot of beef and vegetable stew. Colette hoped James would get there soon. She was starving now.

Colette found Jael on the screened-in porch. She was wrapped in a blanket and sitting in front of an easel, dropping tubes of acrylic paint into a bucket. Colette squinted to inspect the canvas resting on the easel. It was a nearly finished painting of two female figures, one wearing a romantic tutu posing for a portrait, and the other painting the portrait with her back to the viewer. Jael's brush strokes were loose and light-filled, as if she were trying to summon the ballerinas in a Degas. A handwritten note had been taped along the top of the easel: *She worked feverishly, while this temporary talent was still housed within her.*

The message was surprisingly philosophical, but Colette felt that she understood the gist of it. She had felt that way each time she had created a garment or had pulled off a college research paper—and each time she danced well. Her talent was not rightfully hers but had miraculously been on loan to her; she always felt frantic to use it while she still could. Had Jael felt that way even as a professional?

"Hi, Jael," Colette finally said. "I didn't know you were a painter."

Surprised, Jael turned and stood up to give Colette a hug. "So good to see you. I'm not really a painter. I just took it up as an outlet, you know, since I'm not able to dance anymore."

"Well, it looks to me like you're a painter. This is really good."

"Thank you." Jael smiled and re-wrapped herself in her blanket. "Unfortunately, there are always things I'm unhappy with. Painting is so much more difficult than ballet."

Colette laughed. "I suppose it's all relative."

James arrived, looking exhausted. He greeted Colette with a brief kiss before turning to his mother.

"Do you have an ice pack?"

"I'm sure we do. I'll look and see."

"Did you get hurt?" Colette asked.

"Naw, just strained my shoulder a bit." James lowered his voice. "Have you heard back yet?"

"I haven't checked. Would they reply so soon?"

"I think so. They're pretty desperate to find someone. They were going to split the work between volunteers, but they've already run out of people."

"But this is a paid position, right?"

"Yeah. It probably doesn't pay much, but it's better than nothing. Listen... I put in a good word for you. It's probably yours if you want it, but don't feel pressured to do it if you're not interested."

"No," Colette said, her excitement rising. "I'm definitely interested."

Colette checked her phone. Sure enough, she had already received a reply from Myra, the costume mistress. Myra explained that the job would be twenty to twenty-five hours a week and would only last through *Nutcracker* season. Colette would be matching the children with costumes and taking measurements for alterations, as well as executing whatever miscellaneous tasks needed to be done. Little sewing would be involved, but Colette couldn't help but think that her education would work to her advantage. Myra wanted to meet as soon as possible.

"James," Colette whispered. "I think I have a shot at this. I know it's only temporary, but think of how fun it would be! I would be there in the middle of everything! I would get to see you more."

"I know," James said, looking just as excited. "I hope it works out."

Jael returned with an ice pack. "Dinner's ready when you two are."

"Yeah, let's eat," James said.

"Honey?" Jael called. "You ready for dinner?"

When Darrel walked into the dining room, Colette almost didn't recognize him. He was wearing glasses, flannel pajama bottoms, and a pair of shearling slippers.

"Whoa. Are those your comfy clothes, Darrel?" Colette asked, suppressing a giggle. Seeing her boss at home in his pajamas was a special kind of experience.

"Yeah. I call these my loungin' pants," Darrel said. He seemed to appreciate the fact that she had noticed.

Colette looked over at James, who was already eating, completely oblivious to the situation. He had taken off his shirt and fastened the ice pack around his shoulder with a pink, floral tea towel. Meanwhile, Jael was still wrapped in her blanket, shuffling around the kitchen.

"Would you like a roll?" Jael asked. "What's so funny, dear?"

"Oh, nothing," Colette said.

James looked up from his bowl of stew. "Yeah, what?"

"You guys are just so adorable."

Jael observed the three of them and began to laugh. "I guess we are kind of a ragamuffin bunch, aren't we?"

"I feel like I should have worn my Snuggie," Colette replied.

Darrel's face lit up, and he quickly disappeared into the hallway.

"What on earth…" Jael said.

Darrel had immediately returned with a camouflage, fleece blanket. He draped it over Colette's shoulders.

"There you go," Darrel said. "So you won't feel left out."

"Ah. So thoughtful," Colette said, cracking up.

Hunched over and sleepy-eyed, James looked at her and said, "You look good in camo, babe."

"Thanks. That would sound creepy if you weren't so cute."

James grinned. "Hey, why don't you share your news with Mom and Dad?"

Colette tried not to look too annoyed. She hadn't wanted to tell Darrel yet, but now it seemed she had no choice in the matter.

"Well, it's not really *news* yet, but James let me know about an opening at Westmoreland today. They need someone to help out in the costume shop." Colette paused to glance at Darrel. "So, I went ahead and sent in my resume. It would only be through the end of the year. And it's part-time, so I could stay at Tempe's—that is, if I even get the job."

"Well, ain't that something," said Darrel. "Sounds like it's right up your alley."

"Yeah, I think so."

"That's wonderful," Jael said. "It's a great way to get your foot in the door. I'm sure they'll want to keep you once they get to know you."

"They sure will," Darrel added. "She's a hard worker."

Colette smiled but still felt uneasy about the situation. She thought she owed Darrel more of an explanation. "I'm just a little worried about, well—if they do want to hire me—how things will work out at Tempe's. I could probably only work thirty hours, tops. I don't want to mess up everyone's schedules."

"Oh, don't you worry about that," Darrel said.

"I just hate to complicate things."

"Colette, we'll work it out when it comes to it. Just like we've always done. You do what you need to do."

She nodded, feeling truly grateful for Darrel and the freedom his words gave her. James reached for her hand under the table.

"You see? You've got this in the bag."

THE REST OF the evening was perfect. Colette had never felt so comfortable with a family—not even her own. After dinner, they sat by the fire that Darrel had built and held easy conversation. None of them were afraid of silence, which she greatly appreciated. There was something completely satisfying in being able to sit quietly with people she knew and trusted. No one grasped for topics. No one pushed agendas.

Jael eventually produced a photo album and curled herself next to Colette, much like Garçon would have. She spread her blanket over Colette's lap.

"Here's little James," Jael said.

There he was as a chubby, ornery-looking kid with blond hair. In the over-exposed photo, his eyes were a paler shade of aquamarine, but he certainly looked like himself. Colette observed adult James, who was sprawled out on his stomach in front of the fire. His hair was much darker now.

"You were so cute," Colette said. James grunted and lifted his head. He must have been falling asleep.

"Look at Darrel," Jael whispered.

"Oh, wow."

Darrel circa 1993 had a mustache, thick glasses, and was wearing a stiff, trucker hat long before they had become ironically cool. He was holding both Josh and James in his lap and looking quite happy.

There weren't many photos of Jael, but the few Colette saw were lovely. Even in her wind-breaker outfits, Jael was timeless. She looked extremely young, though she would have already been retired by then. Colette tried to imagine what it would be like to sacrifice such a unique career for her family of boys.

"Was it hard to quit dancing?" Colette asked.

"Sometimes," Jael replied. "But it was always worth it. It's different for people now. More women are able to go back to dance after a time. I tried to go back, but I just couldn't do it. At least, I didn't want to."

"Did you miss performing, though?"

"I did. I missed it terribly, but it was also such a difficult lifestyle. Looking back, I wasn't really cut out for it. The only reason I survived was because I simply *had* to dance. I loved it too much. You have to love it completely to be a professional. But, in the end, I found that I loved my boys more."

Jael and Colette both chuckled as they looked at Darrel, now sound asleep in his recliner, and James, who was drooling onto the carpet.

"Can I ask how you and Darrel fell in love?"

Jael smiled. "Well, we met at a business course. At the time, I felt like I needed to get a real college degree. I was kind of going through an identity crisis. It turned out that school wasn't the best idea for me—I felt so out of place there. But I'm glad I didn't quit too early. Darrel sat next to me one night and we got to talking. He had this way of listening that made me feel so special and understood. I was so used to being talked *at*—being directed and scrutinized all the time... Darrel was just very different. Anyway, he took me out for ice cream that same night, and I remember feeling happier than I had in years. He was the kindest person I had ever met. He still is."

"Same here," Colette said.

"Plus," Jael continued, smiling at the memory. "I remember he wasn't too blown away by my career at first. He seemed interested, but not like other people. When some people hear that you're a professional dancer, they assume that you're rich and famous." She paused to laugh. "Or, they take the opposite approach and ask why you don't have a real job."

"Ugh," Colette said, rolling her eyes.

"Darrel didn't ask those kinds of questions. He was more interested in my life outside of ballet, which was really refreshing at the time. I needed someone to see me as a person—a real person who had other things to offer the world. I was actually on the brink of quitting dance, but he saved it for me—rather ironically, I suppose. My career really didn't take off until after we met. And he was always so supportive."

"I'm sure he was," Colette said, still feeling a faint sense of awe that she was cuddled up next to Jael Maier, sharing in her secrets. She could listen to her all evening. "Did you have a favorite role to dance?"

"Probably Juliet," Jael replied. "Or Giselle. I always loved dancing Giselle."

"There's a photo of you from *Giselle* in one of the studios. I always stand by it at the barre. It seems so strange to be talking to you about it now. I'm still a little star struck."

Jael laughed. "Well, as you can see, I'm quite ordinary in person. Not to mention *old.*" Her eyes wandered to her son. "And I'm sure you know by now that James is just a typical young man. Yes, he's extremely talented, but he's also just a good boy who works very hard."

Colette nodded. "That's why I love him."

Jael looked pleasantly surprised. She squeezed Colette's hand. "I can tell that he loves you, too. I've never seen him this way with anyone before."

Colette saved these words in her mind and, when it was time to leave, crouched down on the floor to kiss James on the cheek. She turned back to Jael.

"Good night," Colette whispered. "Thanks for everything. Tell the guys bye for me."

"I will, dear. Drive safely. Oh, and text me when you get home. I'm finally texting now."

Colette laughed and promised she would. She would text Jael Maier when she got home.

CHAPTER TWENTY-ONE

Colette arrived early on the day of her interview. She was told to wait by the front desk, giving her time to try to talk herself into a state of calm. She hadn't been this nervous since seeing James saunter down the stairs at his parents' house. And yet, her fear was not of rejection. Rather, she was terrified because she was certain that she would get the job. By now she had had sufficient time to think it over—to create problems that could happen afterward. Maybe they would expect her to do things she couldn't do. Maybe they would realize that she had nothing to offer. And then she would have to tell James. Making a fool of herself at Tempe's was one thing, but she couldn't bear the thought of disappointing anyone at Westmoreland.

After several rounds of tightening and releasing all of her muscles—from her toes to her jaw—Colette's anxiety turned into impatience. She wanted the appointment to be over, so she could be safe at home. And yet, she couldn't help but be excited for another inside look at Westmoreland, no matter what the outcome.

Freely and lightly, she reminded herself.

When her interviewer finally arrived, Colette relaxed. The woman clomping toward her in Dansko shoes was not a bit intimidating. Colette immediately observed that her personal style was a serious of juxtapositions. She had paired her clogs with a long, nautical striped dress, a fleece jacket, and red polka-dot earrings. Her hair, which was half gray, was crammed back into a giant barrette, while her only makeup was bright red lipstick, which looked rather shocking against her pale skin and bare eyes. But she had a kind face, and it already put Colette at ease.

"I'm so sorry," the woman said, shaking Colette's hand. "I hope you haven't been waiting long. I'm Myra Kelly. My goodness, you're gorgeous!"

"Oh... thank you."

"Just breathtaking." Myra sashayed back to take a good look at her. "I'm so glad James found you. He's such a nice boy. You know, he deserves someone like you."

Colette laughed. "Are you sure? You don't even know me yet."

"Oh, I can already tell you are wonderful. Let's go ahead and go on back. I'll show you where you'll be working!"

So, it was already a done deal? What had James told Myra, exactly? Colette figured she'd better not ask.

The costume shop wasn't as glamorous as Colette had imagined. In fact, she discovered, it was kind of a mess. For housing such beautiful costumes, it was a drab and chaotic space. The dirty floor was sprinkled with trampled sequins, and Myra's office was the most disorganized workspace Colette had ever seen. This wasn't wholly unexpected in light of her eccentricities, but it was clear that Myra was a benign type of crazy. As she showed Colette around the shop, she took every opportunity to share some sort of tangential story. Colette listened attentively, amused at the fact that Myra could somehow make even the most mundane tales sound dramatic.

"This is a rack for *Coppélia* that just arrived," Myra announced. "We'll be altering them eventually, but you know, I can't even *think* about anything until *Nutcracker* season is over. Speaking of that, this whole back room is just for *Nutcracker* costumes. I regret to say, that's where you'll be spending most of your time."

Colette couldn't believe her luck. She grinned like a fool and said, "Looks like fun to me!"

"Bless you, child. We'll see if you still feel that way in a couple of weeks."

Colette pointed to a table piled high with fabric. "What is all that for?"

"Oh, those are for the gala performances. We're making *everything*. Very fun, very exciting, but you'll see it can get quite stressful around here."

"Does that include the one James is choreographing?"

"Why, yes it does! Actually, let me show you something…"

Colette peeked through the fabric while Myra left the room. There were several bright chiffons and rich satins—aqua, Mediterranean blue, royal purple, seafoam green and a deep red. She wondered if they could be for Solomon's Bride. She hoped they were.

"Here are the designs that Liz was working on for James's piece. It's a shame that she won't get to make them herself, but, then again, I can't feel too sorry for her. Did you hear about what happened?"

Colette shook her head. "I just heard she had a baby."

"But do you know who the father is? That *repetiteur* from Paris. Luc de la Coste."

"Really?" Colette had no idea who she was talking about.

"Yes, it was quite the whirlwind romance. He was only here a few weeks before they became serious. He was just completely head over heels for her. I would be concerned, but if you saw the two of them together, it just works!"

"Wow."

"I know. Isn't it just the most romantic thing? Swept away by a handsome choreographer!" Myra's tone turned grave. "Now, if only they'd get married. She'll pretty much be raising that baby by herself. He has to go back to France, you know. "

"Hmm. Sounds like it would make a good novel."

"You're absolutely right! I'll have to remember that when I retire. Anyway, Trinity, my other assistant, will be finishing the work for this one." Myra handed her the sketches. "Aren't the designs gorgeous?"

Colette was astonished. It was as if Liz had been in her head. There was her Shulamite woman, set in watercolor and wearing a flowing veil of blues as brilliant as lapis lazuli. Her head was crowned in a circlet of lilies, her satin bodice embroidered with jewels, and she bore golden cuffs on each arm. The skirt was perhaps the most interesting and, Colette noted, was remarkably like what she had imagined. Liz's drawing showed azure and delicate, seafoam green chiffons draped in many thin, asymmetrical layers, the longest of which fell just above the ankle. Such an ethereal skirt would make Alex's turns even more impressive.

"They're more beautiful than I imagined," Colette said. "They're just perfect."

"Oh? Had you spoken about it with James?"

"Yes. I actually—well, I sort of helped plan the ballet with him—" Colette stopped, amazed. There, at the bottom of the pile, was a page of Tempe's letterhead—a photocopy of her full-length *Cantique* libretto.

"Really?" Myra said. "That's wonderful—"

"No wonder..." Colette said, studying the page. The costume sketches in the margins had been circled, and James's rough handwriting read: *Liz - As close to these as possible. Thx.*

"What is it, dear?"

"This is mine. These are my sketches. James must have given it to her."

"You don't say... They're lovely." Myra looked concerned. "He didn't ask your permission?"

It took Colette a few seconds for her question to sink in. Myra was worried that she was upset that Liz had used her work, which couldn't be farther from the truth.

"He didn't," Colette said, beaming. "But I don't mind at all. I can't believe people actually like what I've done. I can't believe my ideas are going to be on stage. This is incredible..." Colette trailed off, overcome by a sudden bout of emotion. Those drawings weren't even her best work; they were doodles. She had never felt more validated. With tears in her eyes, she looked at Myra and said, "This may sound ridiculous, but this is one of the coolest things that's ever happened to me."

At that, Myra gave her a hug and said, "Oh, that's beautiful. I'm so glad you're here! When can you start?"

CHAPTER TWENTY-TWO

The following weeks flew by in a whirlwind of work, stress and euphoria. Colette could not grasp the fact that she was suddenly working for Westmoreland Ballet. Employment there had been an unarticulated dream, and she felt that it was nothing short of miraculous. Yet, her work was more blue-collar than it had been at Tempe's. After her initial project, most of the tasks she did were menial—spraying pointe shoes, dying hair pieces, washing hosiery and making sure costumes stayed in the correct dressing rooms. But Colette didn't care—not when she had a Westmoreland badge with her name on it. That badge meant that she was an insider, and it could get her practically anywhere.

Myra and Trinity did the real work. They took care of alterations and assisted the dancers once *Nutcracker* began its three-week run. Colette never actually got to see the ballet; she worked during every evening and matinee performance doing the same, repetitive tasks and endless loads of laundry. Sometimes, she had to deal with minor catastrophes in the children's dressing rooms. They always seemed to happen right before curtain.

Although Trinity and Myra were busy, Colette got to know them rather well. They were both outgoing and hardly ever worked in silence, though they were also extremely different from one another. Myra proved to be even more eccentric than Colette had thought during their first meeting. In time, she came to view Myra as a benevolent aristocrat who had been dumped into the wrong century. She enunciated like an old-timey Broadway performer, and everything she spoke of was "delicious" and "delightful" or "horrid" and "so *Derrida*," whatever that meant. She cheerfully prattled on about the same subjects when the *Nutcracker* Party Guests stopped by to get their headpieces pinned.

"Only two more performances this weekend, ladies and gents," she would say. "Then you can break out the sherry."

Colette wondered if anyone besides Myra actually drank sherry.

Trinity, on the other hand, was a little rough around the edges, with multi-colored hair and a lot of tattoos. Every once in a while, Colette caught glimpses of her working on the costume for Solomon's Bride. She watched with fascination as Trinity cut Liz's pattern pieces and hammered out the sewing without much personal interest. It was simply another garment that needed to be done, and she was a seamstress first and foremost. Her vast knowledge of garment construction was intimidating, and she had a habit of reacting violently whenever the equipment was uncooperative.

"Damn this thing to hell!" Trinity would say, smacking the machine as if it were a human head. "Why does this goddamn needle keep unthreading itself?!"

After Colette laughed at one of these outbursts, Trinity took a liking to her. Ironically, she had no patience for the dancers. On several occasions, one of the *corps de ballet* girls would peek into the backstage costume shop with some sort of complaint.

"Can you make this tighter?"

"This is really itchy."

"Can you fix this for tonight?"

Trinity's response was always the same. She would sit silently for several uncomfortable seconds, let out a deep sigh, hold out her hand, and say, "Give it here."

Half the time, she wouldn't even fix the costume. She had a term for this technique—the P.E. Alteration. Colette asked what the *P.E.* stood for.

"Placebo Effect," Trinity replied. "Usually, they try it on and are all like 'Oh, yeah. That's much better. Thanks.' And I haven't even done anything! It's freakin' hilarious."

Colette had to laugh, despite feeling horrified for the dancers. "Hasn't anyone caught on?"

Trinity thought for a second. "Yes," she said. That's all she would divulge on the matter.

Colette wondered if that instance had anything to do with Alex, who seemed to be the one dancer whom Trinity took seriously. She had seen her fix a clasp for Alex on-the-spot with minimal complaint. While Alex had stood waiting, Colette asked her how *Cantique Pas* rehearsals were going.

Alex looked at her directly and replied, "Really well. I love the music."

It was a short response, but at least she seemed sincere. Alex had remained aloof since Colette began working at Westmoreland, but she seemed to be keeping her distance from James. Perhaps he had finally said something to her. Colette didn't really want to know.

The evenings and weekends Colette spent wandering the labyrinth of backstage corridors seemed surreal compared to the weekdays she spent at Tempe's. Now that she was working two jobs, getting to Tempe's on time was more difficult. Darrel was exceedingly patient with her. She was always tired and could never seem to eat a proper meal, but she wouldn't have traded it for anything. Simply being in the midst of a professional ballet company was enough to keep her going, and she loved running into James between scenes. He was usually preoccupied but occasionally stole a kiss before dashing off to wait in the wings. He looked strangely natural in his ridiculous, musty costumes. On the nights when he danced the Spanish role, Colette felt as though she were kissing a prince.

Oddly enough, there was only one thing she missed during this frantic month—dancing. She couldn't remember the last time she had made it to class. Sammy had bravely gone a couple of times without her before finally abandoning it, too. Though Colette's crazy schedule caused her to lose a few pounds, she felt her muscles getting weaker without the exercise. She tried her best to do her own barre workout wherever she was, but it wasn't the same. There was no substitute for a good class.

On his few free evenings, James would come over and teach Colette some steps from the *pas de deux*. They pushed the furniture back and used the living room as a dance floor. Sometimes, Sammy would make popcorn, and she and Garçon would watch from the couch, as if they had no other form of entertainment. Sammy would slouch down, put her feet up, and shout ridiculous feedback at them.

"Gorgeous, darlings! Needs more sensuality, please. I want to see hips thrusting! *Where* are the fawns and pomegranates? This is false advertising."

By late December, Colette could remember nearly all of the choreography, although about a third of it was too advanced for her to do anything but mark the steps. James learned to keep these moments light for her sake. Sometimes, he would assume the female role during the bride's variation. Colette laughed through it every time. Indeed, the whole process of counting through the *Cantique Pas* had been rather comical. Once she saw Alex assume the role with live music, it was another story entirely.

Toward the end of *Nutcracker* performances, Lavoisier requested to see a full run-through in the studio. James invited Colette and she sat next to Lavoisier in a metal folding chair, feeling quite official. They had brought in the concert pianist who would be performing at the gala with them. Colette was excited but also felt nervous for James. She expected that she would hang on his every move, praying that he didn't mess up.

Her fears melted away, however, as soon as those first, mysterious notes were played. James was strong and confident. It was clear that his bride and his audience were in good hands. He acted in character, showing courtly passion and respect for his partner, and his solo variation was kingly. Despite James's nearly perfect technique, Colette's eyes kept darting back to Alexandra.

Alex seemed to know exactly what the music meant. She spoke its language, and she repaid its magic with more magic. Or maybe she was actually Solomon's bride, reincarnate. Whatever the case, her dancing reinstated *Cantique* as a holy song. There was nothing comical about it now. Beauty, sweetness and romance radiated from her fingertips. Her *épaulement* evoked both innocence and wisdom. Her fiery and fluid movements described the unquenchable nature of love. Colette tried her best to restrain her jealousy.

When Alex pantomimed placing a seal on James's arm, her expression was solemn, which surprised Colette. She had pictured this moment being joyful and celebratory, like a twenty-first century engagement. But Alex was interpreting it as something more serious—something like a covenant. With resignation, Colette realized that Alex had the correct idea, and the music seemed to agree. Alex really was an artist, and Colette suddenly remembered why she had been so inspired by the music in the first place. This was why she had wanted to see *Cantique de Salomon* performed—because, with the right choreographer and the right dancers and the right costumes, it could be the most beautiful ballet she had ever seen.

The costumes. Colette had forgotten about them during the run-through. She could hardly imagine the *pas de deux* being better than it already was, but, like Henri had said, *Once the costumes are on—that's when ballets really start to come together.* Colette couldn't wait for the dress rehearsal. Then again, she wished that *she* could somehow be the one wearing the costume, dancing with James and placing an imaginary seal on his arm.

CHAPTER TWENTY-THREE

C olette blotted her lipstick in front of the bathroom mirror. It was Christmas Eve and, in a few minutes, she would be driving to the performing arts center for one last *Nutcracker* matinee. She dressed with extra care like she had on her first day and, in doing so, subconsciously bookended her short experience as a Westmoreland Ballet staff member. She chose a pine-colored knit dress, not because of its festive color, but because she knew she looked good in it. With her berry-red lips and holly-green eyes, she had always looked appropriate in Christmas colors, though she had never been a huge fan of the holiday. Christmas had been marred by childhood memories of a grief-stricken mother and, more recently, frustrating trips to Houston. It was more work than anything. This time, however, she would be spending the holiday with James and his family.

Sammy peeked into the bathroom. "I'm heading out. Can I get a Christmas hug?"

"Yes, please! I'm gonna miss you," Colette said, holding Sammy tightly. "Hope you have fun with your family."

"Thanks. Have a good time with James. I should be back in plenty of time for the gala."

"I'm so excited that you're coming!"

Lavoisier had seen to it that Colette be sent an invitation, and Sammy was to be her date. Christmas with the Brennans, and a fancy New Year's Gala with Sammy—Colette had never been so excited for the holidays.

SHE HAD ALREADY been at the theater for a couple of hours before the company dancers started trickling in, each one especially giddy. They were eager to get this last performance over with. Trinity and Myra were also a little slap-happy.

"Thank goodness it's almost over," Myra said, her speech slurring from the bobby pins hanging out of her mouth. She took one out and held it like a cigarette. "We're in dire need of a break, ladies."

"That's for damn sure," Trinity replied, nodding vigorously. "Tonight, I'm getting in bed with a bottle of Jack and watching *A Muppet Christmas Carol*. Then, I'm sleeping until I wake up. There's your boy, Larsen."

Colette turned around to find James standing in the doorway, dressed in a long-tailed jacket for Party Scene. His eyes surveyed her in her green dress, and his face bore the same expression he had whenever he wanted to kiss her. Something about that face thrilled her. She thought maybe it was a change in his pupils.

"Hi, baby," Colette said.

"Man, you're gorgeous," James said. He wrapped his arms around her waist.

"C'mon, man," said Trinity. "We're right here."

"Sorry." He pulled Colette out into the hallway. "Seriously. You look insanely beautiful today."

"Thank you."

"If I didn't have to be onstage, I'd—"

"Brennan, you coming?"

Colette craned her neck to see Andreas holding the stage door open.

"Just a sec!" James called. He turned back to Colette and leaned in to kiss her but stopped himself. "Dang it. I wish you didn't have that lipstick on."

Colette smiled. "Sorry. I guess you'll just have to wait."

"Come find me at intermission? I miss you."

She nodded as they parted, still stealing glances at each other. Colette stepped back into the costume shop feeling rather seductive and Trinity, seeing the smirk on her face, immediately rolled her eyes.

"What?" Colette asked.

"You two. Are you getting it on in the wings or something?"

"Trinity!" Myra scolded. "For heaven's sake."

"No," Colette said, feeling herself blush.

"*Sure*," Trinity replied. "Just don't get knocked up like Liz."

Colette laughed. "Yeah, okay."

Clearly unsatisfied with Colette's answer, Trinity continued to study her. She set down her sewing and asked, "But you're hitting that, right?"

"That's none of your business," Myra said primly. She frowned at Trinity and added, "Colette, you don't need to tell her anything."

Despite Myra's statement, Colette could sense that she actually wouldn't mind knowing more, either. Reluctant to oblige them, she decided to keep her mouth shut on the matter.

It's not like she hadn't thought about it, though. She and James had been together for over two months now and, while they had certainly done a lot, they hadn't done everything. They each seemed to be holding out for something, and Colette realized that they had never had a proper conversation about it. She knew why she was waiting, but was there a reason why James hadn't pushed it?

Before intermission, Colette tip-toed into the backstage area to watch the end of the act. She quickly realized that she needn't have been so careful. The cast was so excited that they were chatting rather loudly and horsing around in the wings. She could vaguely make out the figures of James and Andreas, who were sparring by the tech booth several feet ahead of her. The people in the closest box seats could probably hear them. Even the dancers on stage were whispering and trying to make each other laugh.

The audience applauded, drowning out the sounds of the celebrating dancers exiting the stage, and Colette was suddenly surrounded by beautiful, sweaty people. The corps dancers weaved around her, brushing fake snow off of their shoulders. As Colette tried to avoid bumping the tutus invading her space, it occurred to her that these people were world-class athletes forced to perform in awkward, constricting clothing. Thanks to her limited dance experience, Colette could imagine how distracting it would be. That was one thing Trinity and Myra didn't quite understand.

James finally saw her and gestured toward her. As Andreas turned to look, his knee buckled; James had struck one final blow to the back of his leg before heading toward Colette. Andreas followed him, limping slightly but laughing. She shook her head.

Dudes are so weird sometimes.

Helena scurried in front of them. She was looking particularly excited and extended her arms out to Colette as if expecting a hug. Afraid that she might crush her, Colette leaned out over Helena's tutu and briefly held her tiny shoulders.

"We were talking about going out for drinks afterward," Helena said. "Can you come?"

"We should have time before dinner," James added.

"Sure," Colette replied. "That sounds fun."

"We always say a final 'fuck you' to *Nutcracker*," Andreas explained.

Colette chuckled. "Is anyone else coming?"

"Nate and Iris said they're in," James answered. "If they're not too beat after Arabian."

"Bah. Those pansies," Andreas said.

Colette was glad that she understood the joke. Lavoisier's Arabian had a reputation for being particularly difficult.

As they continued to chat, Colette could feel a pair of eyes watching them from the water cooler. They belonged to Alex, whose chest was still heaving beneath her Snow Queen costume. Despite her imperious stage makeup, Colette observed a faint look of mortification on her face, as if she were a school girl banished from the gang of cool kids. Apparently James felt awkward about it, too. He finally asked if she would be able to come, as if she had been invited all along.

"I'm afraid not," Alex said. "You'll have to have fun without me." With that, she hurled her cup into the trash can and disappeared into the hallway. Colette thought she would have done the same. She would hate to be invited anywhere out of pity.

On her way back to the costume shop, Colette stopped by the Green Room. She was startled to find that Alex was already there, sitting with her back toward the doorway. She was hunched over, her vertebrae protruding through her costume, and she was holding her head with one hand. The other hand clutched a wad of paper towels. Colette wondered if she was crying, but Alex shifted suddenly, tossed off one of her pointe shoes, and began stuffing the paper towel into it. Her leg flopped to the side, revealing runs in the bottom of her tights from where she had trimmed the toes off. Her foot looked red and swollen, and Colette winced as she watched Alex shove the shoe back over it. She began to tie the ribbons but stopped again to hold her head.

Suddenly, Colette realized that she might actually feel sorry for her. The envy she had been harboring began to subside at the sight of her sitting there, looking so frail and melancholy. Colette had only seen Alex's advantages— her ability as a dancer, her perfectly lean body, and her hours spent with James, dancing in a way that Colette could never experience nor understand. But the defeated stoop of Alex's shoulders seemed to express that none of these things mattered to her at the moment.

But, then again, she's still a stuck-up flirt.

Sensing that someone was watching her, Alex turned around, saw Colette and quickly turned away to wipe the tears from her face. She had been crying, after all. Colette also turned to leave, but it was too late to pretend that she hadn't seen

Just go talk to her, Colette. Just be kind.

"Hey, Alex," Colette said. "Are you doing okay?"

"Yeah, I'm fine," Alex replied, re-focusing on her ribbons.

"...are you sure?"

Alex was forced into silence as her face contorted into tears again. Colette knew that she wanted her to leave. Instead, she closed the door, sat down next to her and waited until she could speak again.

Alex shook her head. "Trust me. You don't want to hear about it."

"Oh." Colette hesitated. "It's not about James, is it?"

"Ha. Oh, James. He adores you, doesn't he?"

"I—I hope so. I adore him."

Alex nodded. "He's a great guy. Everyone thinks so."

They sat quietly for a minute, both staring toward the floor. Colette became fascinated by Alex's sinewy calves, which were practically the same circumference as her lower thighs. It was hard to notice that kind of thing from a distance. She wondered how anyone with legs like that could be unhappy.

"Is there anything I can help with?" Colette asked. "I hate to see you like this."

Colette was surprised at the truth in this statement. Watching Alexandra Vukoja cry was like watching a flower wilt or finding graffiti on a cathedral. There was something unjust about it.

Alex said nothing and began picking at the bit of paper towel in her hand. Moments passed as Colette felt increasingly awkward and unwanted. She had just decided to leave when Alex finally gave in.

"Look," Alex said. "I know Hel—some of the other dancers—they might have been saying things about me. Things that aren't entirely true. James, well, he's a great partner..." She paused, and her eyes rested on Colette's face before darting back to the floor. "You're very lucky."

"I know."

Alex took a deep breath. "I—I hope I haven't made things weird for you. I know *Cantique Pas* was sort of your project."

Weeks before, Colette had imagined up a stinging reply, should she be given the opportunity to triumph over Alex's unrequited love. Now, however, she couldn't do it. At the moment, she wasn't jealous—wasn't even angry. She felt pity for Alex, who was obviously in dire need of some real friends. She decided to put Alex's mind at ease, even if she didn't really mean all of the words she was about to say.

"You haven't made things weird. But, you know, it would be nice if we could get to know each other a little better. You're James's friend, after all."

"Did he say that?" Alex asked, smiling weakly. She looked down at her lap. "I don't feel like any of these people are my friends. But James is so polite that sometimes dancing with him is the only time I feel okay. Honestly... I thought you might take that away from me."

The stage manager's voice boomed over the intercom. "Cast and crew, this is your five-minute call for Act II. Five minutes to curtain for Act II."

They both stood up. Alex wiped her nose and moved toward the door. She still needed to change.

"I won't take it away from you," Colette promised. Alex nodded, her beautiful face looking quite pitiful, and hurried back out into the hallway.

ALTHOUGH IT WAS still early evening, the sky was already pitch black by the time James and Colette left the bar for his parents' house. Their cheeks were flushed from the cold and the drinks and their increasing affection for one another. Colette was usually the funnier of the two, but James was in rare form that night. He kept singing Christmas carols in ridiculous, high-pitched voices, like a boys choir soloist who was past his prime. Colette's face hurt from laughing.

After they had mellowed, James searched for Colette's hand from the driver's seat. She squeezed it back and strained to see his face in the darkness. There was something about him there, smiling the sweetest smile, that made her weak in the knees, and she suddenly remembered her earlier conversation with Trinity.

Are you two getting it on in the wings or something?

Colette almost told him about it and then thought better of it. She didn't want to freak him out. Not now. But then again, they were getting more serious. She was spending Christmas with his family, after all. If she couldn't talk to him about this now, when would she?

"James, I have to ask you about something…" She watched his hand meander to her neck and then down to her thigh, where it rested tentatively, and she began to recall her search through *Song of Solomon*.

> *Your graceful legs are like jewels,*
> *the work of an artist's hands…*

> *…I belong to my beloved,*
> *and his desire is for me.*

He turned to look at her, his gaze resting on her lips. "What is it?"

> *His mouth is sweetness itself;*
> *he is altogether lovely.*

Before she could think about it longer, she blurted, "We need to talk about sex."

James put his hand back on the wheel, and Colette cringed at her poor delivery.

"I didn't mean it like that," Colette added, shaking her head. "Sorry. I mean—everything's fine. I just feel like we should talk about it at least."

Colette watched his face, looking for confirmation that she had successfully recovered from her awkward introduction of the topic. She saw his eyes narrow as he gave the subject serious thought and, as she waited, she took stock of her own reasons for putting it off. His list of past relationships, while short, was longer than hers. Perhaps she would be a disappointment to him in comparison. Or, perhaps he wasn't sure that he loved her yet. She owned that this would be understandable. It was still early and, though she already knew she loved him, she had only admitted her feelings to Jael, not James. She had been waiting for him to say it first.

James cleared his throat and said, "You're right. We should probably talk about it." He paused again, eyes focused, and Colette found herself dying to know his thoughts. As someone so physical and creative, wouldn't sex seem natural to him—even commonplace? If that were the case, why hadn't he wanted it yet? Was there something wrong with her?

As if reading her mind, James smirked at the dashboard and said, "It's definitely not that I don't want to, Colette. I've just been—you know—trying not to."

"Oh," she said, feeling both relieved and puzzled. "Any particular reason?"

"I guess I haven't really thought about it until now." A streetlight illuminated his face for an instant, and Colette saw the muscles in his jaw flicker. He seemed to be faintly upset with himself, and she began to regret bringing up the subject.

"James—"

"I've made some mistakes in the past," he said. He slowed the car to a stop at a red light and turned to look her in the eyes. "I just—want to make sure it happens for the right reasons. I don't want to screw this up."

"You won't screw this up—"

"I love you," James said, his voice steady and sincere. "I love you and I want to do things right—even if it means waiting longer."

Stunned, Colette sat motionless with her hand enveloped in his. Her lips parted as if she were about to reply, but her mind was still replaying his words—still trying to believe that he had really uttered them.

"Is that okay?" James asked. "You look—"

"I love you, too," she said, grinning.

His face relaxed. "I knew it."

"It's green," Colette said. She pointed to the stoplight just as the car behind them honked its horn.

They both chuckled and then fell silent for a while, stealing glances at each other and savoring the moment. James sat contented, with a sly smile on his face, while Colette thought through every word he had said, intending to store them in her mind. Then, she realized that something still needed clarification.

"Um, when you say you've made mistakes in the past, do you mean—oh, crap." Colette cringed and, half-serious, asked, "Do you have a kid?"

"Did I not tell you about him?" James asked, laughing at her horrified expression. "I don't have a kid," he assured her. "No, it's nothing like that."

"Then what is it?"

"I was brought up a certain way. You know—to wait until marriage. My parents and the church kind of hammered that into me, but I ended up ignoring it. I guess it seemed outdated." He glanced at Colette to see if she had a reaction, but she sat still, listening attentively and thrilled to be gaining deeper insight into his mind. "Anyway," he continued. "I at least waited until I was with my girlfriend at Quadrilogy, but I was stupid about it. She was in the relationship for the long haul, and I really wasn't. I knew it, too. And I did it anyway. It just... made everything that much more confusing."

"That doesn't seem that bad to me, James," Colette said, despite the sting of picturing him with someone else. "You were young."

"I know, but I hurt her pretty badly. Plus, she ended up marrying one of my friends there, and I can't help but think—if I were him—that I would wish I had just held off on the whole thing."

Colette nodded. She could understand that. She had already thought about what her past breakups would have been like had no sex been involved— considerably less traumatic, she decided. And a lot less awkward for everyone afterward. The pleasure, which had honestly been disappointing thus far, had not been worth the pain. But she could not imagine ever breaking up with James. Or ever being disappointed with him.

"But besides all of that," he continued. "I guess I've started to see things differently. Like, maybe the waiting thing is actually a way of protecting people. Maybe it's just too important to take lightly."

Colette smiled. "Says the freely and lightly guy."

James chuckled and, looking slightly embarrassed, replied, "I think *Song of Solomon* must be rubbing off on me."

Colette agreed, and she couldn't blame him. The book had changed her, too.

"So," she said, taking a deep breath. "Just so we're on the same page— basically, you're saying you'd like for us to wait until, what—marriage?"

"Yeah," he replied. "Yeah, I am. But how do you feel about that?"

"I—I think it will be difficult," she said. "But I actually like the idea. No harm in trying something new, right? But I have to ask—"

"What?"

"Does that mean that you've been... well, thinking of *marrying* me?"

"Of course." James laughed. "That's the goal, right?"

Colette could have cried. No one had said that to her before. In reality, she had never given anyone a chance to say it. And for James to bring up the prospect of marriage so confidently, so casually—well, it was a nice change. If there had been an officiant in the back seat, she might have married him right then. But there was another question that had been bothering her—

something else she had been too afraid to ask about. Now seemed like as good a time as any.

"James?"

"Yes, my love?"

Colette smiled, though she felt a pang of uneasiness. She clasped her hands together and asked, "Are you not worried about the religion thing at all? We were obviously brought up differently. Don't you think it could be a problem that I don't—well, that I'm not sure *what* I believe?"

James shrugged. "I'm really not worried about it."

"You're not?"

"No," he said, reaching for her cheek. "All I know is that I'm in love with you."

By now, they had pulled up to his parents' driveway, and Colette's heart had never felt so full. The inside of the house was glowing, looking warm and inviting. Through the window, she could see Josh talking to Audrey, who had her hands on her hips. They seemed to be in the midst of one of their tumultuous play-fights, but anyone could tell by looking at them that they were very much in love and always would be. The same went for Jael and Darrel. Whatever this family had, Colette wanted it.

"Do we need to wait here for a while?" James asked.

"No," Colette said. "Let's go in."

CHAPTER TWENTY-FOUR

Something changed after that Christmas with the Brennans. Even with the end of her stint at Westmoreland, Colette felt refreshed and hopeful for her future, uncertain as it was. She knew a few things for sure—she and James were closer than ever, she was in love with his family, and she could not wait to see the *Cantique Pas de Deux* that evening. At the moment, nothing else mattered to her.

She and Sammy arrived at the theater early, both looking beautiful in their different ways. Sammy had styled Colette's hair for her and Colette had done Sammy's makeup. They had taken their time that day, savoring the sacred ritual of preparing for a formal event. As the sky grew dark and the gala drew closer, Colette was bursting with nervous excitement.

James had told her to come find him before the show. She took Sammy with her to the backstage entrance and flashed a guest pass at the unconcerned security guard. Colette had begun to tremble as they marched to James's dressing room, their high heels echoing through the empty halls. She felt as though she were the one about to be onstage.

He answered the door wearing an absurd mixture of warm-ups on top of his rather skimpy Solomon costume. One leg of the yellow sweatpants, which Colette had grown to tolerate, was hiked up and held in place by a ragged-looking leg warmer, and his face bore a slightly frazzled expression underneath his stage makeup. Secretly, Colette loved seeing James in his makeup; he looked pretty damn good in eyeliner.

"Hey, babe," James said, kissing Colette on the cheek. "Hi, Sammy. Thanks for coming. You both look great."

"How is the cuff working?" Colette asked. Trinity had made it to cover James's tattoo.

"Good, I think." He stuck out his arm. "I still put makeup over it just in case."

"You nervous?"

"Just a little."

"I know you'll be great," Colette said. "Well, we can head out. Don't want to distract you."

"Yeah," Sammy said. "See ya, James. Good luck!"

"Thanks," James said. As Sammy turned away, he caught Colette's arm and whispered. "*Hey.* Thanks for everything you've done for this. I realized I never thanked you."

"You're the one who's done everything. You don't need to thank me."

"Yes, I do. This is your ballet, Colette. And I want it to be like how you imagined it. I've gotten a little caught up in my own performance—"

"James, don't worry about it. Seriously." She smiled. "I just can't wait to see you. You're going to be incredible."

He sighed, shook his head and wrapped his arms around her. "I love you so much."

She said she loved him, too, wished him *merde,* and left him alone.

As she and Sammy headed for the lobby, Colette imagined how James would spend his final minutes backstage. He would be shaking out his legs and doing little jumps, popping his knuckles and stretching his neck. He would be whispering to Alex, talking through the last-minute adjustments. And, Colette hated to admit, he would spit into the trash can like any other athlete. She had witnessed that with horror one evening before *Nutcracker.*

They found Jael and Darrel standing at an *hors d'oeuvres* table in the middle of the massive lobby. Jael was effortlessly elegant in her beaded navy gown, and Darrel looked completely different in his black tie get-up—quite handsome, in fact. His thick fingers were holding a cup of cashews, and he was knocking them back as if his life depended on it.

"Wow," Colette said. "You guys look so nice."

"And you are absolutely lovely," Jael said, embracing Colette. "What a stunning dress."

"You look like a glass of champagne," Darrel added.

Colette chuckled and introduced them to Sammy. Darrel quickly wiped the salt off of his fingers.

"Great to meet you, Sammy," Darrel said, shaking her hand. "I've heard a lot about you. You're such a good friend to our girl, here."

Our girl. Colette was proud to have been bestowed such a title.

"Excuse me, Ms. Maier?" A short, bearded man was tapping Jael on the shoulder.

"Yes?"

"Asa Coulter, *Stage Star*. Would you mind answering a few questions about your son's performance?"

Jael graciously agreed, and they stepped to the side, where a photographer was already waiting for her.

"Does that happen a lot?" Sammy asked Darrel.

"Every once in a while," he replied. "Jael's a pro at interviews, though."

Darrel watched his wife with admiration, clearly still captivated by her after their many years together. Colette saw Jael glance at him, and the brief meeting of their eyes communicated something. These two—they seemed to know each other completely. Now, Colette couldn't picture either of them married to anyone else, despite how shocking the pairing had once seemed to her.

Colette could hear bits and pieces of the interview.

"How does it feel to watch your son...? Do you miss the stage...?"

At one point, Jael gestured in her direction, and Colette found the *Stage Star* people looking at her with curiosity. When they were called to take their seats, Jael signed a paper, shook hands with the men, and hurried back to join them.

"They would like to take your picture later," Jael whispered to Colette. "Are you alright with that?"

"I guess," Colette said. "As long as I won't have to answer questions."

Colette settled into her seat and wondered how she had become part of this strange, elite world. Those reporters would quickly realize that she didn't belong there. She wondered if Darrel had felt the same way all these years.

The *Cantique Pas* was last on the program and was preceded by a Lavoisier classic, *Moon Over Delphi,* and another new *pas de deux* called *Zirconium*. Colette watched with impatience, unable to enjoy them fully. She was certain that *Cantique de Salomon* would be better than *Zirconium*, which was created by some guest choreographer from the university. It was a contemporary piece that came off as pretentious—the Emperor's New Clothes kind of dance that Colette couldn't stand. She peeked at Darrel and smiled. He looked bored out of his mind.

Finally, it was time. Colette felt a fluttering in her stomach. She had daydreamed about this night—about what would happen if the whole story had been in a movie. Alex would suffer an injury or food poisoning at the last minute. The understudy couldn't make it for whatever reason. Colette would need to fill in since she knew the part, and she would dance miraculously well. The genuine love between her and James would move the audience to tears. They would receive a standing ovation, and Colette would be featured in the headlines: "The Show Must Go On: Amateur Dancer Saves Westmoreland Performance." Her life wasn't a movie, however, and she reminded herself of the fact more often lately. At least her photograph might be in the *Stage Star*. That was something.

The emcee's voice boomed through the theater. "Ladies and gentlemen. Our final performance this evening has an unusual story. Here to tell it is our very own illustrious Artistic Director, Henri Lavoisier."

The theater erupted in applause as the dapper Lavoisier hobbled over to the microphone. He waited for the throng of enthusiastic benefactors to settle down, cleared his throat, and began to speak. Colette sat on the edge of her seat.

"Thank you, ladies and gentlemen," Lavoisier said. His professional tone seemed to be masking a slight giddiness, and he cleared his throat a second time. "Our next ballet has extraordinary origins, and it is the most important cultural discovery that has ever occurred within our company—perhaps even within our city." He paused, and the audience began to whisper. "It has recently been verified that the music you are about to hear was composed by Iosif Sokoloff sometime during the years 1772 and 1773. Sokoloff, an artist of Jewish-Russian heritage, fled his home country and found himself in Paris both choreographing and composing music for a ballet called *Cantique de Salomon,* which you may know as *Song of Solomon* or *Song of Songs.* It is evident that his work caused an uproar among his own people, many of whom saw the ballet as both a desecration and misinterpretation of the holy book. And, while we know nothing of Sokoloff's choreography, one might imagine that it was overshadowed by the new and exciting *ballets d'action* of his renowned contemporary, Jean-Georges Noverre.

"Sokoloff's *music*, however, is something of genius. Though its notes emanate from a single piano, you will sense a fullness in its melody, as if you were sitting in the midst of a great orchestra. It may bring to mind images, colors, sounds, scents and ethereal whispers of the ancient poetry it represents. Whatever sensations it may inspire, I believe you will agree that, even heard with contemporary ears, this music is timeless—captivating, sumptuous and undeniably beautiful.

"Now, you may recall that Paris during the eighteenth century was in the midst of the Enlightenment, spurred in large part by the famous philosopher

Voltaire. Unfortunately, his writings were often fraught with anti-Semitism, and some of his 'enlightened' followers ran Sokoloff out of Paris shortly after the premiere of *Cantique de Salomon*. It seems our poor composer could please no one. His ballet was suppressed and his music destroyed—but, fortunately, one portion remains…" Lavoisier smiled, and Colette held her breath. "Ladies and gentlemen, here is where the story takes an extraordinary turn. I am delighted to announce that this lost genius is finally receiving his due, thanks to our academy pianist Dunja Kasparova, and the curiosity of a dedicated, adult student here…" Looking thrilled, Sammy elbowed Colette in the arm, and Darrel and Jael leaned forward, beaming at her. "Just a few short months ago, Ms. Kasparova discovered that she was the owner of one of Sokoloff's few remaining works—the *grand pas de deux* from *Cantique de Salomon*…"

The crowd gasped, and Colette looked down to see Dunja near the orchestra pit, grinning and waving both of her thick arms enthusiastically. Her glitzy outfit sparkled in the house lights. Given the news about the music, the appraisal must have gone well.

Lavoisier continued, but Colette could only absorb so many of his words. Her heart was beating so violently that she felt its pulse in her ears. James wasn't kidding. This music was a big deal. And was Henri really talking about her? To all of these people? Why hadn't they warned her?

The sound of her name snapped her back to attention.

"Colette Larsen…" he was saying. "Colette, where are you, my dear?"

"*CoCo*," Sammy said, elbowing her again. "Colette, *stand up!*"

She stood up hesitantly, forced herself to smile, and waved at Lavoisier. Everyone around her applauded. People craned their necks to see her, but she quickly sat back down before they had the chance.

"…Miss Larsen was so struck by the beauty of Sokoloff's music that she shared it with company soloist James Brennan, and they began to re-imagine this forgotten ballet together. You see, she and James happen to be sweethearts…" A pleased murmur spread through the crowd. "…and is there a more perfect way to craft a love story such as this one? I could go on and on about the ballet you are about to watch, but I fear I have postponed our enjoyment long enough. And so, without further ado, I present to you the new *Cantique de Salomon Pas de Deux,* performed by Alexandra Vukoja and James Brennan."

The audience cheered. The lights dimmed again, the curtain went up, and Colette heard that familiar music—the music that had sent chills dancing up and down her spine during *rond de jambe*. Alex was standing center stage, looking like a queen in the costume that Colette had more-or-less designed. When James went to lift Alex in the first *presage*, Colette held her breath.

It wasn't until the end of the *entrée* that Colette was able to relax and enjoy the dance. As she fell further under its spell, she began to forget that James was the dancer she was watching. His movement was somehow beyond himself. And Alexandra was so good that there was no room for envy, only objective wonderment and appreciation. The two danced well together, and it was beautiful. It was *breathtaking*, really. Colette knew that later, James would come back to her as someone quite different—a laid-back guy who could pass for a soccer player or track star.

The entire performance was nearly perfect, except for the very end of James's variation. He did a double *tour* to the knee, but lost his balance on the landing and had to put his hand down to steady himself. Colette cringed and saw Jael clutch Darrel's hand out of the corner of her eye. It was such a tiny mistake. If they had looked away for even a second, they would have missed it. Unfortunately, people seemed to remember only the beginning and end of variations.

"Start well and finish well," Marianne always said.

Poor James, Colette thought. *Why did he put that in there?*

The audience was generous with applause, however, and James continued as if nothing had happened. He was a professional, after all. Colette suddenly felt grateful that she would never have to fill in for Alex. What a nightmare that would be in reality. Even if she could magically dance at Alex's level, she couldn't imagine dealing with the pressure.

The last section, the coda, was the most beautiful of all. Colette had seen it many times in rehearsal, and she had even practiced the steps with James, but she watched it with new eyes that night. She remembered Sammy's concern about *Cantique* coming across as ballet porn, but there was nothing risqué about it now. James's choreography and Alex's regal movement made it clear—these characters were describing love in its purest form. This love was both humble and pre-ordained. It was eternal.

When the dance was finished and they took their *révérence*, the audience rose to its feet. Colette began to cry. After all of James's hard work, after all of this time—it was over. Just like that. It was all so bittersweet. She looked at Jael, who was crying, too, as if the pressure of watching her son had been released in the form of tears. Darrel was too busy whistling to notice.

"Wow," Sammy said. "You were right. That was absolutely gorgeous."

AFTER THE PERFORMANCE, the audience shuffled into the giant dining area for an evening of mingling and cocktails. Colette could hear the patrons reviewing *Cantique* and talking about James as if they knew him. She began to wonder about these strange, wealthy people. Who were they exactly? Did they all live in downtown penthouses overlooking the pitiful suburbs? Had these people, with their diamond jewelry and platinum cuff links—been controlling the lives of people like her—people in the land below?

She eavesdropped on a conversation between a woman in a fur coat and her well-groomed husband.

"Of course the dancing is always *good*," the woman was saying, "but I could hear the wood in her toe shoes. It was so loud! So distracting. And I didn't notice anything special about what's-his-name's music. They should have done *Swan Lake.*"

"Oh, I know," replied the man. "I much preferred the *Zirconium* piece, anyway. More substance."

Colette rolled her eyes. *Wood? Toe shoes? Swan-freaking-Lake? Now, that would be ambitious.*

Maybe these people didn't know as much as she imagined. Maybe they were just rich idiots.

She suddenly felt sorry for the company and for Lavoisier. They just wanted to dance—to make art. And these benefactors, who had old money and new money and professed to know of everything and everyone of importance, were the ones who kept them employed, no matter how ignorant they were of the craft they supported.

Colette had to admit that not all of the Westmoreland patrons were so bad, though. As the evening progressed, she heard more genuine praise for *Cantique.* In fact, the pretentious couple's preference for *Zirconium* turned out to be the last criticism she heard that evening. Others agreed that it was "mesmerizing," "breathtaking" and "so romantic." They spoke of James as if he were a genius and of Alex as if she were a goddess. And they spoke of Iosif Sokoloff. Very few people—or perhaps no one at all—had spoken of him for centuries.

Now, Colette was worried about him. From the sound of it, his life had been extremely difficult and, yet, he had managed to create something incredibly beautiful—something that had moved her in a way that little else had. She wished she could tell him.

She imagined Sokoloff, dressed in his eighteenth-century garb, approaching her in the banquet line. His weary face would betray the trials of his life, but he would have a smile upon his lips. He would bow, take her hand, and speak to her in a mélange of accents.

"I am indebted to you, mademoiselle. You have resurrected my music."

"No, sir," Colette would say. "Your music resurrected itself. I'm just a messenger."

"Scalloped potatoes?"

"Huh?"

"Would you like scalloped potatoes, ma'am?" A member of the catering staff was staring at her with a spoon in his hand.

"Oh, sorry." Colette held up her plate. "Thank you."

Colette shook her head. She really needed to cool it with the daydreaming.

BETWEEN BITES OF prime rib, Colette glimpsed James standing far across the room. He had finally arrived, freshly showered and dressed in his formal attire. She could tell that he was searching for her, and when he caught her eye she stared, awestruck. He had never looked more handsome. When she had first fallen in love with James and his youthful demeanor, she had occasionally fancied him as some sort of Adonis. Now, he looked different— a little weathered, as if performing *Cantique* had suddenly changed him into a full-fledged man—the kind of man who could be both tender-hearted and a warrior if the need arose.

My beloved is radiant and ruddy,
outstanding among ten thousand.

As James made his way over to the table, he was intercepted by Asa, the *Stage Star* journalist, and the photographer summoned Jael and Colette. She took a deep breath and followed them, leaving Sammy and Darrel alone at their table.

"So, I hear you're really into bread bowls..." Sammy began. Colette wished she could listen in on that conversation.

Once they had taken a group photograph, Asa asked Colette one single question: "How does it feel to participate in creating a new ballet?"

"It feels incredible," Colette answered, feeling flushed and self-conscious. "I'm honored to be a part of it."

As they began to wrap up, Alex appeared with the Westmoreland's public relations representative.

"Ah, could you stay for a photo with Miss Vukoja?" Asa asked James.

"Yeah, no problem," James said, extending his arm to escort Alex. Colette and Jael stepped aside, and James and Alex presented sterile smiles to the camera. Alex was a slender column in her black gown and her hair fell to her shoulders in loose waves. She looked much younger with her hair down.

A faint feeling of gratitude toward Alex crept into Colette's heart. Realistically, she was the only dancer at Westmoreland who could have helped James achieve his vision for the *Cantique Pas*. For the first time, Colette considered the fact that Alex was extremely busy, and that there were other leading men in the company. James was a green soloist compared to the partners that she was used to. As a principal, she probably could have refused his experimental project if she wanted to. Colette assumed that she had been too enamored with James to do that, but she also sensed that Alex really believed in his abilities. Maybe she would have wanted to be a part of *Cantique* regardless of her feelings for him.

James let out a deep sigh as they walked back to the dining room. "Glad that's over with," he said. "I'm starving."

"I'm sure you are," Jael replied, patting him on the shoulder. "You did such a great job up there. I'm so proud of you."

"Me, too," Colette said. "You were amazing."

James gave her a kiss and thanked her, but he seemed distracted.

"What's wrong?" Jael admonished, already knowing the answer. James shook his head. "Honey, it was so minor. Hardly anyone noticed."

It took Colette a second to catch on. She had already forgotten about his double *tour* to the wobbly knee.

"I know," James said. "It just sucks. It's not like this was opening night and I'll get a second chance. This was my *only* chance."

"You know as well as I do that there's no such thing as a perfect performance."

"James," Colette added. "You should hear what people are saying about it. They loved it. We are all so proud of you. Seriously."

James nodded, looking a bit more hopeful, and greeted his father as they arrived back at their table.

"There's my boy!" Darrel said. "So proud of you, Jimmy. Excellent job."

That's all Darrel needed to say to his son. James exhaled, hugged his father, and then took Colette by the hand.

As they finished dinner together, others passed by the table to offer their praises. James thanked them graciously and downed champagne whenever it was offered to him. When a group of jovial, retired company members stopped by, they congratulated him on his achievements and promptly swept Jael and Darrel away to their own table. Colette and James watched his parents as they laughed with their old friends, and she wondered if she and James might do the same one day.

As they sat, she noticed James's body begin to relax. His eyes focused on her, and she felt his hand searching for hers.

He whispered in her ear, "Come outside with me for a sec?"

"Why?"

"I wanna talk to you."

"Can it wait?" Colette whispered back. "I don't want to leave Sammy alone."

Colette felt responsible for her, even though Sammy was capable of taking care of herself in a sea of strangers. James agreed, trying his best to be patient. He surveyed the crowd and stood up suddenly, looking resolute.

"Be right back."

Almost as soon as he left, Alex appeared and took his seat.

"Okay if I sit here for a bit?"

"Uh, sure," Colette said. "Great job tonight."

"Thank you so much."

Alex sat smiling at Colette. She looked as if she had something specific to say, yet couldn't work up the nerve. Colette introduced her to Sammy for the sole purpose of breaking the silence.

"So, *Vukoja*," Sammy said. "Is that Croatian?"

"It is," Alex replied. "Are you Croatian?"

"No. My cousin's wife is, though. You look a lot like her, so I just wondered."

"Huh. That's funny."

Another awkward pause followed. Alex gingerly rested her arms on the table before scrapping that idea and moving them back to her lap.

She finally asked Colette, "So, are you coming back to work in the costume shop?"

"I don't think so. It was just for *Nutcracker.*"

"Oh, that's too bad. Myra said you were a great help."

Colette smiled. "That's nice of her."

"Would you like to come back?" Alex asked. "Like, full-time?"

"Well, yeah, if I had the opportunity. That would be a dream come true, actually. But it was pretty clear to me that they don't have the budget for another person."

"I could look into that if you want," Alex said, her voice urgent. "I can talk to the board."

"Oh, you don't have to—"

"No, really. I will."

Colette wondered if this was Alex's way of making amends.

What the heck. I'll take it.

"Okay, sure," Colette said. "If you really want to. Thanks. I appreciate it."

"It's the least I can do," Alex said. Sensing that Colette was bewildered by this display of generosity, Alex added, "Solomon's Bride has been my favorite role I've ever danced."

"Wow. Really?" Sammy asked.

"Really. I can't actually describe why, but I've never felt this way about a performance. There is something really special about the music—even before I knew the story behind it. Thanks for discovering it, Colette."

Her last statement seemed especially personal. Colette realized that it was the first time Alex had called her by name, and she suddenly felt the need to fully forgive her. Maybe she'd even give Alex a hug. Then she wondered if she had consumed too much champagne.

Alex rose to leave, and Colette stood up to give her room to scoot her chair out. To Colette's astonishment, Alex hugged her first, thanked her again, and hurried away.

When James returned, he brought a companion with him—Aaron, a sturdy, thirty-something Friend of the Ballet who had been in Josh's high school class. James introduced him as "his generous financier."

"Someone's got to keep Brennan in tights," Aaron said.

"So, Sammy works downtown in the Main Street building," James said. "Isn't that where you moved?"

"Wow, what a small world," Aaron said. He pulled up a chair next to Sammy. "What floor are you on?"

As Sammy and Aaron chatted, James pulled Colette close to him. "Now can we talk?"

"I guess," Colette whispered. "Did you do that just to get me alone?"

"Yeah."

She smirked and followed him out to the balcony. His calculated introduction of Aaron was surprising, to say the least. Who was this new James?

"Damn it," James said.

"What?" Colette followed his gaze and saw that Helena and Iris were already outside. They were drowning in over-sized coats and surrounded by a haze of cigarette smoke. "What's the big deal?"

"Nothing."

Helena waved them over. "Hey, CoCo! It's all right if I call you that, right? James said that's your nickname."

"Like CoCo Chanel?" Iris asked.

"Oh, well, really my friend Sammy is the only one who calls me that. But you can, too, I guess."

"Cool," Helena said. "I told Iris and Yumi about the wrap skirts you make. We all want one. How much do they cost?"

Colette discussed the matter with them, feeling immensely flattered. Professional dancers wanted her ballet skirts! Ideas flooded her mind—prints and ribbons and color combinations. She couldn't wait to go home and work on them.

She turned to James, "I have new patrons! Isn't this exciting?"

"Yeah," James said, sounding less enthusiastic than she would like. He looked strangely irritated and raised his eyebrows at Helena.

She seemed to recognize the expression. "Well, we'll leave you two alone. Don't forget to text me, CoCo!"

"Thanks, Colette," Iris said, stamping out her cigarette. "Later, Brennan."

Once they were alone, Colette frowned and asked, "*What* is your deal? Why are you being so mean to Helena?"

James laughed and leaned against the balcony rail. "What? I'm not. She'll be fine."

"Okay, psycho."

"I've just really wanted to be alone with you," he said, taking her by both hands.

Colette smiled. "I guess I'll accept that as a good excuse."

He pulled her in closer. "I couldn't stop thinking about you earlier, when I was waiting in the wings. I never get distracted like that."

"Oh," Colette said, flattered. "Sorry."

"I just—I love everything about you and I can't stop thinking that—"

"What?"

"I just want to be with you all the time." His eyes began to water. "I—I want to marry you. Like, right now."

Colette's stomach dropped. She paused to take in his expression. His eyes were earnest and seemed to glow in the moonlight, but the mature, weathered look from before had become faint. With a little disappointment, she realized what was going on with him.

"James," she said, placing her hands on his face. "You're drunk. You should probably stop talking."

He took a step back. "No, I'm not."

"Uh—"

"Okay, maybe a little."

Colette laughed. "You've had a big day. I know you're tired and probably feeling emotional. That's totally fine. I get that. But I'm not sure if you really mean what you're saying. Maybe we should talk about this another time?"

James nodded. "Yeah, okay. You're right. I do mean, them, though. I do mean the things—the things I say. What I'm saying to you right now."

"Okay, baby."

Colette led him back inside and sat him at their table. Sammy and Aaron were so preoccupied that it took them a few minutes to notice.

"I'll get you some coffee," Colette told James. "You're still gonna have to mingle with these people for a while."

"What's the matter?" Sammy asked.

"He's just a little tipsy."

"I'm fine," James insisted.

"Jeez, Brennan," Aaron said. "You're such a lightweight. Sam here has had twice as much as you have!"

"You know it," Sammy said, raising her tumbler. Somehow, she had acquired a glass of whiskey while James and Colette had been away.

"You guys are all crazy," Colette said, grinning. She walked to the bar, all the while ruminating on what James had said. Now, she saw her earlier notion of him as a hardened warrior as being a little ridiculous. She thought maybe his role was rubbing off on him, but he was the same easy-going guy that he had always been—and he was kind of adorable drunk.

And, as it turned out, he wanted to marry her. *Right now,* he said.

Colette liked the idea in theory, but she decided that she was not in a hurry. She had things to do, ballet skirts to make, and Alex had made her a promise. The more Colette thought about that promise, the more excited she became. Though she silently vowed to follow up on the matter, she prevented herself from imagining what would happen if Alex succeeded. She didn't want to jinx it.

ACT III

CHAPTER TWENTY-FIVE

Colette popped her hip and threw her leg up onto the barre. She folded forward to stretch her hamstring, her torso resting on her thigh, and picked lint off of her shin. Despite the frigid February weather, her thick, knit leg warmers were unnecessary that evening. The previous class of teen-aged girls had fogged up the studio before the adults arrived, and the rank scent of sweat clung to the air. Yet, there was promise in that stench. Colette knew she would acclimate to it, and, soon, her own hard work would add to the humidity.

Sammy's perspective was far less romantic. When she walked in, she pinched her nose and proclaimed, "Disgusting! It's like walking into a wall of hot STINK!"

Colette laughed and shifted to face the barre, her right leg now propped up in *à la seconde*. She pulled her right hip down and checked her left foot to make sure it was directly underneath her. She lifted up to stretch sideways toward her leg, and she pulled her shoulder down away from her ear. Even in this simple stretch, there were so many rules—so many things to remember— but Colette found solace in them. These rules would always be familiar to her.

It had been over a month since she and Sammy had started back to class after the New Year's Gala. Although she hated feeling out of shape, Colette had to admit that the winter break had actually been beneficial for her. The knots in her muscles had relaxed, and she was forced to work slowly, going back to basics and correcting old habits. She didn't worry about getting her extension as high as it used to be. Instead, she focused on the things she had learned from watching the company dancers. She paid more attention to her *épaulement* and *port de bras* and listened closely to the music, trying to answer it with her movement. And she was less anxious now. Strangely enough, observing Alex so closely had finally helped Colette remove the pressure she had placed upon her own shoulders. She could never dance like Alex, nor would she ever need to, and that was okay. It meant that, in class, she had nothing to lose. She could try everything. She could fail as many times as she pleased until she got it right—just like she had when she had first fallen in love with ballet.

Colette knew that this class would be particularly challenging, and she could hardly wait for it. Marianne, who had been on leave settling her sister's estate, had finally returned. As sorry as Colette felt for her, she selfishly wished Marianne would have come back sooner. The substitutes were good in their own ways, but Colette and Sammy had both grown weary of their lax attitudes. Those young teachers were just a little too forgiving. Their students needed someone more serious—someone who could whip them back into shape.

Marianne appeared to be equally relieved to see them. After a slow exhale, she said, "It's so good to be back, ladies. How are we feeling? Good? Great. Let's jump on in."

Almost giddy with excitement, Colette turned around to take her preparation. She pulled up through her knees, lengthened her spine, and reminded herself to consciously engage her abdominal muscles. Having already entered into full ballet mode, she was startled to feel Sammy's tap on her shoulder.

"Dude," Sammy whispered. "Check out Tina's leo."

To Colette's chagrin, she saw that Tina was wearing the exact same leotard that James had given her for Christmas. It was by Noverre and was deep burgundy, with a halter neckline and velvet detailing along the bust. While she wouldn't have chosen it for herself, it had ended up being a perfect fit, and it was the nicest piece of dancewear she had ever owned.

James had liked his gift from her, too—well, at least half of it. Darrel had helped her find a power sander that James had his eye on. As she found this to be a boring present, she supplemented it with a nice tracksuit in tasteful charcoal gray. She had seen him wear the jacket, but not the pants. Never the pants.

The music began, and Colette felt a sense of relief and wonder come over her. Why did she love this class so much? Why did these repetitive movements still seem to bring her such comfort—such delight, even after all of this time? Now especially, she knew that she somehow belonged there in that studio, no matter how good or bad her dancing turned out to be. Ballet was in her soul, and these last few, extraordinary months seemed to have affirmed the fact.

Colette remained reverent throughout class, and Marianne, who seemed to be reading her thoughts, gave a long, slow barre. Colette's muscles thanked her. She swept her leg forward *en l'air* and carried it all the way around to arabesque, easily maintaining a 90-degree extension. Not bad. She swept it forward again, enfolded it into *retiré*, and then opened it to *à la seconde*. To her surprise, her leg was above 90 degrees. In fact, it was higher than it had ever been. How had that happened? No one else noticed it, but Colette added this inexplicable extension to her mental list of ballet victories. It was right up there with the time she had managed to hit all of her double *pirouettes*.

It was nice to know that James and Alex had once experienced these small victories, too. Granted, they had been much younger at the time, but Colette reminded herself not to dwell on that fact. Like Sammy often pointed out, they were taking class every day then. Besides, like any discipline, ballet had a spectrum. Comparing herself to a pro was an unfair as a weekend tennis player berating herself for not making it to Wimbledon.

Colette's attention wandered to the pianist. He had replaced Dunja, who had apparently moved on to bigger and better things after her grandfather's music collection was auctioned at Christie's. Colette found that she actually missed Dunja, but she also liked this new guy. He was a talented conservatory student who struck the piano keys with a bold and serious air. His floppy mop of blond hair wobbled as he played, and Colette noticed that his eyes drifted from dancer to dancer, feeding off the quality of their movements. He watched Sammy during *frappé* and matched her sharp beats with quick staccato. *And STRIKE, STRIKE, STRIKE, wrap, back, wrap.* Sammy really did have lovely feet.

Before center, Marianne stopped by Colette's spot at the barre.

"So, I understand congratulations are in order," Marianne said. "I hadn't heard the whole *Cantique* story until this past week. Sounds like it was quite the sensation!"

Colette felt rather proud. People must have been talking. "Thank you. We were very excited about it."

"I had no idea you and James were dating. He's a wonderful young man—and a wonderful dancer."

Tina craned her neck to hear.

"Yes, he is," Colette replied.

"You know, I wish I could say that I remembered that music—and that particular class—but I don't. You have a good ear."

Colette smiled. "I don't know about that."

"You really do," Marianne insisted. "And look what all has come of it. It seems like every day I hear something new about the composer."

"Well, I'm glad the whole thing has been good for him. Even if he's long dead."

Marianne laughed and lowered her voice. "It's good for Westmoreland, too, Colette."

She was right. After the gala, *Cantique* practically exploded. Westmoreland was getting more press than ever, Dunja's rags-to-riches story made national headlines, and James seemed to be doing interviews constantly. Their little *pas de deux* even sparked new debates about the authorship of *Song of Solomon*. Colette devoured every article, feeling partly responsible for any criticism that was laid upon *Cantique*. As it turned out, not everyone was a fan of their literal, romantic interpretation of the text. It was too secular. Too sensual. Others complained about a "boring Bible myth" being placed onto a contemporary stage. It was too archaic. Too irrelevant.

James wasn't bothered, but Colette had to admit that, faced with this handful of critics, she felt relieved at having been uncredited for her role in the ballet's inception. Besides Lavoisier's speech and the *Stage Star* article, Colette had become lost in the shuffle. She appreciated that James tried to include her when he could, but people were more interested in the choreography and in the mystery surrounding Sokoloff's lost ballet. Colette couldn't blame them.

"Alright, ladies," Marianne said. "Take a quick drink and meet up for center. Can I have Colette and Samantha in the front two corners?"

There was a new woman there that night, whom Marianne placed in the middle of the second row so she had people to watch. She was completely out of her depth, but she cheerfully gave it her all. She laughed at her mistakes without embarrassment or apology, and she complimented all of her classmates.

Colette suddenly felt guilty. In all her years there, she had never uttered a single compliment, except maybe to Sammy. She had always been too focused on herself—on her own progress and on her own mistakes.

After class, Colette tasked herself with speaking to the woman. It would be a start.

"Good job tonight," Colette told her in the dressing room. "This class can be kind of intimidating, but you're picking things up quickly."

"Oh, thank you," she said. "I feel so silly. I thought this was a beginning class."

"It's not your fault at all," Sammy added. "It's way more advanced than it should be. They should really change the name."

"Well, that's reassuring. You girls are so good. Do you dance in the company?"

Colette and Sammy locked eyes and burst out laughing.

"No. We're not *that* good," Colette said.

As flattering as it was, the question was rather ridiculous. Could the general public not discern the difference between amateurs and professionals? How sad for the company.

"Oh," said the woman. "Well, I don't really know much about ballet. I just enrolled my daughter in the fall. She would love your skirt. Where did you get it?"

"I made it," Colette replied.

"How neat! Do you make leotards, too?"

Colette shook her head. "No. I think that's too hard for me."

"Oh, you should try it. I'm sure they'd be beautiful."

Sammy was a huge fan of this idea and made it a point to remind Colette for the duration of the car ride home.

"People already love your skirts," Sammy insisted. "Just think about it. You could design your own fabrics. You could customize the style. And you could even cater to us regular adults, you know, people who don't have 'professional ballet' bodies. Think of what a cool business that would be!"

Of course, deep down, Colette also loved the idea, but it seemed to be too ambitious. Who was she to sew custom leotards? She wasn't that good of a seamstress. And how would she even begin to start a real business? The whole thing sounded terrifying.

"I think you need to temper your excitement a bit," Colette said. "Anyway, I need to find something that will make me money *now*. I have, like, two dollars."

"Ask Darrel if he'll invest," Sammy replied.

"Ha!"

"Better yet, ask Alex. She's the one who got your hopes up."

Colette cringed. She had been trying to forget that whole thing.

By now, she had long since returned to Tempe's full-time, and she had heard nothing from Alex about the possibility of continuing her work with the costume shop. A few weeks after the gala, Colette had worked up the nerve to talk to her at Westmoreland. Alex seemed to have forgotten about it, but she apologized and promised that she would look into it as soon as she had an opportunity.

Colette tried not to let the delay bother her. She didn't need a new excuse to distrust Alex, and when weeks went by with still no word from her, Colette couldn't bring herself to ask again. Twice seemed too desperate. Instead, she asked James if he had heard anything, knowing full well that he could not be relied upon to relay the conversational nuance that she demanded. It was Helena who eventually provided Colette with snippets of foreboding information. Liz was back from maternity leave. Alex really had spoken with the board. They saw no reason to hire another person. Lack of funds, blah, blah, blah.

And so, Colette began to give up on the whole idea of trying to stay on at Westmoreland, despite the fact that she had never wanted something so badly. When she divulged her desire to James, he insisted that she call Myra herself and let her know just how much she wanted to work there.

Colette hadn't liked the idea at all. She hated pleading, she hated phone calls, and, besides, what could Myra even do about it? Nothing. There was no job to be had.

Eventually, however, she forced herself to dial Myra's number. She had to try.

"Colette, darling!" Myra had answered. "How are you? We're missing you here." Myra lowered her voice. "Liz is present, but she's *not present*, if you know what I mean. Plus, she looks dreadfully puffy. Childbirth certainly changes a person!"

"Aw, well I'm sure she's exhausted. How's the baby? Have you seen him?"

"Oh, yes. He's precious. Like a ball of dough with eyes. And I swear he cries in a French accent."

Colette laughed and then felt faintly ill. This was her cue. "You know, I miss you guys, too. Do you think—well—would there ever be a chance for another opening?"

Cantique

"I—I just don't know, dear," Myra said. "I'm afraid, well—not any time soon. Not with the budget the way it is."

"Yeah, I figured."

"*Quel dommage!* I'm sorry, Colette. I really am. I would hire you in a heartbeat."

"That's all right. Just keep in mind that I'm interested. You know, if something does come up."

"Oh, you're first on my list."

"Thanks, Myra. I appreciate it. Well, I won't keep you. I'm sure you have work to do."

"Always! Trinity says 'hi.' Oh—excuse me, she says 'hey *biatch.*' You girls!"

Colette imagined Myra shaking her head and peering at Trinity over leopard-print spectacles. She really did miss them terribly. She missed the chaotic shop and her backstage pass and the anticipation of *Cantique*. She missed seeing James in the hallways.

As she resumed her regular schedule at Tempe's, she recalled the time she had returned to work at Oleander after vacationing in the Maldives with her mom and Craig. The trip to paradise had made the office feel more suffocating than ever before. She thought it would have been better had she not gone at all.

Her return to Tempe's felt similar, only she would never wish away her brief employment with Westmoreland Ballet. If anything, it had broken the spell she had been allowing herself to live under since last summer. Tempe's had lost its charm, and Colette grew more restless and irritable with each shift. Its spotted walls were ugly, its fluorescent lights were oppressive, and it always smelled faintly of small engine exhaust. She became less tolerant of the subtle comments and smirks she had grown accustomed to receiving from customers—the kind that implied, *no offense, sweetheart, but you don't know what you're talking about.* Reid and Darrel certainly never made her feel that way, but they could also never understand the toll that it took on her. If anyone had the potential to understand work-related sexism, it would be James, but he seemed to float comfortably above criticism and prejudice, basking in his own endless supply of self-confidence.

But she would have to get used to it. Her conversation with Myra seemed to have sealed her fate. She would be destined to work at Tempe's forever, eventually becoming so wise in the way of tools and hardware that even the most misogynistic of old men would grow to respect her. She would become exactly like Bonnie, and her aged face would resemble a leather jacket that had been in the height-of-fashion three decades ago. Maybe that was okay, though—to have a simple life and an honest job and a kind heart. And, like James had said, she could always dance.

ONCE SHE AND Sammy arrived home from class, Colette immediately left for James's apartment, all the while thinking about how funny he could be, how cute and talented he was, and how lucky she was to see him nearly every day. What did all her troubles matter with him by her side? She loved him, and love is as strong as death.

James greeted her with a passionate kiss that seemed to match the fire she had just been feeling for him. Before she could say a word, he was looking into her eyes the way he did when he had an important announcement. He opened his mouth to speak. Colette wondered if he might propose again. She'd probably say yes this time.

"I've been invited to go on tour," James said, looking overjoyed. "They want me and Alex to tour *Cantique Pas.*"

"Wow, that's great," Colette said, taken aback. "When?"

"We leave in May. The whole summer is already planned—every city seems to want to see it! I've never seen Lavoisier push something like this."

"You're gonna be gone... all summer? With Alex?"

"It looks like it. Isn't it crazy? One day, you're discovering *Cantique* in class, and the next, we're performing it all over the country. Think of how many people will see it! Baby... are you alright?"

Colette had slid down the wall and was sitting in a heap on the creaky floor. Unable to form a response just yet, she observed her surroundings from her low vantage point and became irrationally angry at James for neglecting his dusty baseboards. He was a horrible housekeeper. He was careless. What had he just said? He was going to tour *Cantique.* She should be happy for him.

James joined her on the floor. "Colette?"

"Huh?"

"Are you okay?" He asked. Disappointment crept into his voice. He gazed toward the floor and added, "You don't seem very excited."

"It's just... a long time to be gone."

"I know it is. But I have to do this."

"Yeah." She nodded. "I know you do."

Colette told herself to put on a happy face, to swallow her inexplicable disappointment, to ignore the fact that James didn't seem to mind the prospect of being separated from her, and to resign herself to a life alone again, devoid of much meaning.

Come on, Colette. He'll only be gone for one summer.

She turned to James and placed her hand on his face with the intent of congratulating him. She should tell him how proud and excited she was and that, of course, she would miss him very much. Instead, she burst into tears, told him to dust his freaking baseboards, and went home.

CHAPTER TWENTY-SIX

"Oh no, CoCo. You're not starting this again," Sammy said.

It was now late in May, and Sammy had come home from work to find Colette in bed staring off into space. After seeing Sammy in her doorway, Colette rolled over and clung to the sleeping Garçon beside her. Startled, he awoke and fought to free himself of her grip.

"No, kitty!" Colette shouted as he ran out of the room. "Don't leave me. Love meeeeee!"

"You're a straight-up mess," Sammy said, laughing and crawling into bed with her. "What have you been doing all day?"

Colette looked around her. "I'm not sure."

"Did you talk to James?"

"No." She threw the blankets over her head. "He's too busy."

"Will you see him tonight then?" Sammy asked.

"Why does it matter to you?"

"I'm just a little worried about you two."

Colette emerged from under the covers. "We're fine. And yeah, I'll see him. Jael and Darrel are having a farewell dinner tonight."

"Shouldn't you be getting ready?"

Colette groaned. "Probably. You wanna come? Jael won't mind."

After a few rounds of coaxing, Sammy agreed. The prospect was enough to motivate Colette to finally get out of bed. Maybe she would try to look nice tonight. It would be the last time she would see him for a while, after all.

Colette had grown increasingly anxious ever since that night on the floor of his apartment back in February. A few minutes after she had left so abruptly, James had called her on her way home. His voice sounded hurt and confused. Why was she acting so crazy all of the sudden? What did the baseboards have to do with anything? Colette had no helpful answers. She felt suffocated and weak, as if the parasite had re-latched itself to her chest. It seemed to want to move back in permanently.

They had left that night unresolved, though Colette still thought of it frequently. James had repressed the memory and moved on, but he proceeded to act more cautiously around her. She wondered if maybe he was afraid of her. Colette couldn't bring herself to ask.

Thus, the months leading up to James's departure were not Colette's best. Some nights, she awoke with angry tears, having dreamt that he had forgotten about her entirely. Sometimes, she would find herself on stage, expected to perform as Solomon's Bride wearing only a plain black leotard. No tights. No shoes. No makeup. James would suddenly run off stage, leaving her to improvise the choreography alone.

In her waking hours, Colette saw less and less of him. When he did come over, he was exhausted from spring show rehearsals and the extra work he was doing on *Cantique Pas* publicity. They usually sat on the couch with Garçon and stared at the TV, watching silently until James inevitably fell asleep. Sometimes, Colette would watch him with sympathy. He worked so hard. He just needed a break, poor thing. How could he possibly invest more time to be with her when he couldn't even stay awake?

Other times, she would stare at him with impatience. Did she not matter at all? What kind of relationship was this? He would be leaving soon. Now was the time to be with her—to really talk about things—and their old-school vow of chastity only made her feel less connected with him. She longed for the evenings they spent together a few short months ago when, no matter how tired he was, he would teach her the *pas de deux* and make her laugh.

But Colette told herself not to think of all that. She wanted to be happy tonight. She didn't want the Brennans to detect any slight strain in their relationship. She didn't want to disappoint them.

AUDREY OPENED THE door when they arrived, holding Molly on one hip and looking ecstatic to meet a new guest. Rose and Hunter ran to give Colette hugs. Their enthusiastic greeting felt nice after Colette's day alone in bed. She should really play with those two more, she thought.

"CoCo," Rose said. "Like my new dress?"

"It's *beautiful,* just like you," Colette replied, picking Rose up. "Where's Daddy? Is your Uncle Jimmy here yet?"

"They're outside with Pa." Rose paused, and her eyes widened. "Shooting arrows."

"Arrows?"

"Darrel bought a new target," Jael said, emerging from the kitchen. "It's wonderful to see you again, Sammy. Glad you could join us."

When it was time for dinner, the men came back into the house. Side by side, they all looked alike, although Josh was significantly taller than his dad and brother. He reached a hand out to greet Sammy.

"Sammy English, right?"

"Uh, yeah?" Sammy replied.

"My buddy Aaron told me about you."

"Oh." Sammy nodded, her face flushing pink.

James and Colette exchanged a look, and he made his way over to hold her.

"Is that beanie really necessary?" Colette asked playfully.

James smiled, took it off, and roughed up his hair. He peered into her eyes and—for the first time in a while—Colette felt that she had his full attention.

"I sure am gonna miss you," James said.

Darrel appeared next to them, also demanding a hug.

"Now, I know I just saw you yesterday, but I can't hug you like this in the shop," Darrel said, squeezing Colette tightly. "Don't want to make the others jealous."

She laughed. "Yeah. Hal would throw a fit."

Darrel turned to Sammy. It was her turn for a hug. "Hi, Sam. Great to see you again."

Colette thought she heard air escape from Sammy's lungs. Darrel tended to embrace like a grizzly bear.

"Okay," Jael announced. "Everyone ready for dinner? Josh has volunteered to pray for James."

Darrel nodded in approval, and Josh proceeded to say a prayer for his "baby broseph." His words were surprisingly poetic, and he closed with one line that Colette would never forget.

We trust that You will use his talents to add to the beauty of the world You created.

It was easy to admire a ballerina for embodying divine beauty, but fewer people afforded the same praise to men. That James would have his own beauty to add to the world seemed obvious to his brother, and his masculine affirmation made the fact all the more compelling. As Josh finished, Colette glanced at Darrel, saw him nodding in fervent agreement, and tears began to roll down her cheeks. There was something about these men—something about their confidence.

Jael's hand appeared in front of Colette's still-bowed head, offering her a tissue.

"Josh always makes me cry, too," Jael said.

"I didn't know he had it in him," Colette replied, laughing.

Josh smirked. "I'm just that convincing."

"It was really beautiful," Sammy added.

Audrey patted him on the back. "Isn't he the best?"

AFTER THEY HAD eaten dinner, the women retired to the living room while the men took the kids outside. Sammy was curious to hear more about Jael's ballet days. Jael humbly obliged and eventually produced a box of memorabilia.

"Oh, wow," Colette said. She pulled out a pair of pointe shoes. "This is so fun! Did you always darn the tips of your shoes?"

"Yes. I spent hours and hours sewing pointe shoes. There never seemed to be enough time. Of course, dancers now have so many other options for things. They can spend even more time on technique. I couldn't dance like people do today. They can jump higher, do more turns. It's incredible."

"You were incredible too, though," Sammy insisted. "I've seen you on YouTube. You were so expressive."

Colette agreed. Jael's artistry and consistent, solid technique were more compelling than the acrobatic tricks of some contemporary dancers. Jael Maier would never have made a spectacle of herself. It occurred to Colette that James's choreography seemed to have successfully fused the two styles. *Cantique* was old-world ballet married with fresh athleticism—without pretension and without spectacle. Like his mother, his refusal to sell out to the masses had ironically drawn them in.

Jael watched Colette closely as she continued to inspect her old pointe shoes.

"Would you like to have those, Colette?"

"What?" Colette replied. "No, I couldn't take these!"

"Who else would I leave them to? James certainly doesn't want them."

"What about your granddaughters?"

"Oh, they'll have plenty of keepsakes," Jael said. Audrey nodded in agreement. "I know I have a couple of other pairs around here somewhere. You take them. I want you to have them."

"Well, okay... just if you're sure, though."

Jael smiled. "I'm sure."

"Well, thank you," Colette said. "I would ask you to sign them, but I don't want to be too much of a nerd."

Jael laughed. "I can if you want. Of course, you'll see how old-fashioned they are when you get some of your own."

"Oh, I don't think I'll ever dance *en pointe*," Colette replied, trying to hide a sudden sadness in her voice. Like the young girls at Westmoreland, Colette had felt a longing to earn her first pair of pointe shoes, but she seemed to be waiting for permission that she assumed would never be granted. Pointe at her age? There was no need for that. Her gaze fell back to the shoes. "I'm probably too old to start."

"Nonsense," Jael said. "You could try it if you wanted to. From what James has told me, you're certainly strong enough."

Colette felt as though she had just inherited an unexpected fortune. "Really? You don't think it's silly?"

Jael shook her head. "Not at all. I've known women older than you who have taken pointe class. I don't think it's ever too late to do something that you love. You would just need to be sensible about it."

Colette nodded. She took each of Jael's simple words to heart, and she dared to dream that she might make them a reality. Even Sammy, who had no interest in pointe herself, looked excited for her. Colette vowed to talk to Marianne about it—after she had worked up the courage.

James opened the front door and asked Colette to join him on the porch. She looked apologetically at her companions. She hated to leave their conversation. There were so many more pointe questions to ask.

"You go," Sammy insisted.

"Yes," Audrey agreed. "You two need some time alone before he goes."

James led Colette to the porch swing that he and Darrel had built. It was not particularly beautiful, but it seemed extremely sturdy. They sat close, surrounded by Jael's potted flowers and the sounds of late spring.

"Is Sammy having fun?" James asked.

"Yeah. She's pretty fascinated by your mom. And I knew she and Audrey would hit it off. Hey, what's the deal with Aaron? What did he tell Josh?"

James shrugged. "Beats me. I guess Sammy made an impression on him."

"That's not surprising."

He took Colette's hand. "Hey... so I know things haven't been all that great lately..."

She nodded and felt her eyes begin to water.

"...but I want you to know that I'm still in this for good. I've been distracted, I know. And this summer will probably be rough, but I love you. I want to be with you. Will you... just stick with me for a while?"

"Of course I will," Colette said. It was true that their current situation was not ideal, but she could not imagine James out of her life now. They would just have to deal with the distance for a while. They could do it. Plenty of other people had done it. "Just—please don't forget me while you're away."

James laughed and wiped a tear from her cheek. "How could anyone forget you?"

CHAPTER TWENTY-SEVEN

Tempe's had a different scent during the summer. It was earthy and comforting; a nice departure from the faint stench of frozen sweat and diesel that clung to customers' coats during the winter. When it was nice outside, Darrel would prop open the front door, letting a sweet, floral breeze into the shop. After the flowers quickly sold out, their scent was replaced by the aromas of mulch and topsoil.

There was also a new sound in the shop—that of water flowing through a small fountain in the lawn and garden display. The constant trickling made Colette have to pee, and she cursed the day she had selected the fountain. Weeks before, Darrel, having decided to add variety to the summer inventory, had sought her advice on which garden sculptures to order. Colette seized this rare "creative" opportunity with uncharacteristic enthusiasm. She had clear opinions on the matter, although she hadn't done a day of gardening in her life.

"Go for the animals," she said, pointing to the catalog. "See, this bunny is adorable. And this turtle. People love that crap. And the occasional fairy, as long as it's not the stupid kind. You know what I mean?"

Darrel looked perplexed.

"See this one?" Colette continued. "This is like 'friendly storybook fairy,' but this other one is like 'cheesy fantasy art fairy.' See the difference?"

Darrel nodded slowly. "I think so... Why don't you just mark what you like and I'll send in the order. Oh, and think about how you'd want to set up the display."

"You want me to do the display?"

"Sure. You're artistic. I'm sure you'll make it look real nice."

Darrel also put her in charge of ordering new signage and "sprucin' up" the candy selection. Colette wondered where these extra projects were coming from. Was Darrel trying to keep her preoccupied? Did he sense that she was slowly going crazy without James?

Regardless, Colette didn't mind. She had been doing her best to keep her evenings busy, too. The last thing she needed was an empty shop and a wandering mind.

On this particular day, however, Darrel was not there to give her any extra tasks. She and Travis stood near the front of the shop during the afternoon lull, both staring into space. Colette walked over to turn off the fountain.

"Thank you," Travis said. "I hate that thing. Is that another friend of yours?"

"Huh?"

Travis pointed toward the door. A small, blond woman was shading her eyes and looking into the windows. It was Helena. Colette had not expected her so early.

"You know, this isn't your social club."

"It isn't?" Colette replied. "That's news to me. Now please go away. I don't want you to scare her off."

Travis rolled his eyes and walked over to open the door.

"Good afternoon, ma'am," Travis said, tipping an imaginary hat. "Milady is ready for you."

To Colette's horror, Helena giggled and looked rather enchanted by Travis's gesture. "Why, thank you kind sir," she said. "Hey, CoCo."

"Hey! Let me get your skirt. Just a sec."

Colette pulled a bag out from under the counter and presented it to Helena. When she opened it, her eyes sparkled as if she were looking at a diamond ring.

"Oh, Colette," Helena said. "I *love* it! It's even more beautiful than the first one. Where did you find this fabric?"

"I actually thought it would be fun to dye it myself."

"You didn't! What about the flowers?"

Colette smiled. "Hand-painted. I thought with all of the colors you would be able to wear it with pretty much any leo. I did some others, too. Here, I'll show you."

Colette flipped through the photos on her phone. Travis stood off to the side, his hairy arms enfolded, and craned his neck to see.

"You made all of those?" he asked.

"Yeah."

"Huh. Impressive."

Colette glanced up to see his expression. He looked surprisingly sincere.

"Oh, all of the girls would love these," Helena said. "You are so talented."

"Aw, thanks. Better not quit my day job, though."

"I wish you could." Helena looked around the store, as if just noticing her surroundings. "So, James's dad runs this place?"

"Yep."

"Huh. I could actually see James working here when he retires."

Colette laughed. "He would definitely fit in better than I do."

"Yeah. You're too pretty for this place." Helena glanced at Travis. "No offense."

"None taken," Travis replied.

"CoCo is just so sophisticated. Again, no offense."

"Again, none taken." Travis winked and Helena smiled back, clearly enjoying their strange banter. Colette hoped for Helena's sake that it would end soon.

"Well, I'd better be going," Helena said. "Thanks again for the skirt. I can't wait to wear it! And it was nice to meet you—"

"Travis."

"—Travis. I'm Helena."

"Helena. It's been a pleasure. Come back and see me sometime."

She giggled once more, left the shop, and turned around to wave from outside. Colette shot Travis a foreboding glare.

"Don't get any ideas," she said.

"So, if she's a dancer she's, uh, pretty flexible, right?"

"What you do you think, perv?"

Travis rapped his knuckles on the counter. "No more private transactions on work time, k?"

"No one's even here!" Colette called after him as he walked away. "Man, I hate you."

"Heard that!"

Alone at the register, Colette smiled at the thought of Helena wearing her new skirt to company class. Seeing her face light up as she opened the bag had been more than worth the effort, and Colette wanted to feel that satisfaction again. The idea that something she made might help boost Helena's confidence, or maybe even inspire her dancing—it was incredible, really.

She began to daydream about what it would be like if she *were* to actually quit her day job—to abandon Tempe's in favor of pursuing some crazy, creative business full-time. She would have to sell thousands of skirts to make a living, and that would be impossible. Working for an established dancewear company was really her next-best option, but she had checked on that already. There were no companies nearby, and no one was hiring, anyway. At least, they weren't back when she had first lost her job.

But that had been over a year ago. She had been at Tempe's for *over a year*. Colette cringed at the thought.

Maybe she would just take another look around.

Still seated in front of the empty shop, Colette searched the listings of several brands to no avail. Then, she thought of her leo from James and checked Noverre Dancewear. Her eyes sifted through numerous postings—*Customer Service Representative, Call Center Manager, Vice President of Sales*—until she found something relevant.

Noverre is seeking a creative, hard-working, dance enthusiast for the position of Design & Marketing Assistant. Requirements: B.F.A. Costume Design, Fashion Design, related field or equivalent experience, minimum of two years working in an office setting, ability to collaborate in a team, ability to complete a variety of tasks, proficiency in all major word processing programs...

That was her. She could do those things.

Noverre Dancewear, Inc., Chicago, IL.

Oh. Never mind. She really couldn't move, could she?

SHE CALLED JAMES from her bed around 9 p.m. that evening, which had become their routine. The first few nights apart, they would talk for hours, catching each other up on the mundane details of their days. James would describe each performance to the best of his ability.

"It went pretty well," he would say. "Nailed the double *tours*. The audience seemed to love it. Alex says to tell you 'hi'."

Colette would give her regards in return while hating to think of the countless conversations Alex and James were having without her—the hours and days and weeks they were spending together. Somehow, it was easy for Colette to forget that other dancers and staff were there with them.

As the tour went on, their phone conversations had become increasingly forced.

"Hey," James answered, his voice already sounding fatigued. "Man, I miss you."

"I miss you, too. How did it go today?"

"Fine."

She pressed for more information. They were in Mobile now, making their way westward. Lavoisier had negotiated more performances, and James would be gone another month.

Colette frowned. She was beginning to regret ever telling him about *Cantique*. "Will you *ever* come back?"

"Of course I will."

"Oh, so I finally asked Marianne about pointe."

James yawned. "Oh, yeah? What'd she say?"

"That I would have to take private lessons since I haven't had any experience." Colette sighed. "I can't afford it—or the shoes, for that matter."

"Aw, I'm sorry, babe."

She wondered if he would come up with a different solution to the pointe dilemma, but she heard nothing but another yawn.

"I saw Helena today," Colette said, desperate to keep the conversation going. She heard a door creak in the background, and James's voice became faint.

"Yeah, just leave it there," he said. "I'll take care of it."

"What?" Colette asked.

He resumed his normal volume. "Sorry. What did you say?"

"Who are you talking to?"

"Alex."

"Oh," Colette said. "Are you still at the theater?"

James paused. "No."

"So… are you at the hotel?"

"Yeah."

"Oh."

Colette told herself to leave it at that, even though she wanted to know exactly what he was taking care of. What could Alex be leaving for him?

Don't say anything. Don't make it a big deal.

"How are Nate and Iris?" Colette asked.

"Good. They're on tomorrow. You should see Nate's Solomon. It's insane."

"I'm sure you're just as good," she replied. "Just different."

"I don't know." James laughed. "Their version may be all-around better than ours. Iris is really holding her own."

"Well, they are actually married, James. That has to help."

He didn't have much else to say, and his voice was getting weaker. Colette grasped for more topics. Although she had not intended to mention the Noverre position, she told him anyway. If nothing else, it would keep him on the phone longer.

"It's in Chicago, though?" James asked.

"Yeah."

"That's too bad."

"But I mean, if *you* can go off and pursue *your* dream..." Colette teased.

"Hmph. I'd be all for it if it weren't eight hours away."

"Don't worry. I won't apply. I just like the idea of it."

"I know. You would've been good at it." He yawned again. "Well, babe—"

Colette sighed. "I can let you go."

"That'd probably be good. I love you."

"Love you, too. Talk to you tomorrow night."

Colette rested her head on her pillow while still clutching her phone, as if it were a piece of James. She imagined him sleeping in his hotel, bare-chested and tattooed, probably drooling onto the cheap bed sheets in the most adorable way possible. The thought occurred to her again that maybe she had made him up. Maybe he wasn't real. But then again, if he really were a figment of her imagination, they would have had a much more exciting conversation just now. Imaginary James would have asked her about her day. He would have wanted to hear about Helena's new skirt in detail. He would have encouraged Colette to go for her dreams, wherever they might take her.

But what were her dreams, *really?* To work in a cubicle, just like she had at Oleander? To find a job where designing a garden display was not considered challenging? She really didn't know what she wanted, but she knew that the prospect of working for Noverre was more exciting than anything else going on in her life at the moment. And, now that she really thought about it, it seemed unfair of James to dismiss it so readily. Why did it have to be completely off the table? Maybe she'd apply anyway, just to see what would happen.

Colette sat up, turned on her bedroom lamp, and got to work.

CHAPTER TWENTY-EIGHT

Colette left the dressing room covered in sweat and feeling a little faint. Morning classes were unusual for her, and this one had been a little too difficult. It was an intermediate class taught by a soft-spoken woman who was unexpectedly strict, and it was full of retired professionals, serious amateurs, and home-schooled prodigies.

During center, Colette had gladly relegated herself to the back row. Her new spot gave her a different perspective of the studio, and she found herself scrutinizing the pairs of feet in front of her. Some were outfitted in pointe shoes, some in socks, some in regular ballet flats. Every foot articulated through the same *tendus* a little differently, but all were unusually strong. Years of ballet had turned these feet into something more like hands, and they could communicate in a kind of sign language. Colette looked down at her own and found that they, too, had changed. Then, she realized that she had missed the adagio demonstration. From that point on, she was lucky to keep up with any of the combinations.

Thus, she left Westmoreland glad to have her workout behind her. She could treat herself to brunch on her way home. Today would be a day of treats.

Her phone showed that she had missed two calls from James. She grinned, certain of why he had called her so early, and listened to his message.

"Hey! Just calling to tell you happy birthday. I hope you do something fun today. Wish I could be with you. I love you and, uh, I guess I'll talk to you later. Bye, baby."

To her astonishment, the second voice mail was not from James, but from Alex.

"Hi, Colette. It's Alex... Vukoja. Um, I don't know if you've seen the Pointe Pitch article yet, but I just wanted to let you know that James and I had nothing to do with that. They never interviewed us. I would never have let it happen. I already called and am having them retract it. Just wanted you

to know. Okay. Well, I hope you're doing well. James misses you. Talk to you later."

What the heck was she talking about? Colette hurried to her car, hoping the sinking feeling in her stomach would go away as soon as she figured out what was going on. Why was she hearing this from Alex? James could have at least filled her in himself.

She called James. No answer.

Something told her not to look up the article Alex had mentioned, as if that were possible. Her fingers typed the foreboding terms: *Pointe Pitch James Brennan.* She couldn't help it.

THE ULTIMATE PAS DE DEUX: WESTMORELAND'S ALEXANDRA VUKOJA & JAMES BRENNAN DAZZLE IN CANTIQUE DE SALOMON

by Stacey Walker, Pointe Pitch Blog Contributor
July 9th, 2017, posted at 6:00AM CST

As soon as Westmoreland Ballet stars Alexandra Vukoja and James Brennan graced the stage at the Fort Worth Performing Arts Center Saturday evening, the audience was transported into a garden of timeless romance. No doubt the eager balletomanes had read the rave reviews of Brennan and Vukoja's touring CANTIQUE DE SALOMON PAS DE DEUX, *a musical jewel that has long remained hidden. (See* IOSIF WHO? WESTMORELAND DISCOVERS LOST BALLET.*)*

The dancers Brennan and Vukoja, who are partners both on and off stage, have a palpable chemistry perfect for embodying the ancient tale of King Solomon and his bride. A brilliant technician, Vukoja's performance was inspired, vulnerable and achingly beautiful, while Brennan's variations were confident and compelling, his soaring figure demonstrating danseur bravado at its finest. The eight-minute pas de deux is Brennan's most important choreographic work to date, and he does not disappoint. CANTIQUE'S *classical structure paired with its contemporary flare works well with Brennan's energy and Vukoja's dramatic elegance. It is clear that the partners played to their strengths when crafting the ballet together. Indeed, it is difficult to imagine any other dancers portraying a more intimate duet than this promising power couple. Brennan's King Solomon may have had 1,000 brides, but Vukoja is clearly his favorite...*

Colette couldn't read any more. She wanted to throw up. She rolled down the driver's side window and stared out into the parking lot.

Power couple. Partners on and off stage. Palpable chemistry. Alex must have wanted to make sure that I read the article.

No, she was trying to warn you about it.

But why would she bother to do that? If she hadn't, I never would have known.

James was finally calling.

"Hello?"

"Hey," James said. "Happy birthday! How does it feel to be twenty-seven?"

Colette sat still, suppressing the anger she could feel stirring inside of her.

"Colette? You there?"

"Yeah."

"I guess you saw the *Pointe Pitch* thing?" James said, laughing. "It's ridiculous. Super awkward."

"Yep," she said bitterly, still staring out the car window.

"Hey, don't be upset about it, okay?"

"It's a little hard not to be."

"Well, obviously it was just a stupid mistake on their part. We never even talked to them. I'm sorry you had to see it."

"Well, it sure seems like Alex wanted me to see it."

"You shouldn't be so hard on her," James said. "She was really worried about the whole thing. She insisted on calling you right away, to set things straight. I told her not to bother—that you'd laugh it off—but she wouldn't take no for an answer. You should have seen her."

"You really think I would laugh this off? That writer got her information from *somewhere...* " Colette remembered their early rehearsals—the longing she had seen on Alex's face and James's unwillingness to discuss it. And now he was defending her too much. She shook her head and muttered, "For all I know it could be true."

"What?" James asked. "I can't hear you."

"Are you sure it isn't all true, James?"

"*Hey.* What the hell kind of question is that? We both know that blog is a load of crap, and they're pulling it down any minute now. We can all forget about it."

"That's not the point."

"What is the point, then?"

"The point is that you don't care about this enough. You're so quick to brush things off without thinking about how *I* feel. I can't just 'forget about it' like you can. And I really don't know *what* you've been doing since you've been gone—"

"*Colette!*"

"What?"

"That is a really awful thing to say." He lowered his voice. "Have I given you any reasons not to trust me? You *knew* that I would have to partner with people. This is what I do. Seriously—you need to stop being so jealous all the time—"

"I'm *not* jealous all the time! I don't care that you have to dance with people. When you're with Iris, Yumi, whoever, it's totally fine. I *really* don't care. But this is different—"

"—No, it's not. It's all in your head. You always have to turn it into a bigger deal—"

"Would you quit blaming me? This is YOUR FAULT!"

"WOULD YOU STOP YELLING AT ME?"

"I'M NOT YELLING!"

"Colette—"

"Seriously, James. All you do is think about *your*self and *your* ballet and *your* career. You really don't care about what happens to me—as long as I'm still around to remind you of how awesome you are."

James laughed. "That's ridiculous."

"No, it's not," Collette said, insulted that he could laugh at a time like this. How could he be so unflappable? Did *nothing* matter to him? "If you really cared, you would have called me about this yourself, instead of making me hear it from Alex. What the hell were you thinking?!"

"Colette, I'm about to take class. I can't keep talking about this."

She rolled her eyes. "Sure, class is more important than our relationship."

"That's *not* true."

"It sure feels like it."

"Ugh!" James grunted, exasperated. "Would you just shut the fuck up already?"

Colette fell silent, shocked to find she had actually affected him enough to say such a thing. She felt her anger deepening into wrath, and the only words she could muster were, "Real mature, James."

"Okay," he said. "That's it. I'll talk to you when you've calmed down."

Colette hung up the phone before James could. She skipped the brunch she had been looking forward to and headed straight home, where she spent the entire afternoon in fits of volcanic rage and livid tears. Garçon whined in response and finally ran away to hide in the basement, and Colette sat stewing on her bedroom floor until Sammy came home.

"HAAAAPPPPYY BIRRRTHDAAAAY TOOOO—Good God! What happened?" Sammy asked, horrified.

"It's James," Colette said, her voice wobbling through tears.

"What? Is he okay?" Sammy sat down beside her. "Tell me what happened."

"I just can't do it anymore. Not when he's gone all the time and dancing with her."

Sammy rolled her eyes. "Come on, CoCo. He's coming back. He'll be back before you know it."

"That's not all."

Colette tried to pull up the article for Sammy, but the whole thing had been taken down, as if it never existed. She had at least expected a retraction.

"Well, regardless, I'm unsubscribing from *The Pointe Pitch,*" Sammy said. "They could probably sue them for libel. But obviously James had nothing to do with it. You know that."

"That's not even the point."

"What do you mean?"

"He's *always* been gone all the time—even before the tour. And that's how it will always be. The most we saw each other was when I worked at Westmoreland." Colette shook her head. "I'm starting to think that we rushed into things. I really don't even know him that well."

"Yes, you *do* know him. I could tell what kind of guy he was right away. He would never do anything to hurt you."

"People change."

Sammy frowned, apparently frustrated with Colette's inconsolable attitude. She stood up and said, "Well, I'm sorry all of this happened on your birthday. That really sucks. Honestly, though, I think you're being way too dramatic about the whole thing. But I can see that nothing I say will do any good—"

"*Sammy.*"

"What? It won't. If you *want* to stay stuck in your own personal hell, there's not much I can do about it. And if I didn't know any better, it sounds like you're thinking of breaking up with him." Sammy waited for a response and, when Colette offered none, her face fell in severe disappointment. "Seriously? That's *really* stupid, Colette. James is not dispensable—"

Colette looked up at her, indignant. "You don't understand."

"Maybe I don't, but—"

"He's not perfect, you know."

"Well, he's pretty damn close."

Colette rolled her eyes. "You *would* think that, wouldn't you? You don't know anything."

At that, Sammy left the room, letting the door slam behind her.

Colette remained seated, feeling strangely calm and completely out of tears. Her face was finally dry and felt numb. She had the faint sense that she was not quite herself, and she could function with a hardened heart if needed. She turned off her phone. There was no need to talk to James tonight.

CHAPTER TWENTY-NINE

The following evening, Colette drove to class alone. She had left for Westmoreland straight from Tempe's, partly to avoid Sammy and partly because she was going to do the unspeakable—she was going to try the advanced class.

Sammy wouldn't have wanted to go, anyway. She had once called Advanced Ballet "a death wish," and Colette had more-or-less agreed with her. Now, it seemed like the perfect time to finally give it a shot. She could use the extra challenge. She needed to do something that would demand all of her focus—something that would keep her mind off of James and that horrible *Pointe Pitch* article.

A few glimpses of Darrel that morning had been enough to send her through a series of unwanted emotions. She saw James in his eyes and, oddly enough, heard him in his voice. Darrel's warm demeanor threatened to melt the coldness that had invaded her heart. But then, she remembered James's careless attitude—his flippant words and sudden severity. It all still festered inside of her.

Your son told me to "shut the fuck up" last night.

To Colette's relief, Darrel had spent most of the day in his office, and Hal was scheduled on the floor. Old Hal was not one for chit-chat, and the only acknowledgment he gave her was a brief nod from the break room. Colette nodded back in solidarity, as if to affirm his preference to keep to himself. It had to be nice, really—having no one to bother him, no one to interrupt his thoughts, no one to commandeer his heart.

ONCE COLETTE ARRIVED at Westmoreland, she had to rush to get ready. There would be no slow, warm-up ritual tonight—no foam rollers or tennis balls or stretches. She crammed her hair up into a makeshift bun and changed in a bathroom stall. The ribbon of her wrap skirt grazed the toilet water.

Awesome.

She hurried into class and surveyed the room. No one looked familiar, not even the pianist, and Colette felt like she had just crashed a private party, though she had danced in this particular studio a hundred times. She kept her gaze down and walked toward her usual place at the barre before noticing someone's belongings on the floor, saving the spot. A woman appeared, gave Colette a cool glance and added another item to the pile—a large, mesh bag filled with at least a dozen pointe shoes. Colette gawked at them, unable to guess why so many pairs were necessary. They looked like a school of fish caught in a net, and some were probably dead already, but together they were worth a fortune—over forty ballet classes at least.

There was not enough room to stand behind the woman, so Colette moved to the only free spot along the wall. Once there, she quickly discovered why no one had taken it. There was no mirror, and she would be at the very front for the first side, completely exposed. She considered moving to one of the free-standing barres while she still had the chance, but she couldn't bring herself to. She couldn't walk across the studio again—not when people were already watching her and sensing her awkwardness. No. She'd better stay put and pretend to be confident. She stood up straight.

I will not be intimidated.

The teacher was middle-aged and a retired Westmoreland dancer. He was cordial enough, but also a man of few words who gave combinations only once, and Colette soon realized that she'd better listen hard. Even the *plié* combination was considerably more complicated than what she was used to. By the second *tendu*, she was desperate for someone to watch.

"Quick *tendus en croix*," the teacher instructed. "Hold counts eight, six, four and two. Slow *passé* in eight counts. Change legs. *Tendus en croix*, inside leg, hold counts seven, five, three, and one. *Cou-de-pied* balance with the inside leg for eight counts, don't change. Stand tall. Reverse the whole thing, starting from the back. And-a-one and two and three and four, five, six, seven, hold eight..." He paused to reciprocate the knowing nods of his students. "*Passé* with the inside leg this time, start to the back, holding the odd counts. Balance *sur le cou-de-pied*, outside leg, *soussus*, *soutenu*, straight to the other side."

Intellectually, Colette understood the pattern. It had the same satisfying symmetry of any of Marianne's combinations. But the preparation was longer than the usual four counts, and she had to crane her neck to see when the others started their *tendus*. Once she began, her body could not keep up with the speed of the music. A missed hold sent her off-track just as the teacher turned around to observe her.

"Other foot," he said. "And side, back, side."

"Thanks," Colette said, hoping he would go away.

"How long has it been?"

"Huh?"

"Been a long time since you've danced?"

Colette stopped moving.

What kind of question is that? I danced yesterday. Freaking yesterday.

"A while," she finally said, feeling heat rising to her cheeks. Despite being completely lost, she tried to resume the combination, unaware of what her body was actually doing.

"Oops," the teacher said. "Now you're doing *dégagés. Tendu* stays on the ground."

I know that, you bastard. You think I don't know that?

His face remained serious, and Colette caught amused glances from the other women—all slender and elegant and obnoxiously good. They turned to the other side in perfect unison, as if they had all danced in a professional *corps de ballet* at some point in their lives. Did they really think that she didn't understand *tendu*? Were they all mocking her?

I will not be intimidated, she reminded herself.

The rest of barre was torture. Instead of warming her muscles—instead of building stamina and excitement for center—each exercise made her more flustered. As the steps became increasingly complicated, her technique descended into a mess of turned-in hips and sickled feet and droopy elbows. She couldn't help but watch the others, whose bodies were more graceful than hers, whose nuanced *port de bras* and *épaulement* revealed decades of experience. How old would Colette be by the time she caught up with them? Forty? Fifty?

By *grand battement*, she was on the verge of tears. She tried to talk herself down—to reason herself out of it. Crying in class would be too mortifying to fathom.

You're okay. You're okay. This is really hard, but you're okay. And these women aren't really judging you. They're focusing on their own dancing. They're really not so bad. It's all in your head. Any other day, you could take this class and feel inspired by them, not intimidated. You could watch them dance and say, "That's beautiful. One day I'll dance like that." You need to push yourself, Colette. Marianne always tells you that. You won't grow until you push yourself.

Despite sensing that she should call it a night, she talked herself into staying for center. She hurried to the middle of the back row in an attempt to make herself invisible and staked out dancers to watch. This technique got her through the first combination without any major disasters. Then she heard those dreaded words.

"Okay, let's switch lines."

Colette tried to stay back, but the others motioned her forward. Red-faced, she walked toward the mirror, stood front and center, and waited for the adagio instructions.

Don't screw this up, Colette.

"Hmm. Let's actually start *éffacé*, left foot front. *Chassé* to *attitude. Relevé* or stay flat, extend *arabesque, plié,* arms *allongé. Pas de bourrée...*"

Got it.

"From there, *développé devant*, one, through *passé* two, extend three, hold four. Carry it around five, six, seven, hold *arabesque* on eight..."

Okay. I can do that.

"Eight counts to *promenade* around. Keep that leg high. *Penchée* down one, two..."

No. Not penchée.

"...*enveloppé* seven and eight. Then, we'll reverse all of that, minus the *penchée.*" He hastily marked through the steps before closing *en face.* "*Développé* side, *plié* on five, six, extend higher, close eight. *Développé* the left leg, *plié* five, *fouetté* six to *arabesque*, extend, extend, extend!"

That's a ton of arabesques.

"*Plié, pas de bourrée*, close in *croisé*. Lift the downstage leg front, *tombée* on two—big lunge forward—big *port de bras* over. *Cambré* back, seven and eight. *Plié*, up to *tendu. Plié* to prepare, change the arms, *pirouette en dedans.*" He held his arms in fifth position and shook his head three times, as if expecting triple *pirouettes.* "And close. Start the other side. Right foot should be front. Okay?"

Crap. How did it start again?

There was no time to ask. The teacher nodded to the pianist, and Colette was forced to mimic the others in the mirror. This time, the music was painfully slow. Her muscles trembled with nerves, which made for sad balances and low extensions. She watched the reflections of the others, with their sky-high *développés*, their seamless *promenades*, and their steady *penchées* approaching six o'clock, like Jael's Giselle. Colette glanced in the mirror during her own *penchée* to find her legs closer to 90 degrees and her back down in a rather inelegant position. Mortified, she rushed into the *enveloppé* and waited for the music to catch up, all the while praying that this excruciating combination could somehow end sooner.

It eventually did end, but only after they repeated the whole thing a second time. The teacher fell silent as he thought through the next exercise, and Colette inched her way to the back again, now exhausted and aching all over. If *adagio* was this hard, what about *pirouettes*? What about *petit allegro*? What about *grand allegro*?

Her mind raced through visions of endless *brisés* and *cabrioles* and *entrechats six*. She had never done any of those steps. She imagined the others surrounding her, doing multiple *attitude* turns and *manèges* of double *piqués* and rapid-fire *fouetté* turns while she struggled to link two *chaînés* together.

She could see her bag there in the corner. She could just grab it and leave, but then she would be a quitter. It would mean that the impossible demands of ballet had finally trumped her love for it. Maybe that was actually a good thing, though. Maybe that meant that the delusion was finally over. It was clear that she was not a good dancer. Why had James encouraged her? It was cruel of him, really. To tell her that she was doing well—that she was a natural, that she was strong enough to go *en pointe* if she wanted to, even though it was high time that she move past this fruitless obsession.

The others were marking through the waltz. She saw one of the women do the first *pirouette* full out—only she did three *pirouettes en pointe* and, instead of landing on two feet in fourth position, she calmly rolled down through her standing foot while the other leg floated into *attitude*. Her long limbs created a beautiful line, and the nonchalant look on her face reminded Colette of James on the day he had taught her class.

No big deal, just dancing here.

Colette picked up her bag, crept to the door, and got the hell out of there. Then she called the one person who might be able to make her feel better, even if he could never completely understand her pain—even if she was still angry with him.

"Hey," James answered. "I'm heading to the theater. Can we talk later tonight?"

No, I need you now.

"Colette," James said, not bothering to mask his impatience. "Did you hear me? I don't have time for this right now."

"Oh, yeah." Colette suppressed her tears and added, "I have all the time in the world."

"I don't appreciate the sarcasm. I'll call you when I'm done, okay?"

"Don't bother. There's nothing to talk about."

"Okay," James said. "Bye."

CHAPTER THIRTY

It had been a long time since Colette dreamt of dancing in the open studio—chiffons blowing in the breeze and henna on her feet. This dream was different. She was in a cave illuminated by firelight, watching a shadow dance on the damp rock before her. She felt James's hands lifting her in the same *presage* they had practiced. His grip on her waist and thigh grew tighter and tighter until she felt as though she were suffocating. She tried to look down—to tell him to stop—but her mouth would not open. Blood streamed from where his nails pierced her skin. The firelight flickered, and she finally saw that the hands gripping her did not belong to James.

Colette awoke crying out in panic. She sat up, her heart racing and her chest drenched with sweat, and recalled with horror that she was alone in the house. Sammy had gone to stay with her parents for the weekend. It was childish to be afraid of a nightmare, Colette reminded herself.

It was no use trying to go back to sleep. She turned on her bedroom lamp, and the last conversation with James came flooding back into her mind. He hadn't called her back, and why should he? She had told him not to bother.

Maybe he would *never* call her again. Only when Colette received news via Helena, would she discover that they were finished and that James and Alex were an item. Maybe they had been an item all along.

No, James wouldn't do that. He would never do that.

But maybe Colette had pushed him to it. Maybe her jealousy had caused the very thing that she had feared. Why *wouldn't* he go for Alex? Beautiful, thin, mysterious, incredibly talented Alex. What did Colette have that she didn't have? Really, James would be crazy *not* to—

"Stop being stupid," Colette said.

Poor Alex. If only she knew what a monster I've made her out to be. And poor James. No wonder he thinks I'm acting crazy. Maybe I really am crazy.

Colette considered calling him but knew he would be sleeping. He had probably brushed their arguments aside and fallen asleep instantly, blissfully unaware that Colette was awake and tormented by a gnawing feeling in the pit of her stomach. She knew it was time she should apologize to him, but she didn't feel ready. There was something unsettling about the whole thing—something, she knew deep down, that had nothing to do with James. Why had she been so angry? Why had she handled things so poorly?

The sky gradually grew lighter. When her clock hit 6 a.m., she decided to call him with no clear purpose.

James answered with a groggy voice. "Colette?"

"Hi," Colette said. "Were you asleep?"

"Yeah."

"Sorry."

He sighed deeply, still half-asleep. "What's going on?"

"I just... wanted to talk."

James cleared his throat, and Colette thought she heard his blankets shuffle as if he had decided to sit upright for their conversation. How she wished she could be there with him, face to face.

"Alright," he said.

She was quiet for a while, not knowing where to begin or what she really wanted to say. Why had she called him, again? Just to hear his voice? That was a lame reason.

"Colette," James said. "What did you want to talk about?"

"I know there's nothing going on. And I really do trust you. I'm sorry I freaked out about the article."

"Thank you for saying that. Let's not talk about it anymore, please."

"It's not like that's the only thing that bothered me about it, though. They gave her half the credit for *Cantique*. It's like I don't even exist."

"Colette, I've tried to tell people—"

"I know you have. And the whole thing didn't bother me before, but it's starting to. You called this my ballet once, but now it feels like I didn't have any part in it."

"I'll talk about it more..." He paused to yawn. "About how you noticed the music."

"James... I found you the passage, too. Remember?"

"Huh?"

"I'm the one who found the passage. I read it to you."

"Oh. Right."

"And you used my sketches..."

Had he really forgotten? She thought that he had been impressed—or at least surprised—by what she had to contribute. She thought she had really helped him. But maybe he didn't care at all.

Maybe I mean nothing to him.

"James," Colette said. "Can you answer something for me?"

"Sure," he replied, yawning.

"Why do you love me?"

"Because I just do."

Colette hesitated. "I don't feel like that's a good answer."

"Well, I don't know how else to answer."

"I need specific reasons."

"Ugh," he grunted. "It's six o'clock in the morning."

"If you really love someone enough to want to marry them, you should be able to explain *why*. You should be able to list specifics."

James was quiet. While she waited for him to respond, Colette had a feeling that maybe her demand was a little unfair, after all. What if *she* had to answer such a question? Why did she love James? Just because he was a dancer?

She refocused on the matter at hand. How long had she been waiting on him?

"James!"

"Huh?"

"Did you freaking fall asleep?"

"I don't know."

"Are you going to answer my question?"

He sighed. "Maybe you're right, but I just don't know right now, okay?"

"Maybe I'm right? What is that supposed to mean?"

"What?"

"That sounds like you agree with me—that you should be able to make a list of reasons—and that you can't. So... what does that mean?"

"Colette, this is really aggravating. What do you want me to say? I love you because you're beautiful."

She felt hot tears rolling onto her neck. "Is that really *why*? Because you think I'm *beautiful*? That's not enough. That's really not enough."

After waiting in silence for a painful minute, she realized that he had nothing to add to this revelation. She began to wilt into a profound sadness, her body convulsing from stifled sobs and seething anger.

This is not good. This is not good.

"I can't do this," Colette whispered.

"What?"

"I can't do this anymore."

"Okay, hold on—"

"It'll be better for both of us."

"*Colette!*"

"You can go back to living freely and lightly now. I won't get in your way."

"Wait. *What?*"

"Goodbye, James."

Colette hung up and sobbed harder than she ever had until she felt completely empty. Then she got ready to go to Tempe's. She and Travis had to open, and she couldn't afford to be late.

When she arrived, barefaced, puffy-eyed, and numb-hearted, she braced herself for an inevitable comment.

Travis took one glance at her and said, "You look like hell."

Good, she thought. *It's just as well. I'm over the physical beauty thing. Sick of depending on it; sick of striving for it. Sick of using it as a crutch, even subconsciously. I might as well look like hell and see if I have any other qualities left.*

"Thank you," Colette said, unflinching. She stared him down until he broke eye contact.

"Okay, okay. I'm sorry I said anything. Are you feeling alright?"

"No, I'm not. But I'm already here, so I might as well stay."

"You can leave when Bonnie gets here if you want."

Colette's phone vibrated.

I'm really sorry. I love you and I do have lots of reasons. You know I'm not good at explaining things like you are. Please call me back.

She put it back in her pocket.

"We'll see," she said.

CHAPTER THIRTY-ONE

Colette waited for the call at the kitchen table, surrounded by copies of her application documents in case she would need to reference them. She imagined her interviewer at the other end, where Sammy had just been a few minutes ago, scrutinizing Colette's outfit from across the Formica.

"Do you really need to be that dressed up?" Sammy had asked.

"I guess not," Colette said. She sat up straight and dusted a hair off of her jacket. "But it makes me feel better."

"Right. Remember to smile when you're talking. It will make your voice sound happier." Sammy paused. "Not that I want you to get this job."

Colette recalled that Sammy had given her the same piece of advice during her post-college job search. A lot of good it did back then. She never made the second round of any of those interviews. Well, except for Oleander. Something about this time was different, though. This time, she was completely prepared.

She had spent a ridiculous amount of time on her cover letter, working and re-working it until it was perfect, and it had done its job. It had brought her to the next step. She threw all she had left into her research and, now, she knew Noverre through and through. No one would be handing her a position this time. This wasn't some easy retail job or some personal favor. She would have to fight for this one.

Her phone began to ring. Colette took a deep breath, told herself not to think of James, and answered with a smile on her face.

She acted the part well, aided by the numbness that had overtaken her since her birthday. She was a blank canvas; she might as well paint what Noverre wanted to see, and it seemed to work. The whole thing took less than thirty minutes. Theresa, the hiring manager, was polite, to-the-point and curious about her connection to Westmoreland. Her brief time in the costume shop ended up being a good selling point. Theresa's voice had perked up, and she began asking Colette questions about her personal interest in dance rather than her limited experience with marketing dancewear. At the end of the call, Theresa told her it had been a pleasure, that they would be in touch, and that, hopefully, they would see each other in Chicago for a face-to-face. Colette agreed.

As soon as she set her phone down, she felt an immediate exhaustion set in, accompanied by a sinking feeling in her stomach.

Chicago? What have I done?

No use dwelling on it now. Wait until you hear back.

Her phone rang again before she even left the table. It was Darrel, and she didn't particularly feel like speaking with him but felt obligated to answer. Maybe there was some emergency at Tempe's.

"Hello?"

"Colette, this Darrel. Listen, I don't want to interfere and whatnot, but James told me a little about what's been going on with you two. I just want to say that you don't need to come in to work today if you don't feel like it. I'm sure you could use some time to yourself."

If Darrel had been anyone else, she would have been embarrassed at such an offer. She could still go to work. She wasn't a *complete* basket case.

"Oh, that's okay. I mean, I've been coming in all week, haven't I? I can still come in today."

"I know you can. You're a pro. But don't feel like you have to. I've got things covered here… Colette? You still there?"

"Yeah," she said. She ran her fingers across the edge of the table. "I'm just… trying to think."

"Are you alright, sweetheart?"

She choked back tears and whispered, "I'm fine."

"Are you sure?" Darrel waited. "Colette, why don't you just stay home today. We can plan on seeing you tomorrow."

"Okay," she finally said. "I'll stay home."

"Good. Just lay low. I think that's a good idea. And Jael wants me to make sure you know you're welcome over any time. Any time you wanna talk."

"Okay," Colette whispered. "Thanks, Darrel."

It hadn't occurred to her that James would have told his parents already. Of course he would do that. It would be hard for her to face them now that they were privy to her struggles with their son. But she knew that Darrel and

Jael wouldn't hold it against her. Somehow, they were above all of that, and the thought of their empathy made her cry all the more.

Head aching, she changed into comfortable clothes and thought about what she could do to occupy her time. She couldn't get back into bed, where her mind could wander. There was a mid-morning ballet class, but the last thing she wanted to do was dance. Maybe she would never want to dance again.

She finally resolved to go for a walk when her phone sounded. It was Jael, of all people.

I'm headed to your place if you don't mind. Thought we could go out for tea.

A little shocked, Colette acquiesced. It seemed she had no choice in the matter. Who was she to turn down Jael Maier-Brennan?

Colette tried to fix her running mascara. Her eyes were still puffy, and it was obvious that she had been crying.

Oh well. Jael might as well see me in such a state. It could be the last time she'll see me, anyway.

After Colette met her in the driveway, Jael drove them to the café, which was attached to an antique store down the street from Tempe's. Jael was a slow and careful driver and rested both of her delicate hands upon the steering wheel as if it were a ballet barre. She was doing most of the talking, describing Darrel's house projects and her new paintings. Colette sat quietly, nodding every once in a while. She knew that Jael was prattling on purpose, and she appreciated the pretense. Exchanging niceties had been painful enough.

When they sat down in their corner booth, however, it was clear that Jael's intention was to discuss deeper matters.

"So," Jael said gently. "I'm sure Darrel told you that we spoke with James last night. I hate to hear that things have been difficult between you two. James sounds very worried about you."

"I know," Colette whispered.

"You may not want to talk about it with me, and that's okay. But I want you to know that you can. Darrel and I have a lot of respect for you. We know you take your relationship seriously."

Jael waited patiently as Colette turned her teacup around on its saucer, trying to formulate a response.

"I'm just…" Colette began, "…so confused. I don't know what I'm doing."

"What are you confused about?"

"Well, what did James tell you?"

"Not very much. He told us about the article and that you had been arguing. That you hadn't spoken for several days now." Jael paused to study Colette's downcast face. "He seems to think that you don't want to talk to him at all—that you want to move on. Is that true?"

"I did pretty much tell him that," Colette said. She looked Jael in the eyes, felt mortified at the memories of how she had been treating James, and began to cry. "I'm so sorry. I'm sorry I've messed things up."

"Colette," Jael said. "Let's forget about the fact that James is my son for a minute. His love life is really none of my business, anyway. I want to talk about *you*. Tell me what's been going on."

Colette sat crying for a minute, trying to breathe slowly so she could speak again. She felt so unworthy of Jael's attention, yet she was also in desperate need of it.

"I don't know what my problem is," Colette said. "I love James. I really do. But I've been so unhappy lately. I feel like I have no real purpose. I had plans for my life, you know? Before Oleander kicked me out, I used to be confident—ambitious, even. And sometimes I look around—like at Tempe's—and think *how did I even get here?* It's not like there's anything wrong with my job—and I love Darrel and everything—but I just don't know why I'm there at this point, or how to get out of it. I feel like I have nothing to offer anyone. Least of all, James. He could be doing so much better. I don't understand why he wants to keep me around at all."

Jael sat back suddenly, as if Colette's words had given her an epiphany.

"Colette," she said. "Where do you find your identity?"

"What?"

"Where do you find your identity? In your career? You are *not* what you do for a living. As a dancer, that was especially hard for me to wrap my mind around. It took work to break free from it. I want to spare you from that."

"But you were always a dancer, whether or not you earned a living by it, right? If I could dance like you did, I would definitely identify myself as a dancer."

"Well, I learned that dance is fleeting. Then I became a mother and started to define myself solely by my motherhood. But that's also wrong."

"Why is that?"

"Because these things we love are *gifts*; they are not *who* we are but what we've been given. And even the most beautiful gifts can fail us when we start to idolize them—when we pour *everything* we have into them. Colette, if you stake your self-worth on dance, on your career, on another person, they will all eventually fail you—they'll disappoint you and you'll end up resenting them. There is really only one constant in life, and even He can be puzzling at times."

Colette shifted in her seat. "Honestly… I just don't know what to think about that."

"About what—God?"

"Yeah. James told me once that God gave me a passion for ballet for a reason, but why would He do that? Why would He give me a desire I can't fulfill? Why would He make you great at it and then take it away from you? And why would He send me to work at Tempe's—assuming He actually exists and actually does *send* people places?"

As soon as she asked these final questions, the answers became obvious to her. She recalled the persistent nudge that had compelled her to step into the shop on that muggy summer day. She remembered the day she met James and the day discovered Darrel's family. *She* certainly hadn't sent herself to Tempe's.

"Well," Jael said. "I know why you were supposed to work at Tempe's." She paused to sip her tea. "And regarding your passion for dance, I can think of two reasons why He gave it to you, straight away. One is joy, pure and simple. And if you're really honest with yourself, you feel that joy even without an audience, don't you? You would dance by yourself in an empty room with no mirrors, and you would know deep down that the delight you feel is both a gift to you and a gift to Him. Ballet was my passion for many years, too, and although I tried my best to use it well—to give back to the world, to share beauty that others could enjoy—dancing was never my purpose for *living*. If it was, I would certainly be in trouble now."

Colette exhaled the breath she had been holding and wiped her nose on her sleeve. Jael handed her a napkin, and they both laughed at the amount of snot and tears she was producing.

"Sorry," Colette said, covering her nose. "What's the second reason?"

"Pardon?"

"You said you thought of two reasons why I have a passion for dance?"

"Oh," Jael said, smiling. "Why, to help you fall in love with James. To give you something to share. It led to you becoming part of our family. You know, we had an extra seat that you were meant to fill."

"Jael—" Colette stammered. "That's so sweet. But I don't—I don't think I deserve to be part of your family."

"Nonsense," Jael laughed. "We all love you. James most of all. But, at the end of the day, this is your life. You make your own decisions and you have to do what you know is right."

"I know. I'll talk to him. I just feel like I've really ruined things. Like I can't take it back now."

"Colette, nothing is *ruined.* And I know this matter is not one-sided. I'm under no delusion that my son is perfect. He certainly makes mistakes. But you can always forgive each other. Love covers a multitude of sins."

Colette shifted in her seat again. "Jael..." she said, staring at the flowers on her teacup. "I have to tell you something. I interviewed with Noverre this morning. They might be flying me out to Chicago for a second round. I—I haven't told him yet."

"Well, that's exciting news. I can see how that would complicate things, but you'll just have to see where it leads."

"You don't think I should cancel?"

Jael smiled. "No. There's no harm in going if the opportunity arises. Who knows what will happen. But please tell James. I don't want to be the keeper of secrets between you two."

"I understand. I'll talk to him."

"Good. Colette, I want you to know that Darrel and I see so many good qualities in you. God has a lovely future for you, wherever you end up. You understand me? *Wherever* you end up—here or Chicago, with James or without him. But if you choose to live without him, I want to make sure that your choice is not based off of this feeling that you're having—about not being good enough for him—because that couldn't be farther from the truth. With that being said, I also know that James is a good man, and that he loves you deeply. You two can take your time. You'll figure it out."

CHAPTER THIRTY-TWO

C olette called James once her bags were packed. As she expected, her call went to voice mail. Colette knew he was probably busy, but a pessimistic voice told her that he was screening her calls. After all, why would he want to talk to her? She had practically dumped him, then ignored his calls for over a week. Now he was doing the same. It was only fair.

"Hey, it's me again. I just wanted to talk. I have a few things to tell you. Mainly, that I'm going to Chicago for an interview and then flying down to see my parents. I wasn't planning on going but your dad insisted I take some time off. I'll be there for almost two weeks. I know you'll be in Houston by then. If it works out, I'd really like to see you. Anyway, just please call me back. Bye."

Colette rolled her suitcase into the hallway where Sammy stood waiting.

"No answer?" Sammy asked.

"Nope."

"He'll call you back."

Colette nodded. "We might as well go now, don't you think?"

"Sure. I'm ready when you are."

Sammy drove Colette to the airport. They sat in silence, gazing out into the nearly empty highway on that lazy Sunday afternoon. There had been an awkwardness between them ever since Colette's horrible birthday. Colette had never felt so distant from Sammy, and she knew it was her fault.

"Sam?"

"Yeah."

"I'm sorry I've been such a dick."

Sammy laughed. "Okay, bro."

"But seriously," Colette said, her voice heavy with shame. "I know I haven't been easy to be around lately. And I still feel bad about the things I said to you—"

"Colette, you don't have to keep apologizing. It's okay. I'm over it."

"Still, if you want to fire me as a friend, I understand."

"Oh, you're so fired," Sammy said. She unlocked the car doors. "Now get the fuck out of my car."

They both laughed, but a sudden humility convicted Colette. She imagined herself in Sammy's position, and she realized that she would not have been as forgiving. But Sammy seemed to take everything in stride.

"Sam," Colette said. "What do you even get out of this friendship? You're so amazing. You've always had your life together, and I'm such a loser. You should be hanging out with your fancy work friends."

Sammy laughed and then realized Colette was serious. "You're saying that's a legit concern for you? You're actually distressed about this?"

"I really am. You do all sorts of nice things for me—like taking me to the airport, for instance—and I'm just whiny and boring all the time. Why would you ever want to hang out with me?"

"Jeez, you're not whiny and boring—except for right now! I like hanging out with you because I *like* you. Yeah, you've had a rough time lately, but that doesn't mean I don't want to be around you. As far as my co-workers go, trust me, you have a lot more to offer." Colette looked unconvinced. Sammy rolled her eyes and continued, "Okay, first of all, you're *usually* not needy. You listen better than anyone I know. And you just know me really well. You get me. I have a lot of fun with you. You also make iced tea every day. Is that enough? Need I go on?"

"No, that's good. I feel the same about you." Colette's voice cracked, and tears rolled down her cheeks. "I really don't know what I'd do without you."

"Stop," Sammy whispered. "You're making me cry, too."

They both chuckled, and Colette made a show of drying Sammy's eyes for her. Sammy laughed even harder.

"Hey," Colette said, her voice softening again. "Do you have anything *you* need to talk about? I feel like I haven't had a real conversation with you in forever."

"Naw." Sammy wiped her face again, bit her lower lip, and began to smile. "Well, actually…"

"Yeah?"

"I've sort of been seeing Aaron."

"What? For how long?"

"A couple of weeks now. I would have told you earlier, but it didn't seem like the best timing. I didn't want it to make you sad."

"That wouldn't make me sad! *Sam!* Do you *like* him?"

Sammy hunched over the steering wheel, as if it could help hide the grin on her face, and pulled up to the curb outside the terminal.

"Well, do you?" Colette asked.

"Yeah," Sammy said. "I really do."

"Sammy!" Colette smacked her on the shoulder. "This is so exciting! You have to tell me everything when I get back. I hate that I've been missing out on all the details!"

"I know. Me, too. I so wanted to tell you."

Colette nodded. "I understand... I'm so happy for you, Sam."

"CoCo—"

"I really am, despite the fact that I'm such a mess right now. I needed some good news."

"*Hey*," Sammy said. "You're gonna be all right. I know I don't have the same perspective as you do, but I think you and James belong together. Did you—and be honest—did you *really* want to break up with him?"

Colette closed her eyes. "No."

"Then take it back."

"It's just—more complicated than that."

"Does it have to be, though? I know the distance thing has been hard, but he'll be back soon. And if this Noverre job works out, why couldn't he move to Chicago with you?"

"I couldn't ask him to do that. Besides, I don't think I can just 'take it back.' I've been trying, but he hasn't returned any of my calls."

"None of them?"

"None. Darrel and Jael haven't even heard from him in over a week."

"Huh. That's not good."

"Yeah," Colette said, her eyes watering again. They both got out of the car and met by the trunk. "How can I get him to forgive me when he won't even talk to me?"

"Well, maybe he's just taking time to process everything," Sammy said, trying to look hopeful. She grabbed Colette's suitcase for her, set it on the ground, and hugged her as tightly as she could. "Things are going to work out somehow. I know they will. Good luck tomorrow, and let me know how it goes."

Colette nodded. "I will. Thanks for everything, Sam. I love you so much."

"Love you, too."

THE PLANE RIDE was short. Colette sat in her window seat, clenching her jaw as her mind raced through worse-case scenarios. Maybe James was too hurt to talk to her again. Maybe he had completely forgotten about her. Or maybe he was dead. That's why she hadn't heard from him.

No, she shouldn't think of that. Just the thought made her cry automatically.

What would life without James even be like? Without his youthful charm, his calming presence, his contagious confidence? Who would she tell her secrets to? Whose arms could enfold her the way James's did? And what would Colette's life be like without Darrel and Jael? Without Josh and Audrey and the kids? Colette couldn't bear to imagine it. The loss of James's family would elicit a whole different kind of grief.

But she would have to get used to the idea. After all, it was unlikely that he would want her back now. After growing accustomed to her apparently deceptive beauty, he must have realized that she had nothing to offer him— that she was talentless, direction-less, godless. Despite what Jael and Darrel thought, she would never be good enough for their son. They didn't know how awful she could be.

She shouldn't be thinking of this now, though. She had to focus on tomorrow's interview. For now, she had to pretend that she loved herself enough to get hired. She had to play the impostor—bubbly and ambitious and completely held together.

When she stepped out of the terminal, she saw her name written on a sign in large block letters. Colette greeted the driver, feeling extremely relieved that he hadn't stood her up. She wasn't one to travel on her own.

"Hello, ma'am," he said. "I'm Charles. Looks like we're headin' to the downtown Marriott?"

"Yes, please."

"Great. I'll take your bag. Settle on in. Is James alright?"

Colette's stomach dropped. "Um, excuse me?"

He pointed to the stereo. "James Taylor. 'I seen fire and I seen rain...'"

"Oh, yeah. Sure."

Colette held her phone on her lap for the whole trip, willing it to ring—to see James's name pop up on the screen. It stared back at her in silence, and she tried to occupy her mind elsewhere. She thought of ballet before she had met him—the pressure-free classes and the surprising joy that it had brought her. She would always love to dance, but ballet would never be the same after *Cantique*. There was some deeper respect for it that she had not understood until her conversation with Jael at the café. One particular sentence had haunted her.

You would dance by yourself in an empty room with no mirrors, and you would know deep down that the delight you feel is both a gift to you and a gift to Him.

She knew it was true as soon as she heard it. Now, she wondered at the fact that she knew it was true. What were the implications?

The car pulled up to the hotel, and Colette checked into her room feeling nervous to be alone. Maybe she would order room service and take a bath to calm down—to lessen the weight of her regret by even an ounce. Maybe she would be kind to herself for a change. Maybe she would try to prevent the cruel, poisonous thoughts that seemed to invade her mind so easily. They were suffocating her—pressing on her chest as if aided by some invisible force that wanted her dead.

She slumped down beside the hotel bed, utterly exhausted, and held her face in her hands. The silence in the room seemed thick—palpable, even—as if some hulking figure were standing there watching her, still and mute and close enough to breathe into her ear.

Why do you even bother trying to dance? Why do you bother trying to do anything?

You're talentless, direction-less, godless. And no one would miss you.

It would be so much easier if you just—

"No!" Colette shut her eyes. She pressed one hand to her heart and, with what strength she could muster, whispered, "*Please*. Please help me."

Without knowing why, she began to hum the *Cantique* music, its melody flowing freely without thought or effort. She felt lightness in her chest as the ominous silence dissipated, and thoughts of their own volition began to swirl around her, as though she were in the calm eye of a storm.

For I know the plans I have for you...go into that shop.. love is as strong as death...plans to prosper you...just go into it...jealousy is fierce as the grave...and not to harm you...it burns like a blazing fire...love covers a multitude of sins...rivers cannot sweep it away...plans to give you hope and a future...

She jumped as her phone rang beside her.

"Hello?" Colette answered, her heart pounding.

"Babe? It's me."

CHAPTER THIRTY-THREE

"We're gonna figure this out," James had said, his heart still heavy and his voice weary. "I know things are kind of a mess, but we'll get through it. I just need to see you. I'm so sorry I've been gone so long."

Colette clung to his words. Their conversation was brief, but it had given her hope. He had not forgotten her. From what Colette could gather, James hadn't returned her calls because he was too angry, then too hurt, then too busy, then too tired, and then he hadn't known what to say. But he knew that he loved her, and he would do whatever was needed to make things right between them. They would meet in Houston in a few days. They would talk everything through, face-to-face. They would work things out somehow.

She hoped with all of her heart that James was right. And yet, she felt herself believing that, no matter what happened, she would eventually be okay. Life was too difficult not to trust in that promise, and her troubles were nothing, really—not compared to the suffering of others. What if she were friendless or poverty-stricken? What if she were persecuted, like Iosif Sokoloff? What if her dreams and ideas were mocked not just by her own inner demons, but by nearly everyone around her? Her life was not so bad, and if circumstances suddenly became worse, she would rest in the truth that was becoming clearer with each passing day. God was looking out for her like Darrel watched over Tempe's—with love and ease and with all the time in the world.

Though it was late by the time she went to bed, Colette slept better than she had in weeks. When she awoke the next morning, her interview jumped to the front of her mind, but—to her own astonishment—her usual anxiety had been replaced by a faint sense of comfort. She heard a pitch resonating high above the city noise—the tinkling of distant wind chimes. A breeze seemed to be composing a song through them, and something about the haphazard melody sounded familiar, as if it contained a motif from *Cantique de Salomon.* Her mind drifted in her groggy state.

Maybe it's from Sokoloff's next song.

The bride awakens... and remembers the promise Solomon has made to her.

You need to get up, Colette.

She opened her eyes fully and found beams of sunlight streaming through the slats of the window blinds, summoning her out into the day. She pulled herself out of bed, got herself ready, and left the hotel feeling like she had nothing to lose.

NOVERRE'S OFFICES WERE sleek and full of beautiful things. The first person she saw was a stylish woman about her age, who was chatting with the receptionist, leaning against the desk, and doing slow *petit battement* with high-heeled feet, as if it were a subconscious habit. Colette smiled and immediately pictured herself working there, fitting right in with the other fashionable balletomanes. Together, they would drool over soft knits and feminine prints. They would debate the merits of ballet slippers: canvas versus leather? Split-sole versus full-sole? Ballet pink or flesh tone? They would discuss leotard styles in minute detail, while the rest of the world would barely notice the difference.

"Hi there," the woman said. She ceased her *petit battement*. "Are you my model?"

Colette laughed. "Um, no, I don't think so."

"Oh, well, you look like a dancer, so I just assumed. *Ugh*, where is she?"

"You must be Colette Larsen then," the receptionist said.

"I am," Colette replied. *And I look like a dancer.*

"Welcome. I believe they're ready for you."

The receptionist led Colette into the most beautiful conference room she had ever seen—complete with cases of signed pointe shoes and historic costumes—where a panel of three Noverre staff members greeted her. Her audience was larger than she expected, but she exhaled a steady breath, sat up straight and smiled until the questions began.

It became clear to the interview panel that Colette was in her element. They were fascinated by her eclectic work experience, her passion for ballet, her personal style, her unique skirt designs, and her tie to Westmoreland. She could tell that they genuinely liked her, and her subsequent boost in confidence seemed to inspire her with the perfect answers to their queries.

She felt calm and comfortable, and she knew that with each smile and with each joke and with each anecdote, she was winning them over.

They asked one final question, "Why do you want to work for us?"

"Why *wouldn't* I want to work for you?" Colette replied. "You guys are so cool." They all laughed. "But seriously—this position combines my two greatest passions: fashion design and dance, which also happen to be the two areas where I've had the most experience. I'm confident that I have much to offer here. I practically live and breathe dancewear, and Noverre is the epitome of quality dancewear. Noverre represents everything I love about ballet in particular—the way it combines art and athleticism, beauty and—for lack of a better term—blue collar discipline. I know firsthand how dedicated, how incredibly strong and courageous you have to be to be a dancer. And we need dancers in the world. We need beauty. Noverre understands that, and I would be honored to be a part of a company that inspires and supports dancers the way you do."

Colette was amazed by her own answer and was convinced that she must have been struck by divine inspiration. She studied her interviewers to see if they had detected this supernatural aid, but they were only nodding in approval and taking notes. She was the kind of person they would love to work with, they said. She met all of their qualifications. She was an impressive young lady. It had been a pleasure, and they would be in touch soon.

Before she knew it, it was time to leave Noverre, and time to leave Chicago.

COLETTE SLEPT ON the plane, finally crashing from her late night talking with James and the exertion of the interview. It wasn't until they landed in Houston that she woke. Normally, her thoughts would drift back to her interview to re-hash the details and look for her mistakes, but she found herself wanting to forget about the whole thing. It was over, and all she could do was wait.

After the plane landed, she mindlessly followed the crowd of passengers to baggage claim, where her mother was waiting for her. Colette had never been more relieved to see her.

"You're finally here! Oh, it's so good to see you." Lillian embraced her daughter, and Colette held on longer than usual. "What's wrong, sweetheart?"

"I've had a rough time, Mom," Colette whispered, hugging her again.

"Oh, honey. I'm sorry to hear that. Let's get you something to eat and you can tell me all about it on the way home. Craig is excited to see you. He went out and rented some DVDs from the Redbox. Isn't that fun? And we have a nice merlot to try."

"That sounds great."

"And I have a little surprise for you. Well, *two* surprises actually. We have tickets for tonight—to see James! I hope you don't mind a trip across the city... Oh, no. Should we not have done that?"

"No, no. That's great," Colette said. "That's really nice of you. I—I would love to go."

She hadn't expected to see him so soon. She didn't know how she would handle sitting through *Cantique Pas*, but she would have to try. She wanted to see him. She needed to see him. Now, knowing he was so close, she could hardly wait to see him.

When they arrived at the house, Colette took in her surroundings as if she were a stranger in her parents' home. She had almost forgotten how palatial it was, and it still smelled new. They had packed it full of furniture and decorations that Colette didn't recognize.

"Here's your new room," Lillian said. "Fully redecorated! And... here's your second surprise!" She opened the door to a gigantic walk-in closet, outfitted with a sewing table and a shelf full of fabrics. "I thought you might want to work on some projects while you're here. I saw these chiffons on sale and thought you could do something beautiful with them. Only if you feel like it, of course."

"It's too much," Colette said, feeling a tinge of guilt. Maybe she really should visit more often. "Thanks, Mom. This is really thoughtful of you."

Colette ran her hand across the multicolored fabrics and stopped on one that caught her eye. It was dyed in a painterly pattern, with splashes of plum purple and copper and specks of forest green. It was lovely. It reminded her of someone.

Once Craig arrived home, it was already time to leave for the theater. Colette rode in the back seat of his Lexus and stared out the window into the unfamiliar city. She had to admit—it felt nice to be taken care of. She imagined herself living there in Houston. Her parents would see to it that she wanted for nothing. If she couldn't find a good job on her own, they would find her one. Craig would pay for things. Lillian would dote on her. It sounded nice, but Colette knew that kind of life would not be good for her.

As they entered the theater, Colette's heart leapt into her throat. She had forgotten to warn James that they were coming and, somehow, Craig had managed to get front row seats. Oh well. It was too late to tell him now. With the blinding stage lights, he probably wouldn't be able to see her, anyway.

But he did see her. Colette could tell. There was a moment, barely thirty seconds into the choreography, where James and Alex took a slow *promenade* far downstage. Colette had a clear view of him, and seeing him up close after so long was surreal. He looked a little different. His hair was longer and his muscles seemed thicker, but he was as handsome and familiar as ever. James gestured solemnly out into the audience, proudly displaying his bride, and as he began to turn away, Colette saw him glance back at her over his shoulder. When they had circled all the way around, she saw that he was grinning.

Alex had noticed, too. She followed James's gaze, squinted her eyes for a split second, and she also smiled—a wide and bright smile, as if she were genuinely happy. Colette wasn't sure what it meant, but she noticed that the two had a new energy after that moment. They were all delight and expression, and the audience, sensing that the dancers were truly enjoying themselves, responded in kind.

Having been so familiar with *Cantique*, Colette wondered if it would have little effect on her by now. Despite how much she loved the dance, she had sat through multiple rehearsals, video footage, and the gala performance already. Surely now, she would be too distracted to soak in its beauty. Dance is fleeting, after all.

She was wrong. This time, she did not even consider the fact that James was playing a lover romancing another woman. As she looked out at the stage, lights glinting and music swelling, the same chills ran through her body like sparks. Dance may be fleeting, but she could watch it all day if given the chance.

I helped create this. This is our piece. See how beautiful it is.

As James and Alex took their *reverence*, Colette looked around her. Her parents were both applauding vigorously. Craig looked impressed and Lillian wiped a tear from her cheek. The entire audience rose to its feet, sustaining applause for what seemed like a full minute. James and Alex began a third round of bows and curtsies, their chests still heaving and their skin glinting with sweat. When they finally exited the stage and the house lights went up, Lillian turned to her daughter.

"I think that was the loveliest thing I've ever seen. Oh my—"

"What?"

She pointed toward the curtain. James had emerged, leapt off the stage and in a split second, had lifted Colette up out of her seat. Now a foot above his head, she had a clear view of Alex peeking out from side stage, laughing and waving their direction. Colette waved back.

James set her down and cradled her face in his hands. He was crying. She had never seen him cry before.

"I'm so glad you're here," he said. "I can't tell you how much I've missed you."

"I know," Colette said. "Let's never do this again."

James pulled her head in toward his chest, breathed in the scent of her hair, and whispered, "Can you ever forgive me?"

"Of course," she whispered back, tears rolling down her cheeks. "If you'll forgive me."

James nodded, and Colette felt relief wash over her. She stood there, wrapped comfortably in his arms, until Craig finally cleared his throat.

"Oh," Colette said, wiping her face. "You remember my mom and Craig?"

"Of course. Great to see you guys again." James shook their hands, and Colette began to laugh.

"What?" James asked.

"Your costume."

"Oh, yeah."

James looked practically naked compared to Craig standing there in his suit. What had been appropriate for the stage now looked downright ridiculous. Audience members lingered to watch. Someone flashed a photo, and Colette saw confused theater staff making their way toward him. She supposed that leaping into the audience to greet his girlfriend, while romantic, was not the most professional post-performance gesture.

"James," Colette said. "Do you want to get changed and meet us in the lobby?"

"That's probably a good idea. See you in a bit." James hugged her once more, lifted himself back onto the stage, and disappeared behind the curtain.

CHAPTER THIRTY-FOUR

Colette sat at her mother's glossy kitchen counter, anxiously waiting for James to arrive. Now that the tour was over, he would be spending five whole days with them, uninterrupted, and Colette could hardly wait. They had never been able to spend that kind of time together, and she felt like a teenager on the brink of summer break. But, then again, she had something difficult to tell him.

When Colette greeted James at the door, he whispered, "Holy crap. You didn't tell me they lived in a mansion."

"Yeah, well, I said it was big," Colette replied, feeling a little embarrassed. She led him through the entryway. "No need to whisper. They've gone out to play tennis. It's just us until the afternoon."

"Good," he said with a glint in his eye. He dropped his bags. "It's been so long since I've had you all to myself."

She smiled and felt herself relax into his embrace. It was such a relief to be in his arms again, to feel him cover her with kisses. She kissed him back until she could no longer hold in her news.

"James," Colette said. "I have to tell you something."

"Right now?"

"Yeah, it's kind of urgent."

James tried his hardest to look seductive. "What's more urgent than this?"

Colette laughed. "It really is important."

"Sorry," James said. He followed her into the living room and sat down on the couch. "Go ahead."

Colette exhaled. "Noverre called. They've offered me the job."

"Oh."

"Yeah. I'm supposed to call them back today."

"So... what are you thinking?"

"I honestly don't know. I mean, I *want* to accept it. As much as I don't want to move, I love the idea of working there. I think it would be a great fit for me, even though the prospect of doing office work again isn't thrilling.

237

But I also can't stay at Tempe's my whole life. I've really got to start making something of myself. I'm tired of just… flailing around."

He nodded. "I understand."

"The thing is, I'm not sure where that leaves us. I can't do the distance thing again. I really can't—"

"I know."

"—and the last thing I want to do is ask you to sacrifice your career to move with me."

"Why should you have to sacrifice yours to stay for me, though? That's not fair, either."

"You're more important to me than any job, James. But, honestly, this decision would be easier if I knew—well—exactly how you feel about me. I know you love me, and I won't ask you to give me reasons this time, but—I at least need to know that your love will last." She laughed and added, "I won't always be beautiful, you know."

James's face flushed and his eyes watered. He quickly left the room, grabbed one of his bags from the entryway, and began to rummage through it. "I wrote something for you after that day," he said, producing a piece of notebook paper. "I was such an idiot, Colette." His voice faltered, and he swatted tears away from his face.

"No, I was the idiot—"

"No, you were right. I should have been able to give you good reasons, and I didn't even think about how much it hurt you. I told you, I'm not good with words like you are, but I thought I'd at least try. Here," he said, offering her the paper. "This is what I've got."

Colette observed the page. James had drawn a loose sketch of two dancers. The man held his partner aloft in a majestic *presage*. The woman's hair was dark and wavy, and it flew backward as if blown by a sudden wind. Below the dancers, he had scrawled familiar words.

> *It burns like blazing fire,*
> *like a mighty flame.*
> *Many waters cannot quench love;*
> *rivers cannot sweep it away.*

> *Dear Colette,*

Cantique

I told you that you are beautiful, and I meant it, but I don't think you see that your beauty is not just skin deep. Everything about you is beautiful—your imagination and your clever mind, the way you love your friends, the way you love me despite my faults, the way you dance and the way you dream.

I never told you how scared I was to do Cantique, but I did it anyway because you believed in me and, let's face it, because I really wanted to impress you. I always felt that I was never quite good enough to do the things I've dreamed of, until I met you. You're my muse and inspiration, my partner in life, and I'm simply the man honored to lift you up, for you're destined for heights higher than I can imagine. Please stick with me. I promise that, every day, I will strive to be the man you deserve.

Love you forever,
James

After sprinkling the page with tears, Colette looked up and said, "It looks to me like you have a way with words."

"Well, it took me three days to write the thing."

"Thank you, James. It's really beautiful. But this last part—it's so wrong. You don't need to spend your life trying to be the 'man I deserve.' *I'm* the one who doesn't deserve *you*. I've always felt that way."

He laughed. "That's ridiculous. Maybe we can just agree to disagree."

Colette smiled, shook her head in resignation, and had a clear thought. She should choose James over Noverre. Of course she should. How else would it work out?

"Then I'm not going to take the job," Colette declared.

"No. I don't want you to have to make that decision. I'll go with you. I can start auditioning."

"But—"

"If this is what you really want, I want it, too. I want to see you doing something that you love. I want you to chase your dreams. I've already had plenty of opportunities to do that, and I can still do it in Chicago."

"Are you really sure about that?" Colette asked.

James nodded and took her hand. "Yes, I am."

"Like, one hundred percent? Please be honest."

"Yes," he replied. "One hundred percent. I'm with you."

"We would have to move soon," Colette said, feeling a rush of anxiety. "Like, *really* soon."

"That's fine. I haven't signed my contract yet. Let's do it."

Colette paused, confounded by how apprehensive she still felt about the whole thing. She had thought that James's support would make her decision easier, but her mind was even more restless, rapidly counting through the costs of moving. Sammy. Westmoreland. The Brennans. She would be taking James away from his family and from the work that he loved. It wasn't fair to him.

But, then again, he said he would do it. And who was she to turn down an opportunity like this? Maybe all of the doubt she was feeling was actually self-sabotage. It wouldn't be the first time.

James was still waiting for her to respond, his face full of anticipation, and Colette took a deep breath.

"Alright," she said. "Should I call them now?"

"Up to you."

"I'll do it now."

Colette stood up from the couch and dialed the number with clammy fingers. She felt a tug in her stomach, and a single thought flashed through her mind with each ring.

Freely and lightly. Freely and lightly. Freely and—

"Noverre Dancewear, this is Theresa."

"Hi, Theresa. It's Colette Larsen."

"Oh, hi, Colette! Great to hear from you. So, did you get my message?"

"I did get your message," Colette said.

Freely and lightly.

"And what do you think? Are you interested?"

Colette waited and let herself feel the nagging in her stomach dissolve into a feeling of calm and clarity.

It wasn't self-sabotage. No. This time, it was something else entirely.

She glanced at James, whose eyebrows were raised in confusion. Before Colette could think longer, she began to speak with assurance. "I am very appreciative of the offer and, I would love to work with Noverre, but after thinking about it longer, I've realized that I can't leave my home. I don't believe I'm supposed to move to Chicago right now."

"Oh," Theresa sounded thoroughly surprised. "Okay. Well, everyone will be sorry to hear that. But you seem to be confident in your choice, so I'm glad about that."

James stood up and opened his mouth in protest.

"I know it sounds strange," Colette said, turning away from him. "Believe me, I would love to take this job. I'm just certain that it's not the right time for me, for whatever reason."

"Fair enough. We wish you the best, Colette. And if you happen to change your mind—say within the next thirty minutes—give us a call and we'll chat."

Colette laughed. "That's so generous. Thank you. Thank you for being so understanding."

"No problem. Take care."

"What the heck just happened?" James asked. "Did we not just agree that you would take it? Why are you laughing?"

"Because," Colette said. "This is just like what happened with Tempe's. It's too weird."

"What are you talking about?"

"I had this feeling—this persistent, nagging feeling. Both times. When I called your dad, I had planned to refuse his offer to work there. Instead, I accepted. This time it was the opposite. James, I'm sure about this. I am so sure. I don't know why, and I can't explain it. But believe me, I'm sure."

Bewildered, James sank down into the couch and threw his hands up. "Okay then. If that's what you really think."

"I'm sorry to turn things around on you like this. I really am. But, I know now. I *know* this is how it should be. And you can stay at Westmoreland."

"But what about you?"

Colette shrugged. "I'll be fine. I have a future. I may not know what it is, but, for once, I'm absolutely certain that it won't be disappointing."

Still perplexed, James was silent.

"I just didn't feel quite right about it," Colette continued. "Maybe if I'm patient, I'll find something better. You know, I'd rather create my own pieces than market someone else's anyway. Even if I don't make any money at it."

This James seemed to understand. He studied her face for a while longer before turning his gaze toward the ceiling. He sprawled out on his back, let out a sigh, and opened an arm for her to join him.

Colette tucked herself beside him, her head resting on his shoulder and her mind flitting between thoughts. James had been so willing to make a huge change for her—to leave his near-perfect family behind in a split second decision. She admired him for it, but the more she thought about her choice, the more relief she felt. She needed to live freely and lightly on her own terms, which meant passing on a guaranteed job to remain in a state of uncertainty—or, rather, possibility. For now, her gut told her, this was exactly where she was supposed to be.

"Do you think I'm crazy?" Colette whispered, certain that she wasn't.

"No. I have no room to talk."

"What do you mean?"

"I haven't told you what happened the night I called you—when you were still in Chicago. I had this weird dream. We were performing and—"

"You and Alex?"

"No, you and me. You looked different in the dream, but I knew it was you. We couldn't seem to do anything right. It was like, every time I tried to do a lift, my muscles would fail, and you kept pulling away, like you didn't want me to touch you. I got really frustrated and finally walked off stage. Then all of the sudden this gigantic dude—he was like seven feet tall—was dancing with you and you were incredible. Like, doing all of these impossible jumps. You would just hang in the air—"

"That's awesome. I want to have this dream."

James laughed. "Well, it took a turn. Part of the stage caved in and you fell. You were just lying there unconscious, and I couldn't move to help you. The giant dude could have picked you up, but he kept looking at me and asking, 'You gonna do something, Brennan?'"

"Was the giant dude Andreas?"

"Ha! It sounds like it. But, no, I don't think so. Anyway, I woke up after that and I swear..." James shook his head.

"What?"

"I swear I heard the coda from *Cantique Pas* out of nowhere, and I suddenly felt like I was supposed to pray. So I did. It had been a really long time, but I did it anyway. Then I called you."

Colette sat up. "Wow."

"Yeah. Crazy, huh?"

"It is and it isn't—" Her mind replayed her night alone in the hotel room, and she began to cry again. "You have no idea what's happened to me."

He sat up and held her hand. "What's happened?"

How could she even begin to explain it all? How could she list the countless signs and nudges and gifts she had received over the last year? Over her entire life? They were all coming into focus—all converging on a single, invisible spot, like the lines in a one-point perspective drawing.

There is really only one constant in life, Jael had said. *And even He can be puzzling at times.*

"Your mom happened," Colette finally said, smiling. "She spoke right into my soul."

James chuckled. "She tends to do that."

Colette wiped her eyes. Her last few tears fell onto his forearm, and she ran her fingers across his tattoo.

"This means something else, doesn't it? It has to."

He looked her straight in the eyes and said, "'Keep company with me and you'll learn to live freely and lightly.'"

"Where is that from?"

"It's a verse from *Matthew*," he said. He smiled faintly and added, "From an easy-to-read translation. I was eighteen when I got it, and I really believed it at the time. Then I don't know what happened. I got caught up in myself."

"Why didn't you tell me this before?" Colette asked.

He looked at his arm again. "I um—I actually got a little embarrassed about it, so when people would ask what it meant, I'd give them the short version."

"Are you still embarrassed?"

"No." James let out a sigh and added, "But, looking back, I was stupid to put it there. It's like the least convenient spot for ballet. But I thought I was a bad-ass."

Colette smiled and rested her hand over his heart.

"I love you, James."

"I love you, too, Colette." He kissed her, pulled her up from the couch, and that familiar, sly smile appeared on his face. "Can we do something *fun* now? Surely your parents have a pool or a disc golf course in here somewhere."

"Not quite. But, you know what? I've really been missing class." She rested her left hand on the mantel. "How would you feel about giving me a private lesson?"

"Sure, babe. Let's start with some *pliés*."

CHAPTER THIRTY-FIVE

"**W**ell, what would you two lovebirds like to do tonight?" Lillian asked that evening. "I hope you're hungry, because I planned a feast for dinner."

"Looks like we'll be staying here, then," Colette said, sitting down at the granite counter.

James, who had already made himself at home, was searching through the kitchen cabinets. "Are these up for grabs?" he asked, holding up a bag of croissants.

"Oh, honey," Lillian said. "Help yourself to whatever you can find."

"Will we a have a lot of extra food for dinner?" Colette asked.

"Probably." Lillian opened the refrigerator and began to inventory its contents. "You know me. I couldn't decide between steak or salmon, so I bought both."

"Sweet," James said, plopping down on the stool next to Colette.

"Hey," Colette said. "What's Alex doing tonight? Is she still in town?"

"Uh, yeah. I think her flight leaves tomorrow afternoon. Why?"

"Do you think we should invite her over for dinner?"

Lillian closed the refrigerator door. "What a lovely idea."

James was slow to respond. He tore a croissant in half and studied Colette's expression, as if he were trying to detect evidence of sarcasm or sudden insanity. Colette, however, was completely sincere. She had been feeling quite charitable ever since her phone call with Noverre.

"I just feel bad if she's gonna be alone in her hotel room all night," Colette added.

"Okay," James said, still looking suspicious. "If you really want to."

"That's settles it, then," Lillian said. "Now, where did I put that recipe book?"

As she turned away, James lowered his voice. "What has gotten into you today?"

"Nothing," Colette replied. "I just thought it would be nice to invite her."

"It is nice," he said, his mouth full of croissant. "But are you sure about it?"

"Yes, I'm sure. It'll be fine. She may not want to come, anyway."

James agreed with that assumption, and, as a result, was surprised when Alex accepted the invitation. Once Colette heard the news, she found that she was oddly excited at the prospect of visiting with Alex on her own turf. She helped her mom prepare the meal and the house, hoping that her parents' lifestyle might impress Alex in some way.

While the women worked, James and Craig lounged in the living room, drinking summer shandies and watching a channel that seemed to only play shows about deep-sea fishing. Completely engrossed, neither of them noticed when the doorbell rang, and Colette had to scurry across the foyer with oven mitts still covering her hands.

Suddenly, there she was—Alexandra Vukoja standing on the doorstep with a bottle of wine tucked under her arm. Colette almost didn't recognize her. Without the elegant French twist and the flattering light of the ballet studio, without the stage makeup and the decadence of a costume, Alex looked out of context—maybe even a little meek. Her hair was down and slightly limp, and she wore a simple gray T-shirt and jeans, but she was still beautiful.

After greetings had been exchanged, James and Craig went back to watching *Deep Sea Extreme*, and Colette saw that it would be up to her to keep Alex entertained. She led her to the kitchen counter and Alex sat on a stool, her slender shoulders hunched slightly forward. Her fingers fidgeted as she watched Colette and Lillian finish preparing a fruit salad.

"Are you sure I can't help with anything?" Alex asked.

"Oh, I'm sure," Lillian said, brandishing a large kitchen knife. She decapitated a pineapple and added, "You just relax and keep us company. I have to say—you were stunning the other night. I told Colette that it was the most beautiful dance I've ever seen."

Alex smiled. "Thank you. I love it, too. I never get tired of performing it."

"Even after all this time?" Colette asked.

"Yeah. It's like magic," Alex said. "Now that I've heard the music, I hate to think of my life without it." She locked eyes with Colette, who was noticeably stunned by the depth of this statement. Alex quickly lowered her gaze, as if embarrassed by her confession. "Anyway, it's really nice of you to have me. I was getting a little bored by myself."

"I think I must have seen you having one of those moments," Colette said. "The other night, I saw you smile during the *promenade*."

"Oh, I remember that," Alex said, "But I was actually smiling because I saw *you*."

"Oh."

"I knew you would cheer James up. He was having such a rough time without you this summer. And that was actually our best performance of the tour. Did you know he dances his best when you're in the audience?"

"I didn't," Colette replied. She felt a flutter in her stomach. "But that's really nice to know."

When they finally returned downstairs, Colette was surprised to find the television off and evidence that James, Craig and Lillian had been engaged in a heartfelt discussion of some sort. Lillian was beaming and sitting with her hands tucked between her knees. Her legs shook up and down to some internal rhythm.

"Why are you so excited?" Colette asked.

"Oh, no reason."

Colette cocked her head and exchanged glances with James, who was grinning. Something strange had transpired, but no one seemed to want to clue her in.

"Well," Alex said. "I should probably get going. Thanks so much for the wonderful evening."

"See you back home," Colette said. "Don't forget—wine and doc."

"Right, I won't. Oh, and thanks again for the skirt, Colette. I love it."

CHAPTER THIRTY-SIX

Colette was glad to be home, even if it meant going back to work. She resumed her usual role at the register and typed in her code automatically, as if she hadn't been absent for nearly three weeks. Bonnie, who had been privy to Colette's interview with Noverre, immediately peppered her with questions.

"So, why didn't you take it, then?" Bonnie asked. "Have you gone soft in the head?"

"I don't think so."

"I wouldn't be laughing if I were you. I think you've made a big, fat mistake."

Colette shrugged. "Well, I don't."

"What do you think, Darrel?"

"I think we should leave Colette alone," Darrel said, his eyes buried in inventory papers. "She can make her own decisions, and she did what she thought was right. And that's that."

"He just wants to keep you around, is all."

"I s'pose that's true, too." Darrel finally looked up from his clipboard. "Anyone up for lunch? I could really go for a soup and BLT."

"Captain," Bonnie said. "It's 10 a.m."

"Is it? Well, it sure is. How about some donuts, then?"

"Sure, I'd take one," Colette replied.

"Just one?" Darrel looked worried. "That ballet isn't making you cut back is it? You know, Jimmy eats just as much as the next fella."

Colette laughed and assured him that she wasn't on a diet. Although, she had to admit that she was keeping that evening's class in mind. Among the many lessons that ballet had taught her—discipline, perseverance, patience—it had also taught her to take care of her body. If she wanted to dance her best, she would have to eat well. It was a simple fact. But even the company dancers wouldn't deny themselves an occasional donut.

"Darrel," Colette said. "Why don't you let me get them this time? I owe you about a thousand."

"Aw, you let him get them, hun," Bonnie insisted. "He's got the means. Didn't you know he's got a fortune tucked away?"

Shocked, Colette turned to Darrel and asked, "Is that true?"

"Well," Darrel said, glancing at Bonnie with faint disapproval. "I may have invested in Bread and Pan back in '88."

"No way," Colette said, on the brink of laughter. She covered her mouth.

Darrel shrugged. "I just liked their bread bowls. I had no idea there'd be one on every corner one day."

LATER THAT EVENING, Colette and Sammy found themselves in the midst of one of their best ballet classes. Colette felt particularly svelte and alert, but Sammy—Sammy seemed to have miraculously improved overnight. She held steady *retiré* balances for sixteen counts while the rest of the class wobbled at four and quit at eight. Her *développés* were perfectly placed. Her *grands battements* were completely controlled and higher than usual. Colette knew that the sudden improvement had to be 98 percent mental. After all, technique could only be built gradually. When they finished at the barre, Colette smacked Sammy on the shoulder.

"Who are you all of the sudden? You're killing it tonight!"

"Thanks," Sammy said. She smiled and bit her lower lip. "Just feeling good, I guess."

"Uh huh." Colette studied her face. "Were you and Aaron making out in the elevator again?"

"Maybe."

Colette laughed and turned to face the mirror. Grasping the arch of her foot, she stretched her leg forward, rotated it to the side, and pulled her shin toward her chest until she was standing in a near full-split.

"You're getting bendier," Sammy said. "And you really look like a dancer today, CoCo."

"I do?" She let go of her leg.

"I mean, you've always looked like one. You *are* one. But something about you today—I don't know. You're just fun to watch."

"Aw. Thanks, Sam."

In center, Marianne had them dance her standard *pirouette* combination, which always ended with a *pirouette en dehors*, a *pirouette en dedans*, and a final balance in *passé relevé*, before starting the other side. The class had grown accustomed to it, and even Colette and Sammy had become a little lazy.

Before they repeated the combination, Marianne pointed at Sammy and said, "I want to see you doing all doubles this time. I know you can do them." She turned to Colette. "You, too. There's no reason why you should be doing singles today."

They both nodded, the music began, and Marianne called out the steps.

"*Balancé, balancé, soutenu*, hold. *Tombée pas de bourrée…*"

When it was time for the first *pirouette*, Sammy prepped perfectly and turned not twice, but three times. She landed in fifth position and fist pumped the air.

"*Yes!* Take that, *pirouette!*"

"Good!" Marianne called. "Keep dancing! Don't be late. Let's see that triple again."

Colette smiled and began to watch Sammy instead of focusing on her own dancing. Before she took her preparation, she heard Marianne say, "You, too, Colette. Try for a triple."

The last-minute challenge caught her off guard, but she felt her head instinctively whipping around to the same spot.

One. Two. Three.

Colette smiled in celebration and then, in a split second, completely lost her balance. Before she knew it, she had landed hard on her rear end.

"Well, shit."

Sammy turned around, saw her on the floor, and immediately began to laugh.

"Are you okay?" Marianne asked.

"Yeah," Colette replied, laughing and rubbing her tail bone. "Does that still count as my first triple?"

Marianne chuckled, and the studio door suddenly swung open. The entire class turned to see who had the audacity to interrupt the middle of center. It was Dunja, slightly out of breath and looking the same as ever, but sporting a giant, leather handbag.

"Dunja," Marianne said. "How good to see you! Can I help you with something?"

"Yes. For one moment, may I borrow Miss Colette Larsen?"

Colette scrambled to her feet. "Borrow *me*?"

"Yes. You."

Colette exchanged looks with Sammy and followed Dunja out into the hallway. Dunja wasted no time with pleasantries.

"You help with *Cantique de Salomon* by telling director about my music and by helping with costumes, no?"

"Sort of," Colette replied. "Liz and Trinity really did the costumes."

"But you have ideas. You get ball rolling, so to speak. I owe much to you."

Colette paused to consider this point of view. She *had* gotten the ball rolling, so to speak. Who knew how long she would have sat on that music. Dunja did kind of owe her. Was she going to share her Sokoloff profits with her? Was this her Bread and Pan fortune?

"Well," Colette said. "I guess you could say that."

"You enjoy this? This creation of ballets?"

"...sure."

"You have employment?"

"Yeah. I work at a hardware store."

Dunja smiled. "Okay. We meet back here in hallway, after fifteen minutes."

"Meet here in fifteen minutes?" Colette felt her heart beating faster.

"Yes." Dunja pointed toward the floor by her feet, as if marking that exact spot. "Fifteen minutes."

"Uh, okay."

Colette tiptoed back into the studio, wondering if the conversation she had just had with Dunja had actually happened. But it had to have happened. She couldn't have made it up in her head; it was too strange.

Her concentration now completely broken, Colette did what she could in class. When she had a spare moment, she filled in Marianne and Sammy, who both looked sufficiently intrigued. Marianne excused her after the *sauté* combination, and Colette scampered back out into the hallway, now a mess of sweat and nervous energy.

What in the world is going on?

Dunja hobbled her way toward Colette. "You follow me to conference room. We have meeting."

"What kind of meeting? Why am I going?"

"You'll see," Dunja said flatly. "I think you know some people here."

Cantique

They walked past the back offices to the long conference room, and Colette could see through the window that it was already occupied by several people. Her palms became sweatier, her stomach rumbled. As they entered, she glimpsed her reflection in the glass door and tried to tame the fly-aways framing her face. It was no use.

James was the first person she recognized, then Lavoisier, then Myra, then Lang the ballet master, and the man that she supposed to be the finance director. One face she didn't recognize. What did they all want with her? She waved at Myra, who looked as if she were trying not to smile, and then turned to James, hoping she could glean some meaning from his expression. He was grinning and drumming his fingers on the table as if he were dying to dance.

"Ah, Colette," Lavoisier said. He pointed at the empty chair next to James. "Have a seat."

Colette tried to smooth her hair again. "Sorry, I just came from class."

"You look adorable," James said, kissing her on the cheek.

"Yes, we're all used to sweaty dancers here," Lavoisier said. "I see Marianne has been working you hard."

"Yes," Colette said. "Always."

Lavoisier sat back and clasped his hands together. "So, my dear," he said. "What all has Dunja told you?"

"Oh, not much." Colette glanced at the stone-faced Dunja, who offered no help. "Just that I've been summoned to a meeting. I'm really not sure why I'm here."

"Well, we have some good news to share," said Lavoisier. James leaned forward in his seat and found Colette's hand under the table. "Colette, I am delighted to inform you that, thanks to Dunja's generosity and to the support of a few other gracious donors, we have approved financing to create a full-length *Cantique de Salomon* for our 2019 season."

Colette's pulse quickened, and she felt her head begin to spin. Had he really said what she thought he had? Surely not.

"What..." she whispered, breathless. She turned to James. "Is this for real?"

They all laughed, pleased with Colette's wide-eyed reaction.

"For real," James said.

"It is indeed," said Lavoisier. "As much as I have loved our little *Cantique Pas de Deux,* I have maintained the hope that we might one day

257

turn it into something even more spectacular—something like the three-act ballet you envisioned." He was holding up a paper, and Colette saw that it was covered in her own hand writing. There it was—the outline she had scribbled at Tempe's—the one she had handed to James nearly a year ago. It couldn't be true. "What would you think about that, my dear?"

Colette swallowed. "I think... I think I feel like I might faint." They all laughed again, apparently unconvinced that she might faint. Colette wasn't so sure. "That would be... well, *amazing.*" A full-length *Cantique* seemed like a far-fetched dream, but a full-length using her libretto? It was miraculous, really.

Her mind raced through the visions she had secretly harbored for such an occasion—she saw Alex in her wedding costume, she saw James in his shepherd's disguise and the watchmen in their armor. And she wanted so badly to be a part of it all. Despite a voice in her head warning her not to be so presumptuous, she found herself fervently saying, "Can I help with it somehow? I would really, *really* love to help."

"Fitting you should ask," Lavoisier replied. Colette's stomach fluttered, and she listened closely to his every word. "Now, this situation is quite unusual, but given your role as a catalyst for *Cantique*, we feel it is only natural that you be intimately involved with this project in some capacity."

James squeezed her hand. "You hear that, babe? We all want you to work on *Cantique.* We want you to be on our team."

"Team?" Colette asked, suddenly terrified. "I meant more as a volunteer—"

"Colette." Lavoisier held up her outline again. "This is your work. Your adaptation. And I will only use it with your consent. And, do you see what I see? I see the beginning of a libretto that Max—" he pointed to the man whom Colette hadn't recognized, "—will use to compose the rest of the music. I see sketches that Myra and her staff will work from to design costumes for the entire cast. I see a sensibility to story and to poetry that has already aided James with his choreography. And it will continue to do so as we set the entire ballet. You have already been a vital part of *Cantique* in an unofficial capacity. It is only fitting that we make it official—if you are up for it, of course."

Colette became misty-eyed. Though the fear was still there—and perhaps it always would be—it couldn't keep her from seeing the truth this time.

Lavoisier was right. She really had set something beautiful into motion. And this was a once-in-a-lifetime opportunity. She would be crazy not to accept it.

Emboldened, Colette finally conjured a useful question. "What kind of position would it be exactly?"

"Myra, would you like to take it from here?"

"Of course, Henri." Myra cleared her throat. "Colette, you did such a great job on your work with *Nutcracker.* You're familiar with the shop, and you have the taste and talent to be a stellar costume designer. All you need is more training, which we can give you. This would be your main responsibility—to work alongside Liz and Trinity as a costume assistant. I am assuming, and correct me if I'm wrong, that you would have a special interest in the *Song of Solomon* costumes."

"Yes," Colette replied. "I do. I have tons of ideas."

"That being said, we all feel that you have such a unique perspective and knowledge of *Cantique*—such a personal tie to it—that we want you to also serve as a creative committee member." Myra paused to laugh at Colette's bewildered expression. "Like Henri said, you will be credited for your libretto and so, like all of us, your perspective will be weighed during major artistic decisions."

Colette began to laugh. It was all too much. "I—I don't even know what to say."

"Well," said Lavoisier, "Before you do say anything I should tell you that your position would be full-time, but unfortunately, it will only be guaranteed while the ballet is being produced. But there is always a chance to keep you on if the right financing comes through."

Colette didn't mind in the least. Uncertain as it was, it all still seemed too good to be true.

Lavoisier smiled warmly and added, "You have a real *penchant* for ballet. While I hate to offer you something that is temporary, maybe this is only the beginning. We believe it will lead to many opportunities for you—with Westmoreland, I selfishly hope."

"That would be wonderful. I love ballet. I really do. Second only to James here." Colette poked him in the ribs and had her audience laughing again. "I would love to accept your offer."

Lavoisier stood up and extended a weathered hand, "Well, my dear. That settles it. Welcome aboard. Westmoreland Ballet is honored to have you. And

I expect that you and Myra will make our new ballet as colorful as *La Bayadère*. Only, hopefully with fewer deaths."

"Oh, I will," Colette promised. "And thank you so much. I can't begin to tell you how much this means to me. I really can't believe it."

"It'll sink in once the work begins," Myra said, giving her a hug. "We're so excited to have you."

Once Colette had shaken many hands, and given many more thanks, everyone trickled out of the conference room. Colette held fast to James's arm, depending on him to steady her as they walked down the hallway, lest she begin to float away. James could not stop smiling. When they turned the corner, he lifted her up against a studio door and kissed her as if this were his last and happiest day on earth.

CHAPTER THIRTY-SEVEN

Colette's final day at Tempe's happened to be a Saturday. Sammy had wished her luck and told her not to cry about it. The previous summer, Colette never could have imagined that she would one day be in danger of crying about leaving Tempe's. The decision to work there had been one of random necessity, a temporary solution—nothing to cry about. She confessed that she probably wouldn't miss the work, but she would miss the people. She would miss the magic that seemed to have begun in that place.

Customers were abundant that day, and the hours flew by. Colette was a little disappointed, as she had barely been able to talk to Reid and Bonnie. With Reid's graduation and Bonnie's talk of retirement, it would probably be the last time she would see them together. When the hour neared six o'clock, Darrel called them all up to the front of the store.

"Well, it's close enough to closing time," Darrel said. "Colette, we got you a little something for your last day."

He presented her with a gift bag and a note written in rough scrawl: *To Colette. Thanks for all of your hard work. We'll miss you. Love, The Tempe's Crew.*

"What's this?" Colette asked. "You didn't need to get me anything!"

"Oh, it's just a little something," Darrel replied.

"It's heavy." Colette pulled out the crumpled tissue paper. "A hammer?"

"You never came back to buy the one you wanted. You know, that day you filled out your application." Colette stared at him, holding the hammer like a chef's knife. Was he serious? Darrel finally began to chuckle. "It's supposed to be funny. But I'm sure you could actually use one, too."

"Oh man," Colette said, shaking her head in amazement. "You're the best." Unembarrassed, Colette retold her side of the story from that day, and they all had a good laugh over the matter.

"There's a few other things in there, too," Bonnie said. "From all of us."

Colette pulled out a bag of cinnamon gummy bears, a Noverre gift certificate, and a card signed by all of her coworkers.

> *It's been fun working with you. Thanks for keeping me entertained and for always sharing your cheddar peppers. – Reid*

> *Hun, Tempe's won't be the same without you, but we know you've got bigger and better things to do. Be sure to come back and see us. Love, Bonnie*

> *You're a promising young lady. Best wishes for all your endeavors. Hal Hartman.*

"Aw, Hal!" Colette said. Turns out she wasn't so terrible, after all.

> *You can do anything you set your mind to. Thanks for working with us and putting up with me. Sincerely, Travis*

> *Well, looks like I've lost a great worker but gained a daughter. How did I get so lucky? So proud of you. Love, Darrel.*

By now, Colette had broken her promise to Sammy and was crying profusely. "Thanks so much, you guys," she said, laughing through her sobs. "You all are the best."

Darrel gave her one last task. "Before you get ready to leave, would you check something in the utility closet for me?"

"Sure," she replied, wiping her nose.

"Could you make sure the door to the alley is open?"

"Uh, okay. Why do you need it open?"

"Oh, I'm gonna be moving some stuff out there in a bit."

"Okay then." Colette glanced back at them as she walked away. Bonnie and Reid seemed to know something she didn't.

She inched open the door to the closet, half-expecting something to jump out at her, but it was filled with the same junk as always—meters and electric boxes and stuff she never bothered to try to understand. Once she made it to the opposite side, she unlocked the alley door and heard music—music that had become so familiar that she almost didn't notice it—the adagio from *Cantique de Salomon*. Suddenly, she understood. Her heart racing, she took a deep breath and opened the door.

The alley had been cleared and swept clean. There was a fire blazing in a copper pit, and beyond stood James, framed within an arbor of sparkling lights. He walked over to greet her, his face glowing and starry-eyed, and led her around the fire.

"Good day at work?" he asked.

"Yeah," Colette said. "What are you doing back here?"

"I came to see you. I wanted to ask you something. Hey, are you okay? You look like you've been crying."

"Yeah. I'm good." Colette said, wiping her face. She looked up at the wooden arbor covering them. Text had been burned into its frame, partly obscured beneath the strands of twinkling lights. *Set me as a seal upon your heart...* it read. *As a seal upon your arm. For love is as strong as death...*

"James," Colette whispered. "Did you *make* this?"

He nodded. "I built it for you."

"It's so beautiful." Colette ran her hands over the glossy script. *Many waters cannot quench love, rivers cannot sweep it away.* "How long did this take you?"

James gently turned her to face him. "Baby, don't you want to know what I came here to ask you?"

Colette nodded, and James sank to one knee, as if he had just landed from a double *tour*. "Colette Larsen," he said, producing a ring from his pocket. "I love you more than I ever could have imagined, and I can't wait to spend the rest of my life with you. Will you marry me?"

Trembling and teary-eyed, Colette gave him her hand. "Of course I will."

She pulled him back up to his feet to kiss him, and they heard a sudden throng of cheers coming from inside the shop. Out came Josh, Audrey, Rose, Hunter and Molly, Darrel and Jael, Reid and Bonnie, Travis, Sammy, Aaron, Myra and Trinity, and nearly half of the Westmoreland company dancers.

Colette shrieked and covered her mouth. "How did—"

But Sammy, who was beside herself with excitement, had already thrown herself onto the two of them.

"You're *engaged!!*" Sammy squealed. "It was so hard to play it cool this morning! Let me see your ring."

Colette showed her and realized that she hadn't even had a chance to look at it yet. A large emerald was set in the center and surrounded by a halo of diamonds. Colette looked up at James.

"It matches your eyes," he said. "That's why I picked this one."

"I love it, James. It's perfect."

By then, they were surrounded by admirers. Colette could barely take in her surroundings, but somewhere in the crowd, she could see Jael patiently inching her way toward them.

"Congratulations to both of you," Jael said, smiling through tears. She kissed them both on the cheek.

"Thanks, Mom," James said, looking both proud and ecstatic.

"I can't tell you how pleased I am. What an exciting future you have together."

"Thank you so much," Colette said, reaching to embrace her. "I can't believe *the* Jael Maier is going to be my mother-in-law."

Jael laughed. "Well, I am just as delighted to have you as a daughter. We can talk later. Lots of people want to see you."

Josh, who had been busy bringing out tables and chairs, stopped by to offer hugs.

"You sure you wanna spend the rest of your life with this joker?" Josh asked.

"Pretty sure," Colette replied.

"He's okay, I guess. But seriously, you've both made an excellent choice. Marriage is the funnest." Josh leaned forward so only Colette could hear. "And Audrey is crap-her-pants excited to finally have a sister-in-law. You have no idea."

They spent the next half hour bombarded by congratulations and well-wishes. Colette was deeply thankful for the family and friends there, but she began to grow weary as the time passed. A short while ago, she was saying her farewell to Tempe's, and now all of these people were surrounding her, sharing in one of the most intimate moments of her life. It was all so surreal, and she ached to be alone with James again—to process it all.

Colette felt a tap on her shoulder. It was Alex.

"Just wanted to say congratulations," she said, sincerity showing through her eyes. "You two will make great partners."

"Thank you, Alex. I really appreciate that."

"And I just realized I haven't congratulated you on *Cantique de Salomon.* How exciting that you'll be on staff!"

Colette suddenly remembered Alex's future plans. "What about PNB? You have to stay *now.* You have to stay and dance the role."

"Solomon's Bride?"

"Of course. No one else can do it like you can."

Alex shrugged. "They'll have multiple casts anyway—"

"It doesn't matter. This is your role. I want to see you on opening night."

Alex laughed and looked down at her feet. "I guess I do really want it, if I'm honest."

"Then stay."

"I'll think long and hard. Thanks, Colette—for being so encouraging."

Darrel suddenly called everyone to attention. "I just want to say a quick blessing for Jimmy and Colette, if y'all don't mind. Then Audrey here has been kind enough to bring dessert for everyone."

James took Colette's hand, and together they bowed their heads. She closed her eyes and felt Darrel's words wash over her—comforting her, protecting her, beckoning her to a new and exciting life. She peeked at James's hand, still clasping hers, gave it a squeeze and then saw that he was peeking at her, too.

Once Darrel had finished, the crowd encircling them began to dissipate, and James set out to get drinks. Colette surveyed the group. Sammy and Aaron were chatting with Travis and Helena. Trinity and Iris were hitting up Bonnie for a smoke, and Myra was engrossed in conversation with Jael. While she still had the chance, Colette sneaked over to Darrel, who had managed to find a quiet spot by himself.

She sat beside him and let out a sigh.

"Doing okay, sweetheart?" Darrel asked.

"Yeah," Colette replied. "Couldn't be happier. I'm so lucky. I mean, look at him."

They watched James from across the fire pit. He was looking particularly handsome and was laughing with Josh and Reid, the three of them standing leisurely with beers in hand. Hunter tried to climb up his dad's leg, and James snatched him up with one arm and tossed him into the air.

"Not too close to the fire, guys," Audrey warned from afar.

"You look a little blue, though," Darrel continued. "Are you a bit overwhelmed?"

"Could be," Colette said, her eyes still fixed on James. She felt a pang of familiar anxiety and, though she knew she shouldn't give it a voice, she heard herself laugh and say, "Everything seems too perfect. Even now, I'm paranoid he'll wake up one morning and realize I'm nothing special."

Darrel turned to face her with a look of utter shock upon his face, and Colette immediately regretted her pessimistic relapse. She shifted in her seat, looked him in the eyes, and braced herself to receive Darrel's first reprimand.

"Now, you *listen*," he said. "That's a downright lie from the devil. James is my boy and I love him, but he ain't perfect. Nobody is. You are exactly what he needs, and I can see in his face how much he loves you. I don't know that he ever felt right before you came along. And I—" Darrel's eyes were getting red.

"Oh, stop it!" Colette laughed. "You're making me cry again."

"I couldn't have asked for a better woman for my son, Colette. You came in here and learned faster than anyone. You've worked hard, you've brought such joy to me and Jael. And Josh and Audrey and the kids. Like I said— you're a daughter to me now. And I've never been prouder of Jimmy. You need to stop being so hard on yourself. That's an order."

"Yes sir," Colette said. "You're totally right."

"Damn straight," Darrel said. Colette stared at him, aghast. "What? You didn't think I had any swears in me?"

Colette laughed and threw her arms around him, just like she had with her own father years ago—when she was barely old enough to remember. "Darrel, *thank you*. For everything."

"Don't you mention it, Miss Colette. Now, you go on over to your fiancé."

CHAPTER THIRTY-EIGHT

"**A**re you *sure* you won't need me?" Colette asked.

"Goodness, child," Myra said. "Must I say it again? We'll be fine. You go."

"We've done fine without you all these years," Trinity said. Colette let her jaw drop and pretended to be insulted. "Just kidding, dude. You know I love you." Trinity eyed Colette's jeans and T-shirt. "Are you wearing your work clothes?"

"Of course not. Do you even know me?"

"Better hurry up, then."

"Yeah. See you guys after the show."

Colette made her way to James's dressing room, where she found him massaging his feet with a tennis ball.

"Aw, you're wearing the pants I gave you!" she said.

"Hey, babe," James replied, picking the ball up and throwing it into the trash can. He stood up, fished it out, threw it in again, and repeated the process.

"You nervous?"

"A little."

"You'll be amazing, as always," Colette said, squeezing him tightly. "Damn. I sure like you in that eyeliner."

James laughed. "What a weirdo."

"Will you help me into my dress real quick?" Colette asked.

"Yes, please."

Colette undressed in a frenzy. She slipped into a red silk gown and lifted her hair up as James stepped behind her. "This is so crazy, isn't it?" she asked, quivering at the sudden sensation of James's lips on her neck. She craned her neck to kiss him back. "I can't believe it's finally happening."

James zipped up her dress and shook his head. "Me neither."

"I want to stop and see the girls before I go." She turned around to face him. "Do you need anything?"

"Nope. I think I'm good."

"I know you are." She clasped either side of his face, peered into his eyes and said, "You've got this."

James exhaled. "Thank you." Pulling her in close, he kissed her once more and asked, "Do you think we could—you know—later on tonight?"

Colette smiled. "Of course, baby. If you think you'll still have the energy after this."

"Good point. I guess I'll find out." James grinned. "I love you so much."

"I love you, too. *Merde*. And have fun up there."

Colette stepped back out into the hallway, which was eerily quiet. It was a little too early for the hall to be filled with dancers scurrying to make their cues. Everyone would be in their dressing rooms, doing last minute prep and shaking out nerves before leaving to wait backstage. It was strange to think that all of their work—all of their thoughts and sweat and obsessive attention to detail—would culminate in such a hush. But, soon, music would fill the building, and the ballet they had been long awaiting would begin.

Suddenly, the calm was interrupted by giggles as Iris and Helena burst out of Alex's dressing room.

"Aw, look at CoCo!" Helena exclaimed.

"I was just coming to see you," Colette said. "What's going on in there?"

"Just helping Alex. She's freaking out. Somehow, she managed to lose her Act II shoes, so we brought her a new pair."

"What? How did she do that?"

"I have no idea. She was going on about putting them in her other bag and grabbing the wrong one or whatever—I don't know. I've never seen her this nervous."

"Man. Did you have to drive back to the studio?"

"No," Iris said. "We have the same specs, so I gave her a brand new pair of mine. I always bring extra—you know, like any sane person."

"Has she sewn them yet? She still needs to break them in, too. She won't have time—"

"Her problem now," Iris said. "Hey, how do we look as your Daughters of Jerusalem?"

Colette surveyed the two of them in their flowing gowns of midnight blue. Their loose hair was crowned with the decadent headpieces that Colette had made. She had to admit, they looked perfect.

"You both look gorgeous," she said. "Really stunning. You're going to kill it tonight."

"Aw, thanks," Helena said. "We're feeling pretty great."

"Good. Well, I'm going to peek in on Alex. Hope you girls have fun tonight. She knocked on the dressing room door. "Alex? It's me."

"Thank God. Come in."

"Hey." Colette poked her head through the doorway. "Heard you had a shoe emergency."

Alex turned around to face her. She had a pristine pointe shoe in one hand, a needle and thread in the other, and her eyes were full of panic.

"Colette," she said. "I don't know what my problem is. I'm usually so prepared."

"Wow."

"What?"

"You look so beautiful."

"Only thanks to you." She went back to her sewing and immediately pricked her hand with the needle. "Ouch!"

"Seriously, you look perfect," Colette said, taking the shoe away from her. "I can finish this if you want."

Alex exhaled. "Thank you."

"Is the other one done?"

"Yeah."

Alex handed the finished shoe to her, and Colette checked her placement of the elastic and ribbons against it.

"Huh. I think this is how Iris sews her shoes, too," Colette said, moving the needle with quick precision. "You're practically feet twins."

Alex laughed. "Lucky for me."

"Are you sure the ones you have on are for Act I?" Colette teased.

"Pretty sure."

"I don't mean to add to your stress, but how will you break these in? You barely have any time between acts."

"I don't need to," Alex said. She craned her neck to watch Colette's sewing. "I like to dance on new shoes for The Bride's Dream. I just bend the arch and step on the box a bit."

"You're kidding. What a bad-ass!" Colette tapped the shoe against the dressing table. "These things are rock-hard."

Alex chuckled again. "Thanks for making me laugh, Colette. It makes me feel better."

"No problem," Colette replied, still working the needle as quickly as possible. "You know, I really can't wait to see you on stage."

Alex sighed. "I think that's why I'm so nervous."

"What? Why?"

"This is your ballet. There's so much riding on this for you and James. I feel like I'm bound to mess it up."

Colette looked up from her sewing and saw that Alex was looking at her with pleading intensity, her eyes wide and vulnerable. She couldn't tell if they were brown or had morphed into a deep purple. What had Alex said? She felt bound to mess it up. Alexandra Vukoja felt inadequate.

"That's ridiculous. This is not *my* ballet. It's everyone's ballet. Don't you dare worry about messing it up. You're Alexandra freaking Vukoja. No one can do what you do, and we're all here to watch you do your best. You've rehearsed this thing a hundred times, and I'll be there, cheering you on, no matter what." She snipped the extra thread, gave the ribbons a good tug, and set the shoes on the dressing table. "*Et voila!*" she said, mimicking Myra. "All done. I don't want to brag, but I think I just set a new record."

Alex began to cry.

"No," Colette said. "Don't ruin your makeup!"

"Colette," Alex said, fighting to regain her composure. "Thank you for everything you've done for me—not just tonight, but during this whole production. I couldn't do this without you."

"I really haven't done that much, Alex."

"Yes, you have, and I'll—I'll try my best to make it worth your while." Alex glanced at the clock. "Hey, hadn't you better get to your seat?"

"Yeah. I really should." Colette jumped to her feet and kissed Alex on the cheek. "You'll do great. And don't let James steal the show. *Merde.*"

COLETTE RAN ACROSS the empty lobby as fast as her stilettos allowed. Lavoisier had already begun his introduction when she reached the theater, and the long row of seats she had reserved was now occupied by some of her favorite people in the world.

"Hey guys," she whispered.

"Aunt CoCo's here!" Rose said.

Audrey and Josh waved her in, and she crawled over Hunter, Molly, Jael, Darrel, Aaron and Sammy to take her seat next to her own parents

"It's about time," Sammy said.

Aaron leaned over her, still holding Sammy's hand. "No kidding. We were about to sell your seat."

Haha, Colette mouthed.

"Here's a program, honey."

"Thanks, Mom."

Lavoisier was wrapping up, and Colette knew that soon the air would begin to feel electric—that chills would dance up and down her spine and that the audience would be transported to an ancient place filled with mystery and romance. Soon, they would delight in the bright colors, the sumptuous flowers, the sound of divine beauty manifest in music. The people next to her—her favorite people—they would be able to share in something that she loved dearly, something that would not have happened without her.

Colette flipped through the program, feeling too excited to take much of it in—even her own photograph upon the page. Her eyes finally rested on one line, a sentence from James's biography, and she smiled from ear to ear.

> *Special thanks to my beautiful bride Colette, who imagined and inspired this ballet. Your seal is forever upon my heart.*

She read the line once more as the lights dimmed.

ACKNOWLEDGEMENTS

I owe a huge thanks to my incredible family and sister-editor, Jessica Bahr, as well as all of my early readers—Emilie Beckum, Ashley Castle, Randi Capehart Worley, Olivia Alexander Dull, Kara Evans, Katie Hagedorn, Jennie Hinterreiter, Beth Laird, Beth Yeldell, Katie Yeldell, and the brilliant Kearsten Smith, who should really be a professional editor.

Others to whom I am equally grateful include: Megan Records and New York Book Editors for a thorough manuscript critique when I needed it most. My wonderful copy editor Kerrie McLoughlin for going above and beyond. Shawn Coyne for writing *The Story Grid* and Tim Grahl for starting *The Story Grid Podcast*. I doubt I would have finished this book otherwise. Seth Godin for commanding me (a wide-eyed stranger) to ship my book before I was "ready." Steven Pressfield for writing *The War of Art*, which kickstarted my journey as an author in the first place. And my fellow authors from The Story Grid Workshop—thank you all for your guidance and encouragement.

To all of the amazing teachers, pianists, and adult students at the Kansas City Ballet School—you inspire me during each and every class, and I am so grateful to have a spot at the barre. The same goes for the KCB company dancers and staff, who push themselves tirelessly for the sake of beauty. And to every composer and musician—thank you for the music that compels us to dance.

Finally, to Michael, my incredibly patient husband—I could not have finished this book without your love, encouragement, and steadfast support. Your seal is forever upon my heart.

ABOUT THE AUTHOR

Professional archivist and librarian by day, ballet student by night, Joanna Marsh loves to share her eclectic interests through writing. She is passionate about all forms of art, history, and the creative process.

Joanna holds an M.L.S. degree from Emporia State University and a B.A. in Humanities from Northwest Missouri State University. She resides in Kansas City with her husband Michael and their beloved cat, Caspian. *Cantique* is her first novel. Visit joannamarshbooks.com for more information.

Printed in Great Britain
by Amazon

48006094R00170